I0659204

JOSIAH'S LOVE AND JUSTICE

VOLUME ONE:
FOUR SLAVES

By
Lucas X Black

TABLE OF CONTENTS

ONE

"This is Josiah," Josiah answered his phone.

"Josiah, this is Tim," a vaguely familiar voice said into the phone. "We met at the munch three weeks ago?"

"Yes, okay," Josiah said after a moment of searching his memory. "You and Darla are together, correct? Recently got transferred here?"

"I'm impressed," Tim said on the other end, sounding so. "Look, long story, but I need your services, and pretty soon. Can we meet somewhere and discuss it? I was told you don't do business by phone, and I think that's wisest."

"It's 8:00 now," Josiah said. "Why don't I head back to my office in town and we can meet there? The address is 4389 Henderson. My office is 500, corner of the top floor. I'll be there in … does thirty minutes work for you?"

"Perfectly," Tim said. "Thank you, and I'll see you in thirty."

On his end, Tim rounded up Darla to drive to Josiah's office. As he loaded the address into his GPS, he saw his estimate was correct. GPS told him with current traffic, the drive was 24 minutes.

When the call ended, Josiah raised his voice and called Molly, and in a moment, they were likewise on the road. Their drive was shorter, and they were in Josiah's office ten minutes later, both

1

drinking Cokes while waiting for Tim and Darla.

"You haven't taken on a new client in months," Molly observed.

"Usually, they don't want to pay what I cost," Josiah returned. "This one probably won't bite down either, but that's okay."

A few minutes later, the security guard called the office and Josiah told him to let Tim and Darla come up, and a few minutes after that, they wandered into Josiah's office suite. "Can I offer you refreshments?" Josiah asked. "There's coffee, of course, but cold water, sodas, wine, beer, and I wouldn't be the least bit surprised to find Molly's kept the liquor cabinet fully supplied."

"One of those Cokes would go down well," Tim allowed. "Darla?"

"Water, please?" Darla asked, looking fretful. *As well she ought,* Josiah thought with an inward smirk. *I wonder what she did that her man has brought her to me. I guess I'll find out soon enough.*

Molly handed Tim a Coke and Darla a bottle of Dasani. And then Tim took the bull by the horns. "For reasons I'd rather not get into, I need your services as a beadle, Josiah," he said.

"I see," Josiah returned. "Give me one dollar, please. Each of you, give me one dollar, please."

"Okay," Tim said dubiously. He pulled two singles from his wallet, and handed one to Darla, and they both handed their dollars to Josiah.

"Good," Josiah said. "Now I'm on retainer as your attorney and anything you tell me is completely inviolable."

"Clever," Tim said, and chuckled. "Okay, as you can tell, I'm somewhat older than Darla. I'm 44 years old and she's 25, to put a point on it. I'm only five years younger than her parents, in fact. We wound up taking some of the same classes at a college in Florida and hit it off pretty well, and married right after she graduated. Her parents objected vociferously to the whole thing and disowned her. Meanwhile, I'm afraid it's become apparent that Darla has some growing up to do. So far she hasn't been caught or arrested, but she's been out with new friends smoking one hell of a lot of marijuana and partying to all hours of the night —"

Josiah held up a hand to cut Tim off. "And it threatens your career," he interjected. "You're a lieutenant colonel, perhaps a full colonel, out at the base, and the ethos is if you can't manage and command your family, you can't be trusted with soldiers under your command, and then poof, your career is dust and memory. I'll go a step further with this. General Orton, who commands the base, has gained a rather Puritanical reputation for cashiering anyone for what military regulations see as sexual or marital misconduct. In this past year, eight officers were forced to resign, one was court-martialed for sleeping with a corporal's wife, and any number of senior NCOs were also railroaded out of the service. I understand a couple of them were just into S&M but got reported and were persona non grata pretty well on the spot, so you probably live in base housing and cannot afford the risk of punishing her at home. How am I doing so far?"

"Batting a thousand," Tim said, looking disturbed. "I'm screening for full colonel now and hope to be promoted in the next eighteen months. Have you been keeping a file on me, Mr. Bailey?"

"No," Josiah said. "I didn't need to do that. All I needed to do was be observant and know the lay of the land around here. The West Point ring on your finger told me you're a career officer, but the way you carry and present yourself, I'd have known you're a soldier one way or another. Even in that civilian suit, it's obvious you're military. There's the Purple Heart lapel pin, for instance. The haircut, of course. And I wouldn't be surprised if you even have military creases pressed into your tidy whities, Colonel."

"And Sherlock Holmes with the win," Tim chuckled. "They told us at West Point that we could pretend we were in the Army for the fun until we hit major, and then we knew and they knew they own our ass for the long haul. I could file for retirement tomorrow morning and be gone in six months but … what would I do then? I love the Army, and I'm in it until they tell me to get lost."

"Okay, here's how things work here, Tim," Josiah said. He reached into his desk and came up with a manila envelope. "I will serve as beadle within my own boundaries."

"Explain that, please," Tim said as he opened the envelope.

"It means I won't endeavor to do harm to someone, no matter the offense," Josiah said. "If you want her permanently disfigured or a bone broken, I won't do it. If you want her caned thoroughly and confined on bread and water, assuming there's not some compelling reason to the contrary, I'm in."

"Compelling reason?" Tim asked.

"Let's say she's an insulin-dependent diabetic," Josiah returned. "I won't endanger her health by —"

"Stands to reason," Tim interrupted. Josiah shot a glance at Darla, who looked a bit ill at the topic of discussion. He wondered what brought these two into a union. Darla seemed far more the trophy-wife type who'd marry a descending series of corporate executives. She was seriously that beautiful, tall, athletic, blonde-and-blue. She didn't seem the type – Josiah had encountered many – who would be a camp follower, even for a high-ranking officer.

"What's this about a medical examination, here in the

packet?" Tim wanted to know.

"It comes back to my boundaries and wanting to ensure the safety of the subject placed into my charge," Josiah returned.

"I can probably get a copy of her most recent physical, about three months ago," Tim said.

"No need," Josiah replied.

"If I may?" Molly interjected, and Josiah nodded. "I am a physician, Colonel. We decided it's wisest to keep everything under the radar. I give her the exam. It's standard. Height, weight, BP, ECG, you know the drill. I test the women for pregnancy to be on the safe side. It's basic but thorough. If she busts the physical, the deal is off-the-table, immediately."

"Does she make an appointment with you?" Tim asked.

"There is an exam room in this suite that we've furnished," Molly said. "Without objection, I can do it right here, right now. Any objections, Darla?"

"I ... I guess not," Darla said in a halting voice.

"Come with me, please."

TWO

Darla followed Molly into a locked room, about fifteen feet square, that was indeed a physician's exam room, complete to the table with the stirrups and a little private bathroom. "Strip naked, even your socks," Molly ordered, and Darla, surprised at the sudden brusque shift in the doctor, obeyed, folding her clothes neatly and putting them beside her shoes on a small table. She went through all the ins and outs of the exam. At 5'8", she weighed 150 pounds. Her blood pressure was a smidgen high, as were her other vitals, which Molly laid aside as nervousness, considering the circumstances.

"I don't have to test you to know your BMI is great," Molly said. "I gather you get a lot of exercise?"

"Yes, Ma'am," Darla said, smiling nervously. "I like to bicycle, swim and hike. I used to be into rock climbing but there was a near disaster and I've been phobic about that ever since."

"I understand," Molly said. "Is that where you got this scar on your lower leg?"

"Yes, Ma'am," Darla answered. "Happened when I was fourteen and … well, I was more impressed with my rock climbing ability than I should have been. I didn't break the leg but don't know how I didn't. But it cost eight stitches and I needed a transfusion. My dad nearly had a stroke and Mom grounded me for three months after the stitches came out." She paused a moment. "I guess I sound inane. How bad is this going to be, what he's going to do to me?"

"That's a matter mostly for your master to determine," Molly said. "I'm sure they're discussing this situation while you and I are out of earshot in here. Fortunately for you, you're healthy as a horse. Unfortunately for you, you're healthy as a horse. That means I can't give you an excuse to dodge your fate."

"Jesus," Darla moaned. "Look, you've got to have some idea … how harsh is he with the whip or the cane?"

"I'll put it this way," Molly said. "Everyone who visits him for these services goes away deeply humbled by it."

"Come on, you're his slave," Darla said. "He's lashed you before. How bad is it going to be? I'm trying to brace myself for what's coming."

"I've told you all I can say, probably more than I should," Molly said. "Be glad you're as fit as you are. That's likely to be helpful. Wait here while I see what's going on. Your master might want you to know, but a lot of them prefer to keep it a surprise."

"Okay, unless she's got some sort of cancer that only hits beautiful blondes, I'm sure your Molly is going to give her a clean bill of health," Tim said when the women went into the exam room. "I brought my checkbook, but if you prefer to put it on my card, I have that too." He chuckled. "Beadle Bailey. I guess you've heard all the jokes by now, huh?"

"Yeah, I have," Josiah allowed. "Especially around a military base."

"Then I won't heap them on you all over again," Tim said, digging out his wallet and handing Josiah his debit card.

"So I only have to charge once to your card, let's discuss the specifics," Josiah suggested.

"That makes sense," Tim agreed. "Here's what I have in mind …"

The men spent twenty minutes discussing the specifics when Molly stepped in to report that it was her medical opinion that Darla could be reasonably expected to endure the physical rigors being discussed for her. Finally, Tim and Josiah finalized the plan, and Josiah billed Tim's card for the anticipated session.

"Nice thing about me being an attorney-at-law," Josiah said. "I can call most anything 'legal services' and nobody asks questions. I'll pick her up at your quarters tomorrow at noon, and she'll be set free Sunday afternoon."

"That sounds good," Tim said. "She'll be waiting for you."

"Tell her to get dressed, please," Josiah said to Molly.

THREE

Josiah arrived to the quarters of Lieutenant Colonel Timothy Morris at 12:15 the next day, a Friday, and rang the doorbell. He was greeted by a fretful Darla, dressed in jeans, sneakers, and a polo shirt. She was told to bring nothing, not even her cellular phone, no money, not even a bra or panties or socks, although she'd been told to wear good sneakers, and she appeared, Josiah noted, to have obeyed. She wasn't wearing socks, and by the look of her thin shirt, there was no bra restraining her breasts, and neither was there a panty-line that he could detect. Josiah drove her to a warehouse, where he drove the Mercedes inside, and parked it beside a black cube van.

"Get out and strip down," Josiah ordered. "Leave your clothes on that table, but put your shoes back on."

"We're doing this here?" Darla asked.

Her question was answered by Josiah effortlessly pressing her to the side of the van and smacking her rump four times with a paddle, hard smacks. "You are here to obey, not to ask questions," he grumbled, showing her a pair of scissors, the rugged-looking type that EMTs carry. "One way or another, your clothes are coming off, young lady, and you'll be far happier saving them than me cutting them off you."

"Yes … yes, Sir," Darla said, feeling a bit of fear at his demeanor and self-assuredness. She did as told, and in a moment was naked but for the shoes she put back on at his command.

"If you're hiding anything in your vagina or ass, you'd best remove it now and put that on the table too," Josiah told her. "You're in enough trouble already, and your master has agreed you will suffer added lashes for smuggling contraband."

"Nothing, Sir," Darla said, shamed and looking at the floor. "Master shaved me and warned me he would pay Dr. Molly to sew me closed if I broke your rules."

"You don't want that to happen," Josiah said. This part was a bluff, but Darla didn't need to know that, he considered as he donned a pair of latex gloves. "Okay, turn your toes inward, bend over, grab your ankles, and let's have a look." Darla obeyed and yelped in surprise as his finger entered her, exploring, and then he withdrew his finger and Darla let loose a surprise fart, rancid and loud.

"I'm so sorry," she moaned, blushing and mortified.

"You should be," Josiah said, knowing this one would need some humbling. "By the look of this glove, you should also clean yourself out far better than you do." This was rewarded with a humiliated squeak as Josiah donned fresh gloves and slid two fingers into her vagina, again satisfied she'd smuggled nothing in here either. He next had her stand and used steel cuffs to ratchet her wrists behind her back, and then opened the door to the van and guided her up the steps into the van.

Darla could make out a row of odd-looking seats, facing rearward, with an arrangement of seatbelts, somewhat like a grown-up version of a child safety seat. "These are pilot seats culled from helicopters that were being retired," Josiah explained. "It's rear-facing for your safety. Get in the seat so I can buckle you in." This part was true, but he also wanted her disoriented, so she hadn't a clue where she was from about thirty seconds after leaving the warehouse.

"Yes, Sir," Darla said, approaching the seat on trembling legs, and clumsily sitting. Josiah helped position her, and then tightly secured her in place with the belts and buckles.

He closed the box and got behind the wheel, then took off down the road, taking random turns before getting onto the county highway toward the farm he owned through a buried shell company, and under layers of obfuscation. The farm was huge, and along the perimeter it was overgrown with trees. Darla was unlikely to have the first clue where she was. She was in for a miserable time here before he sent her home Sunday, and that misery would commence in just a couple minutes more.

FOUR

Out of the van after the two-hour ride, Darla walked a bit to stretch her legs. She wondered where she was, and felt distinctly frightened and worried, being out here – wherever this was – and naked but for her shoes. But she knew from the second she began stripping naked in that warehouse that her die was cast. *Besides, I do love Tim, and he's right,* she considered. *I need to grow the fuck up, and I don't think he's close to dumping me, but if he does, I'm fucked. Mom and Dad haven't said a word to me since before I married him, and all the cards I sent them for anniversaries, birthdays, even Christmas, all came back marked Return to Sender. So if he dumps me, I'm homeless.*

"First thing first," Josiah said. "Slaves here are nothing but animals. You get shoes because even horses get shoes, but you're here to be punished, broken, and humbled. You're here to work hard. If you hate me, that's regrettable, but I'm doing what your master asked me to do, but I have resources he really doesn't, so that's okay, since he has tanks and flamethrowers that I don't, right? I'm going to remove your cuffs now. Before you get any big ideas about running away, you need to understand you have no idea where you are, except this place is isolated. You are naked. From here, you are at least a mile's walk through thick woods, including all kinds of snakes and bugs, as well as coyotes, to get off this property, and another two miles more before you even get to a paved road, and it's two miles further still to a neighbor, who is probably more liable to consider you a gift from God and rape you instead of helping you at all."

"I … Sir, I don't want this, but I deserve it," Darla said. "I will not run, Sir Josiah. My master says I deserve this and I guess you and your slave agree with him. I'll take what's coming to me."

"We'll see," Josiah said as he undid her cuffs and led her to a stall in the huge barn, where she saw a cart that she recognized as somewhat of a rickshaw. It was on what looked like very narrow car tires, and the handles had cuffs already on them, in rings. A buggy whip was in a holder beside the rickshaw's seat.

"A draft animal," Darla breathed, shocked.

"A draft animal," Josiah agreed. "Several of my clients are into racing these, so I have an array of these rickshaws here. Go ahead and step into place, grasp the handles."

"Yes, Sir," Darla said fretfully. In position, she felt the cold cuffs ratchet around her wrists, and then felt the rickshaw shift on its front feet while Josiah boarded. She felt every nerve on edge, every sense heightened as she heard her heart thudding loudly in her ears, and the sound of the whip being removed from its holder.

"Now, basic instructions for you," Josiah said. "I mentioned this to Tim and he sounded interested, so he might bring you back here for races sometimes, so this might be important, whether he rides the rickshaw or pays a jockey. I'm going to touch the whip to your back, and that means walk forward. When I touch your left shoulder, it means turn left, right shoulder means turn right. Out on the track, you will stop at the start line, and wait. When the whip hits you – and it's going to hurt – you will start running. The faster you run, the fewer lashes you get. The track is a mile long, and I'm going to run you one hard lap, if you do it right. A normal person walks an average of four miles per hour, a mile in fifteen minutes. I figure, hampered with this rickshaw, you're nevertheless young and seem very physically fit, well-muscled … I figure you should be able to finish a mile in eight minutes. So here's your challenge, animal. I'm going to use a stopwatch. If you finish in eight or less minutes, there'll be a treat for you. If you finish slow, you'll be put on a post for ten lashes plus one per second you were slow."

"Jesus," Darla moaned, and instantly regretted it as the whip slashed across her back, making her yelp. "I'm sorry, Sir," she quickly yelled. "I understand, Sir."

"That's better," Josiah said, and then touched the whip to her back. Darla lifted the handles, noting the rickshaw was thankfully well-balanced, and walked out into the barn. And then he touched her left shoulder and she turned left, and then her back again, and she walked the rickshaw out onto the track until she got to the start line, and then stopped. It was, for her, the first time she'd ever been naked outdoors, and she resisted a hundred urges to hunker down and hide her nakedness, wondering how humiliating it would be to be seen by an audience while being little more than one of those Tennessee walking horses.

She waited what seemed forever, and then the lash crossed her back. She yelped, but had the presence of mind to sprint down the track, running for all she was worthwhile the whip struck her a couple more times to keep her running at her top speed. She yelped a couple times but kept pushing herself, running as fast as she was able with the rickshaw behind her, slowing her down. She made the long arc and got to the second straightaway as the lash kept falling. Darla stumbled and nearly fell, but kept upright and ground her teeth at the pain of the next lash, running like the very devil was chasing her.

She was moving slowly and knew it, and could feel the strain of pulling the load she was pulling. Josiah was tall and strongly built, probably 250 pounds, and the rickshaw probably weighed another hundred or so. Well-balanced or not, it was a heavy load to be pulling, no matter the fitness nut she was. Her arms and shoulders felt the greatest strain, but as she hit the second curve she could feel her legs rapidly weakening. And then disaster struck twenty yards from the finish line as she misstepped and stumbled to her knees, abrading them painfully as the rickshaw came to a halt and the lash started hitting her more rapidly. She fought her way to her feet, sobbing in agony, and started running again, finally passing the start line and then falling again to her knees, gasping in exhaustion.

Josiah dismounted the rickshaw and produced a bottle of cold water from a small cooler under the seat, atop extra weights, and gave it to her with a straw, holding it while she greedily slurped at the water, but taking it away when she'd had about half of it. She looked up at him, wondering what was next.

"Until you took that fall, you were doing well," he said. "But the fall … you finished at eight minutes and four seconds. That's fourteen lashes, slave."

"Y … yes, Sir," Darla groaned, knowing that complaining or whining would only worsen an already bad situation.

"You can have more water afterwards, but I'd rather you not puke all over the place until after I'm done with you," Josiah said as he undid the cuffs, and then grasped her hair and led her to the post at the edge of the track. At his command, she offered her wrists to the cuffs dangling from the post, and felt her wrists bound once again. In spite of her pain, Darla found herself wondering if she'd lost her mind or finally found it, finding herself wallowing in punishment and misery at her master's decree and this evil beadle's hand. But she knew she was guilty of far more than Tim seemed to know about, and to be honest, things she prayed Tim would never learn she'd done.

But those thoughts were dispelled as the whip struck her anew, harsher than before, accompanied by Darla's pained screech. She howled again as the second lash of this punishment found her upper back, and then broke down sobbing as the lash struck her over and again, sparing her no mercy. Eventually, the whipping ended.

For Darla's part, it might have taken fourteen seconds, minutes, hours, or years. She was absorbed in pain and shame and misery and in that span of time (in fact, only about three minutes) knew only pain and humiliation at the hands of the evil beadle her husband and master had brought into the game.

Josiah uncuffed her, and Darla saw that he was erect behind his zipper, and worried she was about to be raped too. But he simply grabbed her sweaty hair and led her back to the barn, and put her into a jail cell in the barn. The cell was equipped with a cot, a big orange bucket, a spool of toilet paper, and two gallon-size bottles of spring water. "This is your home away from home," he said. "Rest in here. You'll want to be well-rested for tomorrow. One of us will bring you food before sundown." He closed the cell door and wandered out of the barn, where he found Molly.

"I see she got your motor running, Mister," Molly said. "I guess as a physician I should help reduce the swelling there as my contribution to humanitarianism."

Josiah chuckled and undid his pants, letting them slide to his ankles, while Molly came to him, fell to her knees, and took his erection fully into her mouth, devouring it while his hands plunged into her black hair. She was talented in the first place, and knew him well, and in moments he was quivering and gasping as he fought back his climax, but in a moment more, he came hard, filling her frantically swallowing mouth with his seed as he groaned loudly against the intensity.

"I hope that helps," Molly said, looking up at him. But Josiah sensed something was wrong, and asked.

"We'll talk about it Sunday after you've cut her loose," Molly answered. "I saw her run. She did pretty good except for the fall she took. I'll go take a look and put some antiseptic on her knees. Maybe Tim will want to race her here."

"He'd be low stakes, I expect," Josiah said. The races took place now and again throughout the year. Each entrant put up a fee (this varied depending on the race) of anywhere from fifty dollars to three thousand dollars, and winner take all. Josiah knew what the military paid (in truth, underpaid, he'd long believed) its members, and doubted Tim could afford to race Darla for high stakes, but he knew how competitive soldiers could be, and could easily see Tim entering Darla for a hundred-dollar race. He filed that thought aside as Molly entered the barn, followed a moment later by a fresh screech from Darla as the burning antiseptic was sprayed onto her knees. Molly came out a moment later, still looking grim, and they went to the big house in her car.

Alone in her cage – a chain-link affair about ten feet by ten and six or so feet high, fenced along the top too to prevent escape, Darla cried long and hard. She felt lower than she could possibly have imagined, and worried what was in store for her. Tim had only told her she would be lashed harshly and worked hard, but had shed no more light upon her fate. She was confused, as well. In spite of all of this, she was also incredibly horny and would have swapped her soul for an orgasm. Tim had told her she wasn't to have another climax until he personally gave her one, pointing out that this time here was punishment. And she felt punished, but there was an undeniable erotic element in all of this, being captive to this handsome couple – Josiah was a good-looking man, and Molly, at forty, looked easily ten years younger – and being naked like this. It shifted the balance of power when she was the only one here that was naked, she realized.

Her fingers drifted to her labia and teased some, but she suspected if she was caught masturbating, there would be hell to pay, and she knew Josiah was devilish enough to make her regret a stolen orgasm for the rest of her life. It would have to wait until night, she

17

decided, when there would be no chance of being caught. Meanwhile, she was in pain. Her back felt like she'd been burned. There was no mirror in here for her to take a look at the damage, so she had no idea how bad it was. She knew she wasn't bleeding. Molly would have sprayed that horrid antiseptic on her back if she had been. God knew it burned like hell when she sprayed that crap on her skinned knees.

Darla was also exhausted. The rickshaw run had worn her out, and she wondered if there was to be more of the same waiting for her over the coming two days here. In a way, she enjoyed the exercise, but she hoped she wasn't subjected to that again. A competitive type in her makeup, Darla hated being measured and found wanting, and damn well knew she'd been a disappointment out on the track. She bent over and picked up a jug of water, and drank deeply of it, and then decided to lie down. She didn't even bother removing her shoes as she lay on her belly, also annoyed because she was one to sleep on her back, but with that recent lashing, that wasn't going to happen.

Molly brought her a surprisingly hearty meal an hour later of two grilled burgers and a healthy helping of fries. "Josiah ran you hard out there on the track," she said. "You'll need fuel to get through your time here, slave. Eat well."

"Yes, Ma'am," Darla said, knowing this wouldn't be a problem. She was half-starved, and devoured all of the first burger and most of the second, along with half the fries and probably a quart of the water. And then her belly cramped with urgent need, and she suddenly knew the bucket in this cage was to be her toilet, not a makeshift chair when turned upside-down. She groaned as she sat on the bucket, mortified when she cut a window-rattling fart, and grunted like a man as she took an enormous shit in the bucket, gagging at the odors wafting up. She stood and wiped, gagging again, and then unrolled half the toilet paper to bury the mess, hoping in vain that it would help contain the odor.

If nothing else, it dampened her arousal. She yawned and decided to try to sleep more. It was warm and still in the barn, and humid, and she was soon sweat-soaked and unable to sleep. Finally, in desperation, she masturbated and came four times before being able, finally, to fall to sleep.

FIVE

"She masturbated like crazy for a while last night," Molly reported to Josiah when he woke at 7:00. Always an early riser, Molly woke even earlier than usual, at 4:00, after a night of fitful sleep, with too much on her mind.

"Tim told me he figured she would," Josiah noted. "It means she gets a repeat of this weekend next month. It also means she'll be caned again tomorrow after we confront her with the accusation."

"Jesus, he's an ornery one, isn't he?" Molly remarked.

"I get the feeling Tim is having some buyer's remorse, to be frank," Josiah said.

"How do you mean?" Molly asked.

"Men have mid-life crises and often get a sporty car or a sporty woman," Josiah said. "In both cases, they tend to cost more than the man can really afford and tend to be really impractical and oftentimes high maintenance. Go out and buy a new Porsche, and it's a great car, but you have to feed it premium gas, for instance, and you don't get tires for it at Wal-Mart. But you love the Porsche and afraid you'll regret it worse if you trade it for something more sensible, so for several years it becomes your tar baby."

"She is amazingly beautiful and sleek," Molly agreed. "But ... yeah, I see where she could be more impressed with herself than anyone around her. I guess this sounds bigoted, but beautiful women like that often don't enjoy good reputations."

20

"Yeah," Josiah allowed. "I got horny around her, but ... I don't think I'd want her in my life. There are simpler ways to give myself an ulcer."

"Oh, come on," Molly said. "In a vacuum, no consequences, you'd fuck her in a heartbeat. It's okay. I would too. I got horny as fuck watching her masturbating down there, and I don't have to be a Philadelphia lawyer to know you would've done the same."

"Well, duh," Josiah said, and chuckled. Molly again gave a weak smile. "Are you going to tell me what's eating you?" he asked.

"Tomorrow, after you've discharged her, I promise," Molly answered, and sighed. "Let's get some breakfast and then go deal with Darla. I figure we can feed her after you've whipped her and run her hard. I'd rather the woman doesn't upchuck all over the place."

"No doubt," Josiah said.

"Okay, up and at 'em," Josiah greeted Darla thirty minutes later. His stomach twisted some at the foulness rising from her bucket, but he stifled that impulse as she stood and looked at him. "You're to be caned this morning, and then to go for another run around the track – two laps this time – a few other activities, and then a long stretch in solitary. If you need to use the bucket, this is your last best chance until you return to your cell, slave."

"Yes, Sir," Darla moaned, knowing a fresh humiliation was warming up for her. She'd never used the john in front of Tim, or any man, but Josiah was showing no sign of affording her privacy. And she realized she really had to go, both ways. She went to the bucket and turned her back to her audience, then sat and relieved herself, trying not to sob in her humiliation as she expelled more foulness into the orange bucket. It took a while, but finally she finished, and clumsily wiped herself and stood.

"If I let you come out of there without cuffs on, will you cooperate or make us regret it?" Josiah asked.

"I'll cooperate, Sir," Darla said, trying to stifle her irritation. *Where the fuck do you think a buck naked woman, with no idea where she is, is going to run?*

"Very well," Josiah said, and opened the cage.

"Come with me," Molly ordered, and Darla followed her from the barn to the track. This time they stopped at a railing, and Darla spotted the tie-down rings littered about the otherwise unassuming section of fence. She didn't require Dick-and-Jane direction when Molly pointed to the railing, and simply bent over, offering her wrists and ankles toward the rings. In a few seconds, her wrists were again in cuffs, this time pulled tightly toward the rings with ropes, and then her ankles were bound in leather cuffs and likewise pulled toward lower rings. Splinters poked her lower belly, but Darla correctly suspected she was soon to have far greater concerns on her plate.

Josiah approached a moment later with a cane in his hand. He hunkered down in front of Darla so she could see the evil length of rattan soon to be her undoing. "Your master and I discussed this caning," he said. "He assures me you're strong enough to endure a long and brutal session, and by the look of you, he's probably correct. But it's been my policy that I would rather go a bit more easily on a new charge here. To put a point on it, my policy for new clients is their slaves are not to be lashed greater than fifty strokes in one session, nor more than one hundred in any 24-hour period. This isn't to say you don't deserve worse, but since you're more or less a first offender, it goes a bit easier on you. You are to be lashed thirty-six strokes this morning, and will be awarded an additional twenty-four this afternoon for a total of sixty lashes today. Tim has authorized me to lash you further as I see fit for any failings in your deportment while under my stewardship, so I am going to suggest you proceed on your best behavior. Now, tell me the truth, slave. Have you been caned before today?"

"No, Sir," Darla said. "Tim has used his belt on me, and paddled me. He's flogged me to tears a few times, but never used a cane on me. It was always a threat but never carried out, Sir."

"Perhaps you should have heeded his threats, and avoided being a guest here," Josiah remarked. "In a moment, Molly will gag you. This isn't to stifle your outcries, since I frankly find those to be sexy to my ears and humiliating to the slave, but it is to protect you so that if you bite down, you're not going to shatter your teeth. Molly?"

Molly came toward Darla with a ball gag in her hands, and buckled it in place. The gag was hollow through the center so the girl could breathe, and Molly would monitor her from the head anyway. One this was done, she went to her car and produced a heart monitor and defibrillator unit from the trunk, a Physio-Control Lifepak 15, and attached leads to the young woman to monitor her heart throughout the process. While Molly didn't anticipate anything going wrong, she'd rather all three of them were safe than sorry.

"Sinus rhythm, rate is 120," she reported. "A bit accelerated, but I guess the girl is somewhat nervous."

"Then let's begin," Josiah said. He circled around Darla, noting her trembling, and touched the cane to her rump to gauge his aim. Darla had read about the cane, and seen many videos of canings, and knew this was going to be terrible, but guessed correctly that she wasn't the least bit prepared for what was coming her way. She bit down hard on the gag, and clenched her fists, praying she could endure this beating. A second later, the first stroke landed across the middle of her rump. The cane, long, thin, and dense, left an instant welt on her. Darla, all pride and propriety out the window, screamed at the agony. Josiah lashed again and again, growing highly erect as he continued the slave's punishment. Thoroughly stuck in place, Darla couldn't evade that evil rattan. All she could do was endure the lashing and scream at nearly every stroke until her voice was gone about 25 lashes into the exercise.

Done, Josiah inspected his handiwork, seeing several welts on the right had gone blue. He knew she would be feeling this for some time to come as Molly approached him, smiled at the welted ass Darla was now sporting, and fell again to her knees and took his member into her mouth, grasping his ass as she sucked him down. In a moment, Josiah trembled as he came hard in Molly's mouth while she desperately swallowed.

"There, that should let you concentrate better," she purred in his ear as she stood. "Shall I hitch her to the rickshaw?"

"Yes, do that, please," Josiah said. "I'll be back in a moment."

Molly busied herself with the pain-weakened slave while Josiah stepped around the barn and took a huge leak. When Josiah returned, Darla was in place, cuffed to the handles of the rickshaw. Molly even produced a hair tie to keep Darla's golden hair out of the whip's way, Josiah saw with dark amusement.

"You'll run two laps around the track and be done in fifteen minutes or less," Molly said. "I will start the stopwatch when the whip hits your back. If you're slow, as happened yesterday, you will be assessed ten lashes plus one per second that you went over your allotted time. Understood, slave?"

"Yes, Ma'am," Darla grunted in a hoarse voice. Molly

produced a stopwatch, and nodded to Josiah. A moment later, a fierce lash crossed Darla's back, and she began sprinting along the track, spurred on by harsh lashes every several seconds to ensure she was running for all she was worth. For her part, Darla was indeed giving it her all, grunting in pain every time that evil whip found her upper back, and as she was halfway around the first lap, caught her stride, a difficult thing to do when hampered with the rickshaw.

She continued her run, picking up speed with her newfound pace, and the lashes fell fewer and further between as she started the second lap, racing along well. She crossed the finish line, winded, and slowly came to a stop, turning lazy figure-eights as her breathing slowed. Josiah shot a questioning look at Molly, who gave a thumbs-up, meaning the girl had made her time goal and would avoid more lashes at the post. *Good*, Josiah decided. *She still has plenty more coming, and sometimes they need to eat the carrot dangling from that stick, right?*

"Okay, you made your time," he said. "Take us back to the barn."

"Yes, Sir," Darla replied, and began an easy trot to the barn, backing the rickshaw into its stall. Molly released Darla's cuffs and led her to a clearing a hundred or so yards from the barn. A trailer was in the clearing, and had some tools in it, a shovel, a wheelbarrow, a ladder, a hatchet and a saw.

"Okay, start digging," Molly ordered. "I want the hole dug six feet cubed. Fill the wheelbarrow, and then dump it into the trailer. If you come across roots, there's a hatchet and a saw. I'll bring breakfast to you and some water. Get working."

"Yes, Ma'am," Darla said. She began digging, hating the tedium, and sensing it was busywork. She saw privates all the time whitewashing rocks around various buildings at the base when there was little else for them to be doing, and got the idea that's why she was going to be probably all day digging this pit.

But she considered it was better than sitting in the cage in that hot and airless barn, and kept herself busy digging. A few minutes later, as she dumped the first wheelbarrow full of dirt into the trailer, Josiah and Molly showed up together in a battered International Harvester pickup truck, one that looked like it had been used by Lewis and Clark. The truck was mostly primer and rust, but still bore a few patches of faded baby-blue paint. They parked the truck and slid an ice chest from the bed.

"Take a few and get some food into you, and some water," Josiah said.

"Thank you, Sir," Darla answered. Josiah handed her a smaller Playmate ice chest, in which she found four breakfast tacos and salsa, and she devoured three of them before stopping for a bottle of cold water from the ice chest. She drank the water, gobbled down the fourth taco, and then drank a second bottle of water.

"Okay, get busy," Josiah ordered. "There's plenty of water for you – I packed a 24-bottle case in there on ice – so you won't go thirsty. We'll bring you lunch later. I expect to see one hell of a lot of dirt in that trailer by then, if you have a clue what's good for you."

"I'll be on it, Sir," Darla promised. She hated this kind of work, but would rather this than yet another lashing, which this evil son of a bitch seemed to have in an unending supply. She shut off her thoughts and just focused on her work … fill the wheelbarrow, dump it in the trailer, rinse, repeat. She stopped periodically for a drink of water, and soon had her hole six feet square and over a foot deep when she encountered a thick root, perhaps as big around as her upper arm. She dug under it as much as she could and then got the hatchet and started chopping, but the hatchet bounced more than it chopped. She got the saw, which she saw was actually almost a new pruning saw, and began sawing through the root, first at the proximal end, and then the distal, finally getting it free and tossing it into the trailer as Josiah returned again in the derelict farm truck, bearing lunch.

"May I ask the purpose of this pit?" Darla asked as she unwrapped a thick sandwich.

"There's no routine garbage service out this way – we're way out in the middle of nowhere here – so you're digging a burn pit," Josiah answered. "When it's done, we'll have slaves on punishment detail here burning trash. And eventually the pit gets too full of things that just won't burn, things like metal or glass, and then a slave will fill this pit back in."

"I see, Sir," Darla said. She finished her sandwich and balled the foil, then put it in a trash bag in the bed of the old IH truck, and got some water, drinking a bottle down and groaning.

"Hard work can be painful," Josiah observed.

"I figure I'll be over this in about two weeks," Darla said, and chuckled a bit.

"You deserve it," Josiah ventured.

"I do," Darla agreed, now in a grim tone. "I fucked up and this is the price I pay. I won't fuck up again."

"I should hope not," Josiah said. "Okay, the game's about to start on TV and it's hot out here. You get busy again and one of us will fetch you later."

He fired up the truck and drove off, quite pleased with himself and, at the house, stripped naked and dove into the pool with Molly, paddling about on the warm day and just taking it easy. Back at the clearing, Darla fumed as she dug, pissed off at Josiah and his arrogance while she dug harder and harder, getting to about three feet and pondering the ladder. She dumped the dirt into the wagon and went back to the pit, and suddenly doubled over and vomited into the pit, shivering with a sudden chill. She also had a sudden throbbing headache and guessed it was heat exhaustion. The ice chest was in shade at the foot of an ancient oak tree, and she fetched water and gingerly sat on the ice chest, sipping at the water slowly, so she wouldn't vomit again, and praying she wasn't in further trouble. But she knew herself well enough to know if she didn't cool down and get this rest, they would find her face-planted in the pit she was digging. She finished the bottle of water, and pulled out two more bottles. One of these she drank. The other she left sitting in the grass to warm up a bit.

A few minutes later she started feeling a smidgen better and became aware of the sounds of water splashing a bit. She walked toward that sound and came across a pond with a rudimentary fishing pier. By the look of a flood gauge a hundred or so yards out, she saw it was eleven feet deep. The pond itself was more or less oval, probably three hundred yards by five hundred.

Darla knew she might get in trouble, but she knew she needed to cool down from getting overheated, and decided sometimes it was wiser asking forgiveness than permission, so she removed her shoes and waded out into the water, sighing as it soothed her light sunburn and cooled her body overall.

While she liked swimming, she was too tired to really swim, and after submerging, just floated about for a few minutes. She didn't have a watch but counted to a thousand, guessing that was about fifteen minutes, and then reluctantly returned ashore, put her shoes on, feeling much better, and returned to work.

She made a mental note to take more frequent breaks, and began shoveling more dirt, wishing she could simply move the trailer to the edge of the pit and fill it directly. She realized she could have done that before starting to fill it, but doubted she could push the thing now, with probably a good ton of damp dirt in it. Every three wheelbarrow loads, she sat for a count of two hundred Mississippi and drank more water. Consequently, she got far less work done than she had early in, but she hoped something would be better than nothing.

Three hours later, as she struck another thick root, Josiah and Molly arrived together in the truck. Darla stood and looked at them as they stepped to the pit and inspected her work. Molly was impressed that the young woman had moved as much dirt as she had, but Josiah had expected the girl to have gotten another foot deeper.

"You seem to have slowed down after lunch," Josiah remarked.

"Permission to speak and ... well, to confess, Sir? Darla asked. Josiah nodded. "Sir, I started developing what I think is heat exhaustion. I threw up, developed a headache, was suddenly weak and worn down. I drank water and sat in the shade, then heard the waves of the pond back there and took a brief soak. After I got back to work, I forced myself to take a short break more often."

"I guess I should be glad you got lucky and I'm not trying to explain to your master how it is that you're dead of cottonmouth bites and floating in that pond," Josiah said. "Or eaten by an alligator."

"Jesus," Darla said, looking sick at this reply.

"I don't want to think how many cottonmouths I've killed out there," Josiah said. "I know over the last five years I've killed eleven gators out there. The alligator tails are at least good to eat. I've grilled a lot of those. What I'm saying, slave, is you got lucky. Don't ever go swimming in that pond again. It's good for fishing but never for swimming."

"Yes, Sir," Darla said, feeling unsettled at this news. "I didn't know, Sir. I just needed to cool down."

"Walk on back to the barn," Josiah ordered. "You have a second caning today, on orders of your master, and then time in your cage."

"Yes, Sir," Darla answered. "Christ, I hope I don't die from it."

"A caning?" Josiah asked. "Thus far there are no notches carved in my cane, Darla, and I don't propose to kill you either."

"Yes, Sir," Darla said.

"I need to examine her first," Molly announced. "I know she's worked hard, but she doesn't look good. Get in the bed of the truck, Darla."

At the barn, Molly had Darla sit on a chair, and then rolled out a cart of medical equipment to examine her. She spent about ten minutes doing this, and then surprised Darla by setting up an IV bag.

"She's dehydrated, overheated ... I have to give her a medical disqualification from further activity," Molly announced to Josiah. "I think a liter of normal saline and a good meal will help, but she obviously overdid it with that shovel. Let me guess ... you didn't want to get in trouble for slacking, so you ignored thirst and the heat and kept pushing yourself, right?"

"Yes, Ma'am," Darla said. "I threw up right after lunch, and felt faint. So I sat in the shade and drank water to cool down and then went for a little swim. I guess I got hotter than I realized until ... well ..."

"It happens," Molly said. "Okay, well, you're excused from any further activity until morning. I'm going to start an IV on you that'll take overnight to run. We'll see how you're doing by morning. Josiah, I think a fan is indicated for her as well. It stays warm overnight and I want to keep her relatively cool."

"I can manage that," Josiah said. "Cool air better or just air?"

"Cool, I think," Molly said. "If she gets too cold she can use her blanket."

"I'm on it," Josiah said. He went off to another area of the spacious barn while Molly busied herself starting the IV on Darla and then taping it in place. She pointed Darla to the cage and used a carabiner to hang the bag high. A few minutes later, Josiah appeared with a wagon. In the wagon was an ice chest with a squirrel cage blower attached to it. He slid the cord of the fan through a hole and then exited the cage and plugged it into the wall. Almost instantly, chilly air began blowing from the ice chest.

"It's a simple air conditioner, if inefficient," Josiah explained. "You fill the chest with ice. The blower blows in regular air that chills as it travels to the vent here, and ta-daa, cool air."

"That's good, and thank you, Sir," Darla said. "I was afraid I'd be in worse trouble."

"No," Josiah said. "I can't blame you for what you can't control. You couldn't control the sun, and overestimated yourself. It happens. The idea is to return you to your master chastened, but still healthy. The IV will help. Your supper is in the truck, but I'm going to run back to the house and bring you some orange juice since your electrolytes are probably off-kilter now."

"Do you like guacamole?" Molly asked Darla.

"No, Ma'am," Darla said. "I never got a taste for avocado."

"Pity," Molly said. "They're loaded with potassium. Okay, orange juice it is. Bring her a banana or two as well, please, Josiah."

"Back in a few minutes," Josiah promised, and then he left in the battered truck.

"We'll have to let your master know what happened and learn how he wants to proceed," Molly said. "He's liable to send you here for another weekend. But that's up to him."

"Yes, Ma'am," Darla replied. "I have to say I wish he wouldn't, but … yeah, he probably will."

"Good bet," Molly confirmed. Just then, they heard the rumble of thunder and Molly looked outside to see flashes of lightning far off. "At least the rain will make it a bit cooler tonight. I hope thunder doesn't frighten you."

"No, Ma'am," Darla said, and managed a smile. "I love thunderstorms. I keep wanting to buy the equipment to get good photos of lightning."

"Better you than me," Molly said, and snorted. "I like them until they're right over me, and then they scare the hell out of me. Whenever you get photos, I'd love to see them."

"I'll do my best to get them to you," Darla promised.

Just then, Josiah returned with orange juice and three bananas for Darla, who ate and drank like it might be her last chance in this lifetime. Molly checked Darla one final time and then she and Josiah returned to the house.

SIX

"Tim, this is Josiah," Josiah said into the phone a few minutes later, right as a loud crack of thunder erupted nearby.

"How goes it?" Tim asked carefully.

"Mostly, as planned," Josiah allowed. "But today's end-of-day element couldn't be done. She had a bout of heat exhaustion and is resting now with an IV of … what's that stuff again, Molly?"

"Ringer's Lactate," Molly supplied.

"Ringer's," Tim repeated. "I know it well. I got seconded to Quartermaster a while back for about three months and wound up ordering enough of it to float a big boat. But I don't know much about it, other than field medics seem to go through a lot of it."

Molly spoke up. "It's a volume expander, Colonel, full of electrolytes your Darla lost while sweating. Field medics would indeed use a lot of it for wounded soldiers. Consequently she's weakened and feels like hell. The IV will help some with that, and we fed her orange juice and bananas to get a bit more potassium into her."

"So our afternoon plans fell off the rails for that," Josiah chimed in. "If you want her to come another weekend, we can arrange that. I'll leave that decision to you."

"Send her home tomorrow, as planned," Tim decided. "I'll consider how to proceed. Thank you, Josiah."

33

"Welcome," Josiah returned, and he heard a click. Tim had ended the call. Josiah raised his brows in slight surprise, but then shrugged and reached for the TV remote.

"We need to talk," Molly said.

Finally, Josiah thought, *I get to know what's been bothering her.*

SEVEN

"I really fucked up," Molly said.

"What happened?" Josiah asked.

"You know, all of medical school, and then internship and residency, all too easily beat the humanity right out of a person," Molly said. "You learn to be cold, unfeeling, a stone. You don't reprimand gently. Lord, I had skin like an alligator about three months into my internship, and if anything, it only toughened ever since."

Josiah was silent, knowing Molly was leading up to the point, and prompting her wouldn't really speed her along. Molly finally spoke again. "Wednesday, an aide in the office fucked something up. It was minor, really. We got a new form for recording vital signs and she transposed the respirations and pulse on it, so it showed she was breathing 82 times per minute with a pulse of 16. In the grand scheme of things, not a big fat hairy deal, but I blew a headpipe at her, read the poor girl the riot act until she was in tears. She fled the office sobbing and never returned. Leigh Murphy called her and she flat said she didn't care if they tripled her pay, she was never coming to any office again where I am. Now, in and of itself, that's not a big deal, although Leigh wasn't happy with me. The girl – her name was Haiylee Lewis, spelled H-A-I-Y-L-E-E, for God's sake – was a sweet girl but a dimwit, and aides are a dime a dozen anyway." She fell silent again for a long moment while Josiah waited her out.

"So this morning, I had a patient named Ann Smith, without an 'e,'" Molly continued. "We have another patient named Anne

Smith, with the 'e' on it. They're both the same age, 62 years old. So I got the chart for my patient, and a sheet was in there with orders for the other patient, and I got pissed off. I mean, there are no excuses for mistakes there, but still, it wasn't a huge thing. My patient has one set of conditions and the other patient has an altogether different set, and I'd have had to have been brain-dead to have confused the two, since a hip will never be a wrist. But I went right into Betty Murchison's office – she's handled all medical records there for years now, and other than this, had done a really good job – and I lit into her like a Marine DI, just ate her ass totally. She didn't burst into tears, but she stood up midpoint, told me she was able to retire, and was doing so immediately. She picked up her purse, threw a few personal things into a box, and marched right out."

"I see," Josiah said in an even tone.

"Okay, okay," Molly grumbled. "I know that means 'cut to the chase, already.' Yesterday, shortly after Betty walked off, a memo went out to all the partners in the practice that there was a meeting scheduled for 5:00. I was too busy to give it any thought. But the upshot of it was that I was the subject of the meeting. Leigh said my abusiveness toward subordinates had grown to intolerable proportions. The upshot of it all was that I'm suspended for the next two weeks. After that I am to work a week, and then the partners will meet to decide whether I can remain at the practice or if I am to be fired. If I'm fired, the practice buys out my portion of the partnership – you probably remember all that from the contract – and I'm out in the cold to either establish my own practice or to join another practice. Leigh flat-out said if the choice was hers alone she'd have excluded me a year ago."

"I can see why you're disturbed," Josiah ventured.

"Bullshit," Molly said. "Josiah, your intelligence is why I was always drawn to you, despite all our differences. If you're half as bright as I think you are, you're thinking it's high time I got a comeuppance for my bitchy ways, even as you're wondering what's the next move, right? I'm good at blowing you, but made it plain early in with you that I'm not the slave type, and there will be no discipline or servitude, and anything more intense than you whacking my ass with a ping-pong paddle was off the table, and you can punish those little mattress bunnies sent here to your heart's content so long as you don't fuck them, and if I was standing in your shoes I'd be gleeful and gloating."

"You really think that little of me?" Josiah asked. "That's disappointing, Molly, but I accept that. You'll need a good attorney. Since we're married, it would be a terrible idea for me to represent you —"

"No," Molly interrupted. "I'll accept what the partners decide when they meet about me, good or bad."

"So what is it you need from me?" Josiah asked, confused.

Molly looked away and took a deep breath. She took another breath and then knelt on both knees, and looked him directly in the eyes. "What's happening to Darla and a dozen other unfortunates who've come here," she said. "I'm suspended from the office for the coming two weeks, and I deserve to spend it in penal servitude. I'm asking you to enslave me and … put your mind to work. Teach me my lesson so maybe I can salvage my career in the week I'll have there to prove myself."

"Wow," Josiah said, honestly surprised for the first time in a long time.

"Look, what happened at work was … a lot of shit come to a head, and I've lost all moral right to ride this high horse, abusing those under me and abusing your trust," Molly said.

"My trust?" Josiah asked.

"It's time I came clean," Molly replied. "Christ, you're going to want to whip the skin right off me." She fell silent again, and again, Josiah waited in equal silence, unwilling to prompt her, but taking guesses as to what was going on here, guesses that were indeed hurtful.

"Before we go further, may I go to the bathroom?" Molly asked.

"Yes, you may," Josiah said smoothly. He'd never heard her ask permission for anything before, and sensed a newfound and genuine contrition in her, and wondered what more he was about to learn. Molly gracefully rose and exited the den while Josiah waited, considering and discarding the notion of a glass of Scotch. He sensed this wasn't the time to be drinking.

A moment later, Molly returned, and Josiah gaped in astonishment. She was stark naked and trembling as she handed him steel handcuffs and turned her back to him, offering her wrists to be cuffed. "Mas ... Master, please cuff me before I run out of guts," she said.

"Okay," Josiah answered, and in a moment cuffed her hands behind her back.

"Thank you," Molly said, again in that meek tone Josiah had never heard coming from her. She knelt again, looked him briefly in the eyes, and then looked down at the floor. "Master, now that I'm helpless, it's time to confess. I've ... I've been sleeping around on you for a year now. At first it was a couple of patients, hot young men only happy to get their rocks off with me. And a few hot young women. Mostly it happened in the exam rooms. But two of them became a bit more regular over the last six or so months."

"Jesus Christ," Josiah exclaimed in shock.

"Master, I want a clean break," Molly said. "I'm begging you to do whatever it takes to ensure there's no question in my mind or yours, when I return to the office, that I am utterly owned by you. If you can forgive me and wish to keep me, I would even ask that you brand me like I'm no more to you than a head of cattle. And I … Master, I've lost the right to exact any demands on you. Maybe it would even do me some good to see you fucking someone younger and hotter and prettier than me, to remind me I can be gotten rid of here too."

"Too?" Josiah asked.

"The hard reality is there's only a slim chance I won't be dissociated from the practice in three weeks, Sir. Leigh holds considerable influence – to illustrate, my stake in the practice is around seven percent and hers is about twenty-five percent – so she doesn't need to rally much of a vote to send me away. The contract specifies that the practice cuts me a check for my stake in it within fifteen business days of the dissociation, buying me out, and I'm gone like I was never there, Sir."

"It sounds like you've painted yourself into a corner," Josiah ventured.

"I was willingly swishing the brush, but yes, Sir," Molly said.

"Go wait beside the truck," Josiah ordered. Molly trembled anew, but did as bidden, kneeling in the mud beside the truck as the furious storm's rains chilled her. A few minutes later, Josiah assisted her into the bed of the truck, and then drove off to a far-away clearing on the grounds, where a small cabin was set up along the shore of another pond.

Molly knew this cabin well. Josiah seldom came here, since it was a place to get away from it all, while he considered this entire farm to be a getaway. But Molly spent time out here. The cabin was, in truth, bigger than their house in the city, and more comfortable. But Molly knew, nice as it was, that this was her prison and dungeon for a while. Josiah helped her from the truck and held her arm as she clumsily climbed the steps onto the porch and then into the house.

EIGHT

"I'm going to remove your handcuffs now," Josiah said. "Once I've done that, you will approach that post. I will cuff you to it and give you the first of what I assure you will be many epic lashings."

"Jesus, this is really happening," Molly whispered, barely audibly, as the cuffs came off.

"Yes, it really is," Josiah said. "Approach the post, animal."

"Jesus ... y ... yes... yes, Master," Molly managed to say, approaching the post on trembling legs. She raised her wrists toward iron rings embedded in the post, rings Josiah had told her were probably originally placed for lanterns. But he'd mentioned to her then that they'd be handy for bondage as required, and she'd chuckled, telling him not for her. She couldn't find amusement in this irony, but recognized the irony nonetheless.

Josiah cuffed her wrists to the rings, using an extra set of cuffs he'd brought, and then used long belts to strap her to the post at her thighs, calves, and lower back, sticking her tightly in place while she closed her eyes and tried to find strength to endure what she admitted even to herself was sure to be far less than she deserved.

"You couldn't survive what you deserve, not all in one session," Josiah said. "But you are under two weeks of penal servitude that I will extend as I deem necessary. Is there a problem with this?"

"No, Master ... I deserve no say in my fate, Sir," Molly said in a quavering voice.

"You will be horsewhipped forty lashes right now, and I will then bend you over for a fifty-lash caning, after which I intend on buggering you before putting you in confinement for the evening," Josiah said. "Do you request a gag?"

"I ... I do, Master," Molly whispered, near terror at his sentence, but reminding herself again that she deserved worse than he would ever do to her. Just then, Josiah's phone rang and he looked curiously at the screen to see the number was from the medical practice.

"Don't go anywhere," Josiah said, and walked to the study and answered the call.

NINE

"This is Leigh Murphy," Josiah heard.

"What can I do for you, Dr. Murphy?" Josiah asked a bit warily.

"Can we meet and talk privately?" she asked.

"About?" Josiah asked.

"About Molly, and about me, you ... a lot of things," Murphy said. "Mr. Bailey, she's been ... well, I'd really rather not discuss this over the phone."

"It's apparently so important that you're calling me from the office on a Saturday night," Josiah ventured.

"I think we should talk," Murphy repeated.

"Well, perhaps we should," Josiah agreed. "I'm —"

"At your ranch outside of town," Murphy interrupted.

"Yes, in fact, I am," Josiah agreed. "I gather you know where it is, then?"

"I do," Murphy confirmed. "Is Molly still there too?"

"She won't be near us," Josiah said. "She's in a separate cabin right now."

"Twenty minutes?" Murphy asked.

43

"That works," Josiah said, and hung up. He went into the main living room of the cabin.

"This will have to wait for a time," he said. "Can I trust you'll be here and cooperative, or are you going to bolt on me?"

"I swear I'll be here, Master," Molly answered. "If you wish to bind me, I deserve it, but I will take what you give, Sir."

"Then remain here, on your knees," Josiah ordered. "If you need to use the john, hold it or let it go right where you are, but you are to remain on your knees on that spot, animal. Understood?"

"Yes, Master," Molly said. "I … thank you for giving me this chance, Master. I love you. I hope someday I'll deserve your love."

"Time will tell," Josiah said. He went out to the truck and drove through the pouring rain to the main house, glad the truck was a four-wheel-drive since he suspected he'd need it if the rain kept up much longer. Making a mental note to call his secretary Monday and cancel appointments for the coming two weeks, he parked the truck and went into the house, removing his shoes in the mud room and then going to the kitchen to build a pot of coffee that instinct told him he'd want before long. While it brewed, he changed into dry clothes before catching a chill.

"Thank you for letting me come see you," Murphy said when she arrived. "Lord, it's not fit for man nor beast out there tonight, is it?"

"I shook off like a dog a while ago," Josiah said, chuckling. "Look, you're a bit smaller than Molly, so if you want to change into something dry, I think she's got a dozen scrub suits here, even. We could toss your clothes in the dryer before you catch a chill in here."

"Interesting hospitality, offering me the chance to get naked out here in the middle of nowhere," she said, and flashed a disarming grin. "But yes, I think I'll take you up on that offer, Mr. Bailey."

"Josiah, please," Josiah said.

"Only if you call me Leigh," she returned.

"Deal," Josiah agreed. "Let me show you her wardrobe."

Ten minutes later, Josiah heard the dryer start, and then Leigh returned, wearing a light blue scrub suit and, so far as Josiah could tell – there were no tell-tale panty-lines or bra-lines under the thin fabric – nothing else, not even shoes. He wondered if she'd come here to seduce him or exactly what her angle was.

"There's coffee, tea, sodas, or if you want something stronger, plenty of goodies in the bar here," he said.

"I shouldn't, but ... I will," Leigh said, going to the bar and pouring a healthy glass of Jim Beam and tossing in a few ice cubes. "That way I can try to persuade myself it was the liquor made me do it."

"This sounds ... interesting," Josiah said.

"Josiah, do you know about Molly being in trouble at the practice?" Leigh asked.

"She told me she's suspended two weeks, due back to work a week, and then there will be a meeting as to whether to separate her from the practice," Josiah answered.

"She's always been ... bitchy ... but this past year or so she's moved toward insufferable," Leigh remarked. "I figure you're her master, and should be kept up-to-speed on how she's behaving, so you can address it directly with her."

"Wow," Josiah said. "What leads you to these conclusions, Leigh?"

Leigh sighed and took a long swallow of her whiskey, and then set the glass aside. "I have a lot I need to tell you, and I hope you hear me all the way through before you lose your temper and send me away."

"Lay it out there," Josiah said, looking her in the eye.

"I learned about you two being in BDSM by happenstance, and asked a few questions around the community, where I learned you're a well-respected dominant, and that you work as a beadle – lovely blonde you have stashed in that barn, by the way – and then I'm afraid I ... and this is where I am in deep trouble ... I got snoopy and crossed lines."

"Keep going," Josiah said evenly after she paused for a long moment. "Obviously I need to beef up the fence here."

"Yes, Sir," she said. "My curiosity got the better of me. I guess it makes me a good doctor, but not necessarily a good person. I hired a PI to look into you and Molly, and to follow you for ... several ... weekends. You two seemed to come here a lot, often with this slave or that. The ownership of the property is really convoluted, but I have to admit, cleverly handled, by the way. Yes, I've been on your property here a few times, including this morning."

"So what brings you here now?" Josiah asked. "If you're trying to blackmail us —"

"On the contrary," Leigh interrupted. "Look, I'm here because ... Jesus, this is going to take some explaining." She paused and took a breath, exhaled, took another, and exhaled again. "I guess I'm what you'd call a switch, Josiah. I'm not really dominant, but have one young man and one young woman who bottom to me, but ... I enjoy it, but it's not entirely for me, and they're both irregular trysts. I guess you could call them booty calls, even. I have a dom online who lives several hours away. Or maybe he's simply my judge? When I fuck up – which is too often, and I think he's grown tired of me – he sentences me and I have to go to a local dominatrix to be punished to his sentence. Three weeks ago it was eighty strokes of the cane and four hours upright on my knees, for instance."

"Intense," Josiah allowed.

"The marks only faded a few days ago," Leigh confirmed. She shook her head. "I think the marks from this matter will be longer lasting."

"If you came here asking me to intervene or petition your … your judge … for lenience, you're barking up the wrong tree," Josiah said. He maintained a calm demeanor but was furious with this woman. "If you're trying to leverage it with Molly's career, still the wrong tree," he added.

"Neither," Leigh returned. "Sir, he ordered me to come to you, confess, and submit to your punishment, whatever you determine is right or fair, for the coming week that I'm on vacation from work. I had it scheduled for several months and was going to take a longish road trip, but … well, here I am. The residents at the practice should be delighted to ply their trade with two attending physicians out of the office. The truth is, I think he doesn't have much interest in me, Sir, and I think he's hopeful that you'll decide you want me entirely, or that you'll beat me so badly I decide I want out of this lifestyle, but I guess if you return me to him, he's honorable enough to take me back and not leave me in the cold."

"And who is this luminary who's punted you onto my field?" Josiah wanted to know.

"His name is Blake Rogers," Leigh said, and produced an index card from her pocket, handing it to him. "This is his phone number and e-mail address. He figured you might be surprised and want to discuss this with him."

"I only might, huh?" Josiah remarked. He stood and went to a closet, and produced a set of handcuffs, earplugs, earmuffs, and a blindfold. Leigh's eyes widened and she trembled, but she faced him. "I'm going to cuff you, deafen you, and blind you, so you don't snoop around or sneak off while I speak with your judge, and then I'll decide what to do with you, which may well include simply having you arrested for criminal trespass."

"I understand, Sir," Leigh said. In a moment, she was cuffed and on her knees, and then the earplugs went in her ears, the blindfold went over her eyes, and the muffs went over her ears. Josiah placed her on her belly on a sofa, and tied her ankles together. She was going nowhere. That done, he went into his study and dialed the number on the card.

TEN

"Hello," a deep male voice answered on the second ring. "Would you be Mr. Bailey?"

"I am," Josiah said.

"I am Blake Rogers," the man responded. "It's a pleasure to 'meet' you, so to speak. I gather Leigh is there and has made a clean breast of everything?"

"You may assume so," Josiah said. "I suppose I'm trying to get confirmation."

"She said the word on you is you don't like discussing things by phone, and I completely get that," Rogers remarked. "I'd like to e-mail some things to you, then, if I may."

"Sure," Josiah said. "It's Beadle.Bailey@usa.com if you wish to send something."

"Moment, please," Rogers said. Josiah could hear the rapid typing on the other end. "Okay, you have mail, Mr. Bailey."

"Before I review what you sent, will you tell me why you don't just take her on?" Josiah asked. "She's beyond beautiful and obviously smart as hell. She tells me she thinks you hope I take her on as mine, ultimately."

"She's perceptive too," Rogers observed. "Mr. Bailey, I'm dying of the cancer here. They don't know what's brought it on, but there's not a damn thing they can do for it. The docs say if I'm lucky

I have about eight months left. Frankly, I hope I'm highly unlucky and have only about a day or two. I haven't told her this for ... well, for a variety of reasons ... but it's better if I'm in her past."

"Regrettable," Josiah said.

"We're all born so that God can stomp us like cockroaches on some cosmic dance floor," Rogers said with a sardonic chuckle. "But I hope part of your punishment of her is that she's yours for at least the coming year, perhaps two years. She knows I'm not interested in her 'that way,' and she thinks I'm married – I'm not married and she'd be shocked to learn I'm actually homosexual – so I saw to it that she never grew emotionally invested in me, Mr. Bailey. Besides, I've required videos of her other sessions. I agree, she's lovely, even smoking hot, but nothing that would appeal to me. I'm sure you understand."

"I'll keep that in mind," Josiah said.

"Mr. Bailey, I've been an observer of the human condition and people in general my whole life," Rogers said. "I've never met anyone more devoted or more in need of what it is you offer. I know your wife works with her, but ... well, some things aren't for me to say. But Leigh wants to serve the two of you. I think you'll find her taste for servitude and discipline and humiliation runs deep. I think that's why she did what she did with regard to you and your Molly. She wanted to give you very good reason to break and enslave her. I think she'd give up everything, even her career, for the right master, Mr. Bailey. I know her earning potential is probably small potatoes in your view, so I'm not so concerned about any avarice on your part ..." he chuckled "... even if you are a lawyer."

"I'll keep that in mind as well," Josiah said.

"Review what I sent you in e-mail, Mr. Bailey," Rogers said. "But feel free to call me back any time if you have questions or want advice. But give me about thirty minutes to run to the john and whack up with some more drugs. I'm not sure if the morphine or marijuana works better, but both together are really soothing. The marijuana is illegal as hell here, but the courts are so slow that I'd be dead most of a year before my case came up."

"Yeah, we lawyers like it like that," Josiah agreed. "Passions and memories aren't as sharp, mistakes get made, and the innocent aren't wrongly convicted."

Rogers snorted amusement at this. "Take care, Mr. Bailey, and thank you for this," he said, and ended the call.

Josiah brought up his e-mail and saw that Rogers had sent him a trainload of varying files. One was a document of Leigh's offenses going back the four years he had supervised her. Josiah counted the entries and found fifty-one, which averaged once monthly, and considered that she was habitual in her offenses. Three were to do with moving violations in traffic, including one epic ticket for driving forty over the limit in her Mercedes. Josiah wondered how she managed to keep her license after that, but she somehow did. That particular offense cost her $800.00 in fines and found her paying it off with a dollar-a-lash caning that went through twenty sessions administered by Madam Lucretia every Monday, Wednesday and Saturday until her punishment was fully applied. Any missed sessions – he saw there were two of these, one documented as a work emergency and the other weather-related – meant the lashes tripled in the following session from forty to one hundred twenty. And by the look of it, she was punished a dollar per lash and paid Lucretia roughly two bucks per lash for doing the job. It was an expensive ticket indeed. Josiah tapped on his ten-key and saw that across her four years, Lucretia had laid roughly 5,000 cane strokes to Leigh in addition to other punishments, including one harsh flogging of fifty lashes laid to Leigh's naked back, and other variants of paddle, strap, and even an old-school birching to Leigh's breasts and belly. Each offense report began with a scan of a typed and printed confession and request of punishment from Leigh, and signed by her. She kept these in a file at her home, Rogers noted, and suggested she hand the folder over to him.

There were several photos of Leigh bound and bearing marks, including a full frontal shot of the birching, which had left her scratched and bleeding in a few places. That photo included her red face, tear-streaked with snot dripping from her nose. Josiah found himself aroused looking at the photos, and then opened the video of a caning delivered to Leigh eight months before, a session of one hundred strokes for snooping on a man that interested her.

Josiah knew Lucretia, and had even seen her in action. At one session in a public dungeon, she had whipped her slave Tony, a muscular and handsome specimen, until he screamed for mercy. He'd heard later that she'd taken him to a gay S&M party and tied him bent over with a box of condoms beside him and left him there several hours in a free-for-all. Tony wasn't only straight, but had been known for his homophobia. There had been, before that night three years before, a certain arrogant swagger to Tony that had been entirely absent ever since. Lucretia had thoroughly broken the man. Lucretia, at about 6'3", was a tall and beautiful black woman. Josiah remembered hearing she'd played in the WNBA for three or four seasons back when, but left when she saw that pay wasn't near what she could get doing other things, like being a professional dominatrix. He filed these thoughts aside and turned his attention to the loaded video.

"Get in here," Lucretia snarled. "Little Miss High and Mighty is in trouble again, isn't she?"

"Yes, Ma'am," Leigh said, off camera. And then she stepped into view, wearing what Josiah saw was a paper scrub suit, tear-away and disposable. Leigh knelt before Lucretia, and looked at the floor, Josiah guessed at some point between the mistress' feet.

"Out in the world you might be some sort of a big shot, but in here, you're just a slave who's really not worth even feeding," Lucretia sneered. "Your master doesn't want you. You're an albatross around his neck, Miss High and Mighty. He even asked me about selling you on his behalf – Asian buyers are a hot market for slim and pretty blondes – but I told him you'd wreck my reputation with your untamed behavior. I'm sick of you and so is your master, so I have to tell you I'm going to enjoy beating you today. A hundred strokes of the cane. That should make your ass swell up nicely. I'm going to do my best to make you bleed, girl. What are you?"

"I'm a worthless cunt, Miss," Leigh said in a meek tone, one that surprised Josiah. While he'd had little interaction with her, he'd always found her to be rather bold. In Lucretia's dungeon, she reminded him of a scared dog showing its belly to its betters.

"That's right, and I'm going to enjoy bringing you down," Lucretia sneered.

"I know, Miss," Leigh said in a low and shamed voice.

"I don't even know why I bother reprimanding you," Lucretia said. "You're like a stupid sheep that keeps getting in the same trouble over and over again. Stand up!"

Leigh stood and Lucretia forced her over a bench, and then strapped her in place, still in the paper scrub suit. Josiah wondered after that, but left the curiosity to the side. He knew and liked Lucretia, and was certain she had her reasons. In minutes, those reasons became clearer as the caning began, each lash punctuated by an agonized howl from the victim. The paper garment wasn't designed for these stresses, and soon split open, revealing glimpses of welted rump. Lucretia, meanwhile, was remorseless and machine-like in her lashing of Leigh, whose right buttock soon turned purple under the persistent assault of the cane. The lashing wore the pants away as Leigh's rump swelled under the caning. At around fifty strokes, the woman stopped crying and wailing, only grunting with each lash, broken of her tears, even.

Finally, the last lash cut into the tatters and fibers of Leigh's pants, and Lucretia idly wiped the cane and set it aside before unbinding the hapless slave. But even so, it wasn't over for Leigh. Lucretia grasped her hair and pulled her down to a kneel.

"Your dom wanted you buggered, buggered hard, to drive this lesson home, but I can't do that without violating prostitution laws," she said. "So you're going to get a big ass plug in you, and you're going to do the dirty work, and it stays in you for twenty-four hours or until he lets you remove it. I'm going to lubricate it and put it on this low stool. You're going to position yourself where the tip is just inside you, and then on my command you're going to fall on it, let your weight force it up into you, cunt."

"Oh, God," Leigh whispered. "Yes, Miss."

"And to ensure compliance, you'll be my guest in a cell here for that duration," Lucretia continued, as though Leigh hadn't spoken at all. She set an impressive plug on a short stool, and on her command, Leigh positioned herself for impalement. On the next command, Leigh screamed as she threw her legs forward, letting gravity do its evil. She sobbed for a long moment and then Lucretia ordered the woman onto all fours and had her crawl into a cage. A plate was on the floor of the cage with some sort of goop Josiah correctly guessed was pureed food, and another with water. Leigh's hands were cuffed behind her back and she was left alone in the cage, where she slept at first, too spent to do much else. And there, the video ended.

"Wow," Josiah said to himself. Leigh was obviously a discipline seeker with self-control issues, he reflected. Already, he knew Molly would approve of him doing what he wanted with her. He was debating how to proceed when his phone rang again.

"Grand Central, this is Josiah," he answered, guessing this call was also to do with Leigh.

"This is Lucretia, Josiah," Lucretia said. "Blake just called me and suggested you and I should talk. Can we meet?"

"Yeah, if you feel like braving the storm to come out to the farm," Josiah allowed. "I have three charges here and I shouldn't leave the grounds."

"Jesus, you're busier than I am," Lucretia chuckled. "What the hell, I'm only fifteen minutes from there. Do you need me to bring anything?"

"Only yourself," Josiah said. "I'm getting hungry and about to throw a nuke 'em dinner in the microwave. If you're hungry —"

"How about if I bring supper?" she interrupted. "My boy cooked enough to feed an army. We were supposed to have a get-together here tonight but the rain ..."

"That would be good," Josiah said.

"Fifteen minutes," Lucretia repeated.

ELEVEN

"Thanks for letting us come over," Lucretia said as she entered Josiah's living room. He had removed Leigh to an upstairs room, still deaf and blind, so he could meet with Lucretia out of her earshot. Josiah smiled and hugged Lucretia and nodded to her boy Tony, who generally wasn't permitted to speak or shake hands with his betters, which was virtually everybody, in Lucretia's view. Built along the lines of an NFL linebacker he had once aspired to be, he was completely broken and in her thrall.

"So let's talk," Josiah said.

"First, let's eat, please," Lucretia suggested. "Tony cooked a good meal and I'm half-starved."

"Sounds good," Josiah agreed.

The dinner, served by Tony on Josiah's plates, was indeed amazing, grilled pork chops, grilled asparagus, baked potatoes and corn on the cob, all followed by key lime pie that Tony had made. Josiah raved about it, and Tony smiled, flattered.

"He has a talent in the kitchen," Lucretia allowed. "Jesus, I'd be the size of this house if I had him cook like this all the time. Tony, clear the table and wash the dishes while we discuss business."

"It will be done, Mistress," Tony said in a hoarse voice, the first words he'd spoken since arrival.

"Shall we repair to my study?" Josiah asked, and Lucretia nodded.

"I feel badly about this," Lucretia said a moment later in the study. "Leigh … she's complex and complicated."

"I noticed," Josiah said.

"So she asked about you and Molly, and I figured she was just curious," Lucretia went on. "So I told her about you two, what little I know, that is. I was furious with her when Blake called me to tell me she'd stalked you and all the rest, but pleased that he handed her off to you to deal with her as you see fit."

"Oh, it runs deeper than that," Josiah said.

"I'm almost afraid to ask," Lucretia remarked.

"We don't talk much about what we do, so I'll ask you up-front, do you know what Leigh does for a living?"

"I figure it has to pay well, considering the car she drives, but no," Lucretia answered.

"She is a physician," Josiah said. "So is Molly. They're both shareholders in the same medical office."

"Holy shit," Lucretia muttered. "I knew Molly was a doctor, but only that much. I know you're a lawyer, for that matter. I'd no idea about Leigh."

"We tend to be private even with one another," Josiah remarked. "In any event, she saw us at a dungeon event but I never saw her, and I think Molly would've said something if she'd seen Leigh there. So Leigh … anyway, it sounds like she's at least honest when she realizes she needs to confess. She's upstairs in a blindfold and earplugs, handcuffed. I didn't tell her you're coming here. She knows I spoke with Blake, but not what was said. He's indicated he thinks it'd be best if she remained under my supervision."

"He's dying with some kind of cancer, he told me a few months ago," Lucretia said. "I think he'd rather pass her off to someone now — he offered her to me, but I didn't want her, I'm only seldom into women except for income — than up and die on her and leave her wondering what the hell happened with him."

"I suppose it never occurred to anyone to ask me first," Josiah said, but he didn't editorialize.

"If I'd known I would have given you a warning," Lucretia said. "I thought back on it and she was casual enough in asking about you and Molly that I honestly figured it was just idle curiosity, but I had no idea she already knew Molly, which would have been — it obviously was — a game-changer."

"I can't blame you for it," Josiah said after a detectable pause. "Shit, I have no idea how Molly's going to see this." He debated inwardly with himself, and then looked into Lucretia's eyes. "I'm not asking you to tell me what to do here, because the decisions are entirely mine, but … can I trust in your confidentiality?"

"Give me a dollar," Lucretia said. Josiah, chuckling, reached into his billfold, didn't find a single or even a five, and handed her a ten.

"Time for me to flip up a card," Lucretia said. "When I left basketball, I used that money to go to law school, and became an attorney. I didn't like being an attorney, but I have found that shield … useful … in what I do now. So you're now my client and I'm honor-bound not to reveal jack-shit you tell me to anyone. And I owe you nine bucks. It's in my purse out in the car." She chuckled and flashed him a bright and disarming grin.

"Maybe I should've partnered up with you a couple years ago," Josiah chuckled. "I've had more than one client who needed a woman more than a man —"

"Vice versa, as witness Leigh," Lucretia interjected. "She seriously needs a dom, a master, to yank her into place and keep her there. I think if Blake wasn't ill, he'd be just the guy to do it – he told me he told you about the cancer, or I couldn't have told you, by the way – but he's pushing up daisies too soon, and I admire him for doing his best to try to cut her loose without hurting her heart or sacrificing his privacy to her. God knows what she'd do if she thought she could rush up to him with a basket of chemo."

"She wouldn't," Josiah offered. "So long as it's just us lawyers talking ... give me a dollar since we're both staying honest here." Lucretia handed him back his ten, and Josiah chuckled. "Okay, now that we're both on retainer to one another and can blab to our heart's content ... they're in a sports medicine clinic. They deal with healthy people who are hurt, not with the aged or infirm. Molly loves it, but admits it's not always so challenging since it tends to be straightforward stuff they do there. On the other hand, there are few complications since most of the clients are under fifty. It also means she's very capable of treating our clientele out here."

"Blake says Leigh told him you're entertaining a particularly tasty guest out here this weekend," Lucretia smirked. "He thinks she got somewhat of a girl crush on your guest."

"She goes home in the morning," Josiah said. "But yeah, she's a beauty."

"Gotta be hard not to fuck them," Lucretia ventured. "I've met many of your clients – people talk, sometimes too much – and a number of them are incredibly sexy ones, male and female."

"Well, it wouldn't be a good idea, for a wide range of reasons, although I agree that in a vacuum, I can think of twenty or more I'd fuck in a heartbeat, if there were no consequences," Josiah returned. "It'd be fun for the moment, but emotions get in the way, to say nothing of rape allegations or prostitution allegations and jealousy ...

it's not worth the headaches just to get my rocks off, especially when Molly is always willing to relieve those urges."

"Then I guess you're living the dream," Lucretia said. "How is Molly going to feel about all this with Leigh?"

"That, my dear, is anyone's guess," Josiah said. "She's sure to be furious about Leigh's intrusions, and their relationship is ... touchy ... recently. It's to the point that Molly might sell out of her share of the practice and seek a new venture."

"Jesus, it sounds like you got handed a bomb," Lucretia said.

"Potentially," Josiah agreed. "I'm usually good at knowing how Molly will think or regard a situation, but on this ... all bets are off, Lucretia. I think I'd be as wise betting at craps. I can easily see a half-dozen scenarios on how Molly will handle this news, and they're probably all wrong guesses."

"Look, I have nowhere to be until late tomorrow afternoon, a 5:45 with a client," Lucretia said. "If you need me to stay and moderate or referee this, in case it gets out of hand, I can. I'll just send Tony to wait in the car until things settle out."

"Let me consider that," Josiah said. "I don't want to get too deeply into it, but ... Molly turned submissive on me right before this shit with Leigh came to my attention. It's a long story, but that's one hell of a big change already without throwing Leigh into the mix. Let's complicate this even further, why don't we? The apparent signal event that triggered this sea change in Molly involves the issue with Leigh."

"Do you think they orchestrated it somehow or another?" Lucretia asked.

"Usually the simplest answer, in this case 'no,' is the correct one," Josiah said. "At the same time, I generally don't hold much faith in coincidence. But I'm leaning 70/30 toward 'no' on this one."

"Makes sense," Lucretia said.

"Do you want to see Leigh?" Josiah asked.

"She's blindfolded and ear-muffed right now?" Lucretia asked.

"Yep," Josiah confirmed.

"Why not wait until the big reveal?" Lucretia suggested. "I assume Molly is elsewhere on the grounds?"

"Yeah, she's in a guest house here – a nice cabin, actually, and supposed to be waiting naked on her knees."

"I don't think you want to walk in this Godawful weather," Lucretia said.

"We can put Leigh in the bed of that beat-up old truck out front," Josiah said. "Sometimes slaves need to be made miserable, and I don't know many people who like being out in a harsh storm like this one."

"I like that idea," Lucretia offered. "Let me tell Tony to stay in the kitchen."

TWELVE

Leigh was cooperative as she was stashed in the bed of the truck as the storm raged, although she squeaked a bit as thunder struck nearby, piercing through the sound-deadening qualities of her earplugs and muffs. Once she was in the bed of the truck, Josiah and Lucretia got into the cab and closed the doors in unison, and Josiah fired up the old motor and drove slowly through rain and mud to the guest house.

Josiah went into the guest house and found Molly still on her knees, but fidgeting. He hurriedly blindfolded her, and then put plugs in her ears and muffs over her ears, and then gestured to Lucretia to lead Leigh inside. Lucretia stopped Leigh on the porch and cut her scrub suit to tatters, making her as naked as Molly, and then led her into the house and put her on her knees, four feet from Molly.

At Josiah's gesture, the muffs and plugs came off of both women. "Silence," Josiah commanded, and neither woman spoke.

"Nod or shake your head when I ask a question," Josiah spoke again. "Understood?" Both penitents nodded.

"Did you act alone?" Josiah asked. "Shake your head if the answer is no, or nod if the answer is yes. God help you if and when I learned there's a lie."

He watched as Leigh first, and then Molly, nodded.

"Are there ulterior motives you're trying to conceal from me in some attempt to saddle me with a *fait accompli?*" Josiah asked next. Both physicians shook their heads. Molly looked genuinely confused.

"Fascinating," Josiah remarked. He stepped behind Molly, and beckoned to Lucretia to remove Leigh's blindfold at the same time he removed Molly's, and heard Molly gasp as she saw Leigh, and then moan as she realized she was naked and bound before her colleague and nemesis.

"What is this?" Molly sputtered, sounding angry.

"Molly, Leigh came over with somewhat of a confession," Josiah said. "It seems she's been snooping into our business and even stalking us. She apparently has been sneaking onto the property and has even seen some of our activities with our guest out in the barn."

"I'm … I'm here to be punished, Molly," Leigh said. "I made a complete confession to Josiah, and will serve a term of at least the coming week here, punished as he sees fit to do. It's a long story, but I'm here at the orders of my dom."

"Your dom?" Molly echoed. "Fascinating." She sighed and looked at Josiah. "Master, this is what I deserve, and I have no right to object to anything you choose to do. I told you that and I'm sticking to it."

"I'm … what's going on here?" Leigh asked.

"Molly made her own confessions to me tonight, and is now enslaved to me," Josiah said. "Among other surrenders she has made, I now have sexual freedom, or the freedom to add on slaves."

"My dom won't object to anything," Leigh said. "I think he's honestly hoping you just keep me, Sir. So … I'm yours sexually as well, Josiah. Am I to call you Master for this coming week?"

Josiah was surprised to see Lucretia nodding from behind

Leigh, but decided to take her advice. "Yes, you are, slave," he said.

"Thank you … Master," Leigh said softly, and Josiah saw a tear leaking from her eye.

"You're welcome," Josiah said automatically. "I understand from Blake and from Lucretia that you require frequent and vigorous whippings."

"I … Master, I doubt I'll be a problem after this," Leigh said.

"Why is that?" Josiah pursued.

"Sir, for the first time in my life I'll be punished by the person I've wronged, for one," Leigh said. "And … Master, my spying on you was despicable, but it's resulted in me gaining huge respect for you. Miss Lucretia is harsh on me, and I'm fond of her, but that's commerce, just business. I guess it's no different than what you're doing to that slave out in the barn. Lucretia … it's not from her heart, I guess. I'm saying this poorly, but … she doesn't really care how I behave."

"And you think I'm going to love you?" Josiah asked.

"Master, for now, I need you to hate me, to treat me like dirt, even to whip me bloody, and … I'm begging you to use me hard, work me hard, punish me hard … and fuck me hard."

"Bet on it," Josiah said. "You slaves are both going to have your assholes widened."

"Master, may I be prepared with a plug to loosen me?" Leigh asked.

"Me too, Master," Molly chimed in. "Leigh, he's a horny one most all of the time. A year ago he came eight times in one day, and three times a day isn't at all unusual with him. We're going to get ridden. Or, well, you're younger and prettier, so you'll get ridden, at least."

"Not to worry, Molly," Josiah said. "You'll get plenty too, slave."

"Yes, Master," Molly said.

"Okay, if you both need plugs, I need to go to the big house to retrieve them," Josiah said. Since sometimes slaves came for his services with no equipment at all, Josiah had a stockpile of items he had purchased, which he invoiced to clients at cost-plus-twenty-percent. He had all kinds of gear in one big bedroom of the big house, which had become his storeroom.

"Master, if I may?" Molly asked. Josiah gestured for her to speak. "Sir, I ... I took the liberty of bringing a lot of items to this house in anticipation of this. I didn't double the items, since I didn't know about Leigh, but I figured I would be buggered. I brought a stash of plugs and lube, Sir, as well as canes, whips ... I'm sorry. I was so nervous I forgot to tell you, Master."

"Slaves, stand up," Josiah ordered. He assisted Molly and Lucretia assisted Leigh. Josiah removed Molly's cuffs, and Lucretia dipped into her pocket and came up with a handcuff key for Leigh, and removed her cuffs.

"Which room?" Josiah asked Molly.

"Up the stairs, the bedroom at the head of the stairs, Master," Molly said.

"Lucretia, a moment of privacy, please?" Josiah asked. Lucretia nodded and the two went up the stairs to the room Molly had designated.

"Because of a variety of reasons, I want to make a sisterhood of those two," Josiah said a moment later when they were upstairs. "Unfortunately for one or both of them, that is going to mean a little bit of trickery."

"Let me guess," Lucretia said. "You want each of them to choose a plug, but they learn too late that they chose their sister's plug, right?"

"Yep," Josiah said, not at all surprised at how perceptive Lucretia was. It was hardly inspired thinking when dealing with two slaves.

"I'll take Leigh first, and will hide her choice until you're ready to unravel it for them," Lucretia said.

"Good enough," Josiah returned.

They went down the stairs and Leigh, unsurprisingly, chose a plug that was large, larger than Josiah's erection. And then Josiah led Molly up the stairs. "Choose one," Josiah ordered.

Molly looked over the collection of plugs, and finally selected a mid-sized plug, on that wasn't as tiny as a suppository, but would never be mistaken for a hard erection. *Tough luck for Leigh, but not surprising this was Molly's choice,* he considered as he put her chosen plug into a bag and led Molly down the stairs.

"You two are going to have to learn to get along with one another, and to become sisters, for at least the coming week that Leigh is here, and longer, should I decide to extend Leigh's punishment or to include her in my life beyond," Josiah announced. "You each chose the plug that will go into your sister. Leigh chose a very large one for you, Molly. It's going to hurt going into you, I won't lie. But at the same time, it'll make things more pleasant on both of us when I do bugger you. As you've said, I tend to be a horny one, so it's entirely possible I'll bugger both of you tonight. Leigh, Molly chose a somewhat smaller plug for you. It will be more comfortable, but I'm afraid it'll make things rougher for you when I bugger you later. Molly, I saw Leigh take a plug by impaling herself, falling onto it to force it into her. I'll give you the choice of that, or having it harshly rammed into you."

"Rammed, please, Master," Molly said. "That way the choice is rightly out of my hands."

"All fours," Josiah ordered, and Molly swallowed as her eyes widened, but she obeyed, arching her back to tilt her bottom up in an offering.

"I'm ... I'm ready, Master," she said.

"Leigh, hurt her," Josiah ordered.

"Jesus ... y ... yes, Master," Leigh said. She knelt down behind Molly. "I'm sorry, Molly."

"Stop!" Josiah ordered, and Leigh looked at him in confusion.

"May I interject?" Lucretia asked, and Josiah nodded.

"Both of you slaves listen up, because what I'm about to say is liable to solve a lot of grief for you two as things progress," Lucretia began. "You are to be as sisters, and loyal to one another for that, but your first and greatest loyalty is to your master. So when you told Molly you were sorry, you were disrespecting your master in so doing, Leigh. He knows you're about to hurt Molly. He ordered you to do so, and Molly deserves no apology. You two are slaves being punished, and you'd best both warm up to that in a huge hurry."

"Yes, Ma'am," Molly said.

"Yes, Miss," Leigh chimed in.

"Leigh, stand up and bend over the back of that sofa," Josiah said, unbuckling his belt.

"I deserve it, Master," Leigh said, and bent over as ordered.

"You'd best not move a muscle," Josiah said. "If you evade, there will be a horsewhipping for you tonight, slave."

"Yes, Master," Leigh said. Josiah lashed her with the belt, making a loud smacking sound as Leigh hissed in pain. Josiah whipped Leigh nine more strokes and then buckled his belt. He shot a glance at Lucretia and saw she looked transfixed, mesmerized by the scene, and wondered after that.

"Recover and hurt Molly now," Josiah ordered.

Leigh stood, weepy and red-faced, and nodded. She knelt behind Molly, who was trembling, and lubricated the intruder. She parted Molly's buttocks and put just the tip into her bottom, and realized how she should do this to please Josiah as she positioned herself, placing the base of the plug over her pelvic bone and then thrusting her hips forward, hard, and forcing the plug into her sister, who screamed out and began sobbing. But to Molly's credit, Josiah noted, she didn't beg for mercy or make an objection.

"Thank you, Master and Sister," Molly managed to say. "Sir, may I kiss my sister to show her my gratitude?"

"You may," Josiah said. Molly rose and knee-walked to Leigh, and cradled Leigh's face in her hands, and then tenderly kissed the woman.

"Thank you for helping to discipline me, Sister," Molly said.

"You're … you're welcome," Leigh returned. Josiah didn't miss the red flush on Leigh's upper chest, nor a similar flush on Molly's. If he had to guess, something quite similar was going on with Lucretia as well, judging by her facial expression.

"Leigh, position yourself to be plugged," Josiah ordered, and in a moment Leigh was face-down-ass-up. "Molly, force it into her."

Molly did to Leigh what had been done to herself, but the plug slipped a bit and the base got Molly's clitoris, and she instantly arched her back, nipples pointing toward the ceiling, and shuddered her way through an intense orgasm.

"Ooooh God!" Leigh cried out, understanding what had happened, and she suddenly curled into a fetal position as she erupted with her own orgasm, cumming so hard that the plug shot out of her bottom.

"You two really need to learn better control," Josiah said. "Girls being punished are not to climax, are they?"

"I'm ...Master, I'm sorry," Leigh said.

"May I have a moment with you?" Lucretia asked Josiah.

THIRTEEN

"You suddenly have three very horny women on your hands, big guy," Lucretia said in the upstairs room. "Right about now I want to rip your clothes off and fuck you until one of us dies."

"I don't think I'd object," Josiah chuckled.

"Here's what I have in mind, if you're game ..." Lucretia began. She spoke for several minutes while Josiah nodded, feeling harder and harder. He liked how she thought, and figured it would be of huge benefit to everyone here.

"You're sure?" he asked.

"Josiah, I don't get the need to bottom very often, but it's there in me and rises up from time to time. It did tonight," Lucretia said. "Ordinarily, when that happens, I go see another dominatrix I know and she puts me through my paces. I do the same for her once in a while. But that involves an airplane ride, you know. Besides, this property is your kingdom. Visiting royalty still is subject to your law, right? Besides, it'll do Tony good too, I think."

"Okay," Josiah said. "I'm ... let's run by the barn because I want to look in on our charge, and then we'll go get Tony."

Out on the porch, Lucretia stripped naked and offered her wrists behind her back for cuffing. Josiah cuffed her and walked her toward the truck and helped her into the bed, and they drove off toward the barn. He parked the truck outside the barn so the rain would continue to fall on Lucretia, and then went into the barn to look in on Darla. She was sleeping and the IV seemed to be flowing well into her. He decided not to wake her, and went back out to the truck. Lightning flashed bright and close, followed a split-second later by a mighty boom of thunder, and chuckled as Lucretia cried out in surprise and maybe a bit of fear.

He drove to the big house where he found Tony kneeling in the living room. "A message from your mistress," Josiah said, and handed Tony an envelope with a letter in it from Lucretia.

Tony's brows rose in surprise as he read the letter. "Mistress is in trouble, Sir?" he asked.

"She is," Josiah confirmed. "You saw the letter and I read it before she put it in the envelope. Now, are you going to give me trouble, boy?"

"No ... Jesus ... no, Master," Tony said. The letter had told him that Lucretia offended Josiah and that she agreed all on his land should be subject to his law, and she was to be punished, and he was to witness it and do nothing to interfere, on pain of his own punishment. Tony had awful memories of being a glory hole at a gay dungeon club not nearly long enough in the past, and would obey his mistress in all ways. He rose and stripped from his clothes, and turned his back to Josiah, offering his wrists for cuffs.

"Master, how bad will it be for her?" Tony asked.

"I'm going to hurt her, make her cry, maybe even bleed," Josiah said. "And I'm going to fuck her hard so she knows who's the boss out here."

"Thank God you've cuffed me," Tony said.

"When we get in the truck, your ankles will be cuffed too, boy," Josiah said.

"Yes, Master," Tony said. "Sir ... will you consider beating

71

me instead, even ten times what Mistress is about to receive? Even put me on the post and horsewhip me, Master ... but please, not Mistress."

"No, but maybe I'll take you back to the leathermen for a glory hole again," Josiah said, and Tony shivered. Even so, he impressed Josiah.

"Even that, if it saves Mistress, Master," he said barely above a whisper.

"Part of her punishment is you bearing witness to her undoing," Josiah said. "She's humiliated that this is going to happen, but that's the point of it."

"Yes, Master," Tony said. Josiah led him out to the truck, and once he was in the bed of the truck, cuffed his ankles while he gaped at his bedraggled owner, looking about like something the cat dragged in. By the time Josiah got back to the cabin, Lucretia and Tony were chilled and soaked to the skin. He led them into the house and Molly and Leigh gaped at the naked arrivals.

"I have to be punished too for speaking out of turn here," Lucretia said. "On this property, Josiah is the undisputed master here, and I'm to be beaten and fucked, humiliated in front of three other slaves, two of whom have been under my thumb."

"Molly and Leigh, I'm going to beat her harshly and then fuck her," Josiah announced. "If she cums, she is to be horsewhipped and caged in the rain overnight. After it's done, one of you slaves will be chosen to suck me clean and the other to lick my seed out of her. You two are due one hell of a lot of punishment already and you don't want to earn more, so the only person who's going to cum is me. Understood?"

"Yes, Master," Leigh and Molly said. Josiah grasped Lucretia's hair and pulled her to her knees, and looked fiercely into her eyes.

"I understand, Master," she said in a meek tone.

"Tony?"

"I can't jack off with my hands cuffed like this, Master," he said, and Lucretia frowned, cut her eyes toward Tony, and then looked up at Josiah and nodded.

"Molly, go start sucking on Tony's dick," Josiah decided. "Get him right to the edge of a cum. And don't tell me this is new territory to you."

"It … yes, Master," Molly said.

"No … please … no," Tony begged.

"Master, may I?" Lucretia asked, and Josiah nodded.

"Tony, this is your master's order and you will submit or so help me God you'll be a glory hole for the leathermen every time they meet for the next year."

"Yes, Mistress," Tony moaned.

"Just Lucretia … I'm a slave here right now, just like you."

"God," Tony wept. "Yes, Lucretia."

"When Tony is particularly good, I give him a handjob," Lucretia said. "He's not allowed to fuck, so I think his head might explode with Molly's mouth on him. And he knows that no matter what happens here or who ordered it, when he cums he'll be savagely punished by me. Well-played, Master."

"He's about to be broken a bit more," Josiah said as Tony cried out when Molly took him fully into her mouth. He tried backing away but got to the wall and could back up no further, and

Molly was relentless in her oral attentions. Finally, right as Tony was quivering, Molly released his throbbing member.

"Leigh, finish him off with your hands," Josiah ordered. "Make him jizz on the floor there."

"Yes, Master," Leigh said. Josiah kept a straight face as he saw Molly wince. She'd seen him do this before with other males sent here and knew what was coming for poor Tony. In four strokes of Leigh's hand, Tony cried out as his seed erupted in a big puddle on the floor. He was still panting and trying to come to his senses when Josiah approached and gave a hard smack to Tony's balls, putting the big man on his knees, groaning in misery.

"Lick it up," Josiah commanded.

Tony groaned but began lapping up his spilled seed, swallowing and gagging, but he managed not to vomit. Finally, his mess was licked off the floor.

"Who's in charge of you here, Tony?" Josiah asked with quiet menace.

"You are, Master," Tony whispered.

"You remember that, boy," Josiah said. "Lucretia, go get a cane for your punishment. Stand and I'll remove your handcuffs."

In a moment, Lucretia was back, bearing what Josiah thought was a particularly evil cane, a thin one that was about a meter long. But this session, while presented to the other slaves as a punishment, was really by Lucretia's desire, and if this was what she felt she needed or wanted, then so be it. They'd worked out the details before Lucretia removed her attire on the porch, attire that Josiah was sure was dripping wet by about now.

"Will I have to restrain you?" Josiah asked.

"No, Master," Lucretia said. "I know the punishment doubles if I evade, even on the last stroke."

"Bend over, slave," Josiah ordered, and Lucretia bent over the back of the sofa, as Leigh had done earlier. "Thirty lashes." This was actually the only thing they didn't negotiate, the number of lashes. Lucretia told Josiah it was better that it was out of her hands, because she felt far more submissive with it that way, asking only that it be no more than one hundred strokes.

"Master is lenient, thank you," Lucretia said. Josiah slashed the cane into Lucretia's round brown rump, and she hissed, but remained still, although he saw her fists grasping the cushions of the sofa. Josiah was not gentle, lashing her at a slow tempo, driving the cane to a blur on every stroke while Lucretia hissed and groaned, and finally yelped. Tony wept helplessly as he watched the display, and he saw Molly looking grim and Leigh torn between arousal and fear. Finally, all thirty strokes were laid in, and Josiah could see the swelling and welts, which looked very sexy to him. And then he grasped Lucretia by the hair and led her near Tony before telling her to get on all fours.

"I want him to see what a master will do to you," Josiah said. He stripped from his own clothes and parted her labia, and then thrust hard into Lucretia, his hips slamming against her battered rump. Lucretia cried out, but this didn't sound like a cry of displeasure, not in the least. He thrust hard, pounding in and out of her while she clenched her fists. Josiah knew she came when she cried out and clenched hard at his thrusting member, and then he erupted into her, shuddering as his seed spurted deep into her. He wondered if she'd confess her climax or pretend it hadn't happened. That consequence was a real one, but he decided not to push it if she didn't confess.

"So I have a die here I'm going to cast," Josiah said. If it comes up an odd number, Leigh will suck me clean while Molly licks my seed from Lucretia. If it comes up even, vice versa. Josiah picked up the die and dropped it on the floor, and rolled three. "Leigh, get over here. Molly, clean her out completely."

Lucretia rolled onto her back and opened her thighs while Leigh greedily took Josiah's still-hard member into her mouth, sucking it clean of Lucretia's juices and his cum. There was a refractory period where a man cannot catch a fresh erection, and Josiah's member withered in Leigh's mouth. Fortunately for Josiah, that refractory period was a short one, and he was confident he would be buggering Leigh before the evening's activities concluded. Molly finished cleaning out Lucretia and looked a bit green at the new experience. Lucretia looked sweated and spent, but knelt before Josiah.

"Master, I confess I came when you fucked me," she said in a quiet and trembling voice.

"What are your consequences for that?" Josiah asked.

"I am to be horsewhipped on my back a minimum of twelve lashes to a maximum of fifty, Master," she admitted.

"That is my decree," Josiah agreed. "Leigh, cuff her to the post there. Molly, I saw my whip up there. Bring it down."

Lucretia was docile but trembling as Leigh cuffed her in place, and Molly returned soon with the coiled whip, which she knelt and handed up to Josiah. "I think twenty lashes should do," Josiah said. "Do you request a gag?"

"No, Master," Lucretia said. "I ... I'll be shamed more for screaming, Sir. I deserve this. Obviously I need to learn better self-control."

"Obviously," Josiah agreed. He slashed the whip across her back. Lucretia didn't cry or yelp. She screamed as the burning lash cut across her, and screamed anew as the second and then third lashes bit into her. Josiah continued the whipping, noticing on the sixth lash that Leigh was counting them out loud, and wondered why. Lucretia was a sobbing mess before it was halfway done, but never begged for mercy. It took only about four minutes to lay in all twenty lashes, and Josiah could see Lucretia was broken by it. She hadn't bled, but she was thoroughly welted, and for her sake, Josiah hoped she liked sleeping on her belly, or she was in for a horrible night.

"Release her from the post," he ordered Leigh. She and Molly both had to help Lucretia stand for a long moment before she had her strength back, and then Lucretia crawled to Josiah and kissed his feet.

"Thank you, Master," she said. "I'll try to do better moving forward, Sir."

"I have two other slaves to punish now," Josiah said. "You may rest, but you are not to speak to Tony. In fact, I don't want you on the same side of the room as him. Understood?"

"I understand, Master," Lucretia said. Josiah stroked her hair and then leaned down and kissed her. She kissed him back and he sensed … something.

"Leigh, Molly, one of you will be horsewhipped thirty lashes, and the other will be buggered," Josiah said. "Tomorrow, we'll do the reverse of that."

"Master, I know you want Leigh, and maybe I need to know that you have sexual options that can exclude me," Molly said, approaching the post on trembling knees. "Besides, as horribly as she's behaved, I've been far worse, Sir."

"Chain her to the post, Leigh," Josiah ordered.

"Master, may I examine her physically, and Lucretia, to ensure they're healthy enough to undergo this?" Leigh requested. "And may Molly do a like examination of me, Sir?"

"That sounds wise," Josiah said.

"Master, the medical gear is out in the barn," Molly said. "Because of the rain I suggest we go there rather than risk the electronics getting wet."

"Okay, all of you get in the bed of the truck," Josiah ordered. Tony, cuffed, had to be assisted to his feet.

"Master, I … I accept what happened," he said. "I won't get violent or run if you wish to remove my chains, Sir. But if you want me chained, it is your right to do."

"Remove his cuffs," Josiah ordered Molly, handing her the key. In a moment, Tony was free of the cuffs and knelt down.

"Thank you for trusting me, Master," he said.

"Let's go get these exams done," Josiah ordered.

FOURTEEN

Darla woke and at first tried covering herself, but seemed to realize Josiah was the only one clothed, and watched the goings-on. "Is the IV helping?" Molly asked her.

"Yes, Ma'am," Darla said. "Thank you."

"Heat exhaustion?" Leigh asked, and Molly nodded.

"She overdid it out there and didn't drink enough water," Molly said.

"I saw she looked a bit weak, and then went for her swim. Lucky a gator or snake didn't get her," Leigh offered.

"She was told exactly that," Molly agreed. "It interrupted her plan of punishment. I'd guess her master will have to send her back out here again."

"May I ask why you're naked?" Darla asked.

"For the same reason you are," Molly said. "Master's policy is that if you're a slave here, clothes are unnecessary."

"Wow ... I see," Darla said. "You're all being punished."

"Lucretia already was, and so was Tony," Molly said. "Leigh and I are next. We just decided a round of physicals was important before pursuing things any further."

"Come on over here, Molly," Leigh said, switching from slave to doctor in a heartbeat. She spent fifteen minutes examining Molly, and a like amount of time on Lucretia and then Tony.

"Jesus, if everyone was as healthy as you three, I'd have to get a job selling toothbrushes door-to-door," Leigh said, and chuckled. "Okay, my turn, Molly."

Molly did the same physical that Leigh had done on her, the same she had done on Darla. "Your pulse and BP are a bit elevated, but I'm taking the events surrounding us into account," she said. "I'm afraid there's nothing I can do. You're terminal. I estimate you only have about sixty years left, so you should make peace with your people, and get your affairs in order."

"Okay, everyone's good, then," Josiah said. He wasn't surprised. Tony's build told Josiah that he spent a lot of time in a gym staying buffed and toned, and one look at a naked Lucretia told him the same. Leigh was also well-built, if not as athletic as Tony and Lucretia, and Molly likewise kept in decent shape. "Back in the truck."

"Would you rather do this in the barn?" Lucretia asked.

"No, at the cabin," Josiah said. In a moment, the slaves were in the truck, and a moment later they were getting freshly drenched in the driving storm. Josiah was beginning to wonder if he should abort this evening and get everyone to higher ground somewhere, but decided they'd be okay. The main house was built on high ground, as was the parking area there. And he kept one room in the main house full of emergency provisions, including about a hundred gallons of bottled water, and a camp stove, and several cases of canned goods and MREs. Several propane bottles were out on the back porch. It was enough to provision Josiah and Molly for most of a year, so even extending it through six people would keep them all fed for at least a month. Worst case scenario, flooding would strand them here for three or four days.

FIFTEEN

"Master, may I ask why we didn't do this in the barn?" Lucretia asked.

"If I may, Master?" Molly asked, and Josiah nodded. "We've kept a policy of not involving clients in our personal doings. The five of us here are personal, not business. None of us paid Master money for this. Darla's master did pay for this. So we're careful about keeping a wall between the two things. Since buggery, a sex act, will happen, Darla is not to witness it. Now, I'll freely admit Master has enjoyed many a blowjob from me right after lashing a client, if the client is blindfolded and clueless. But … it's been his policy all along not to involve sexually with clients, even ones as amazingly hot as Darla out there."

"She is a slice of eye candy," Lucretia agreed. "What's the story on her?"

"And now we're at another policy," Josiah said. "The first thing I do with any clients for my beadle services is to have them pay me a dollar up-front. Out in the world, I am an attorney, and that means I cannot discuss the business of my clientele, even out of school. So the story on Darla is only that she is here for my beadle services."

"I'm sorry, I didn't know, Master," Lucretia said.

"Should the rest of us do that as well, Master?" Leigh asked. "Pay you a buck up front so you're covered? I hadn't thought of that, but it makes a lot of sense, Sir."

81

"Yeah, it would probably be for the best, but I'm guessing you all left your money in your other pants," Josiah said, straight-faced. He was surprised when Tony barked a loud laugh at this quip.

"Sorry, Sir, that just got my funny bone," he said.

"It was supposed to," Josiah returned. "Okay, Leigh, bind Molly to the post. It's time she began being broken."

"Master, Tony can do that," Lucretia said. "He's probably more experienced. I've used him as my minion many times at my place, Sir."

"Fair enough," Josiah said. "Tony, bind her."

"Yes, Master," Tony said, and pushed Molly into the post while he lifted her hands overhead to be cuffed. He strapped her legs to the post, and then swept Molly's hair over her shoulder to fully bare her back.

"Molly, you saw what a lesser whipping did to Lucretia," Josiah said. "I think in about five minutes you're going to be forever a different woman, a broken slave, and you're well advised to stay broken to my will."

"Yes ... yes, Master," Molly choked out, trembling fresh. Josiah replaced the cracker on his whip and slashed the whip into her. Molly shrieked at the agony, and eight lashes in, fainted from the combined pain and fear. Josiah was prepared for this. He'd had more than one client faint out here for one reason or another, and simply had Leigh bust an ammonia ampoule under Molly's nose. Molly groaned, but woke, and the lashing continued, the welts rising red on her pale and tender skin. Four of the lashes made her bleed, but the wounds weren't deep, more like cat-scratches than anything else. Finally it was done. She was in a swoon, utterly spent from her lashing, and Josiah sensed he'd gotten all from her he was going to get this night. Tony helped her from the post and helped her stand until she regained strength, and finally she came to.

"Th … thank you, Master," she croaked out in a hoarse voice.

"I hope you really mean that," Josiah said.

"I do, Master," Molly whispered, weeping.

"Leigh, you know what's next, now don't you?" Josiah asked.

"Yes, Master," Leigh said, and immediately positioned herself. Josiah removed his clothes and then removed her plug, lubricating his erection, and then he thrust hard into her, and Leigh cried out. Josiah found her tight, but loosened enough by the plug that he lasted a while, plundering her harshly, punishing her rectum, before erupting his seed deeply into her bowels while she sobbed. He didn't sense that she came, and he was pleased as he drew out of her. He saw Lucretia whispering to Tony, who nodded with a grim expression. In a moment, Tony was back with soapy water and rags, and on his knees before Josiah, washing his member clean of Leigh's filth.

Tony did a thorough and gentle job of it, and Josiah decided to needle him a bit. "I might just have to keep you for this purpose, boy."

"Is Master satisfied?" he managed to ask.

"Yes, just pat it dry and that should be good," Josiah said.

"As Master wishes," Tony said, and used a dry towel to pat down Josiah's clean member.

"Okay, I want you all sleeping separately tonight," Josiah announced. "Molly, you've already established a room here, so take that one. Show Leigh the guest room at the other end of the hall, and she'll stay there. Tony, there's a mother-in-law apartment through that door. Lucretia, you may sleep in the room where the supplies are. Dismissed."

The four scattered to their designated rooms, and Josiah went into the kitchen, found a bottle of bourbon in a cabinet, and poured a glass of it. He took about ten minutes, sipping at the whiskey, and then went on a round of interviews.

SIXTEEN

Since it was downstairs, his first stop was to talk with Tony, who he found in the shower, cleaning himself. "Does Master have more requirements?" he asked.

"No, just monitoring," Josiah said. "I know this evening has been somewhat of a shocker for you."

"It has, Master," Tony agreed. "But Mistress told me many times that a slave isn't challenged by doing what he wanted to do anyway, but by following orders he doesn't like, and that was ... well ... the entire visit here so far."

"Hopefully the shower is at least pleasant," Josiah remarked.

"I ... I'm sorry ... yes, Sir, it's a good shower," Tony said, looking afraid that he'd talked too much.

"Get a good night's sleep, Tony," Josiah said. "Take another shower if you want."

"Thank you. Good night, Sir," Tony said.

Josiah went up the stairs to Leigh's room, where he found her curled on the bed in a fetal position, weeping. "Do you want to talk about it?" he asked.

"It's ... Master, that's the first time I was ever fucked in my

85

ass," Leigh said. "It's a love-hate thing going on as far as that goes, and I'm trying … trying to sort it out. I think I'm going to hate being horsewhipped tomorrow. I can't believe how fast it undid Lucretia and Molly, and I don't have illusions I'll take it any better simply because I'm more accustomed to being whipped. I'm smarter than to believe that, Master. But … at the same time, I want it and need it and deserve it, and in a weird way I feel honored that you're doing this for me rather than sending me packing. I mean … Jesus, I'm going to sound arrogant, but this isn't the time for falsity, is it?"

"No, it really isn't," Josiah agreed.

"I know I'm … attractive," Leigh said. "God knows I get hit on enough by male patients, and a surprising number of female patients, at the practice, as well as one doctor there who asks me out a few times yearly. I always told him no, and always will. He's a nice man, but a milquetoast, and I know I need a strong master, like Blake has been, like you obviously are. So I came here pretty sure of myself that you'd want me. But … I saw that girl Darla and nearly backed out. Putting her next to me is like putting a Ferrari next to Mom's minivan, and you weren't at all sexual with her. But here I am, surrounded by women far more appealing than me, yet you're giving me the chance, and I feel honored, especially considering what I did to get here."

"I wonder how honored you'll feel tomorrow when the horsewhipping happens," Josiah said.

"In truth, I'll probably be wishing I'd just leapt off a skyscraper instead of coming to you, but … I deserve it and I think I'll learn from it," Leigh said. "I like Miss Lucretia and she's hell with her punishments, but I keep coming back to the fact that she's a contractor doing a job. You're an offended master punishing a woman who might want to be your slave. The dynamic is a huge difference in my heart, Master. And I guess, maybe for the first time since medical school, I'm afraid I've bitten off more than I can chew, and there's nothing I can do for it but my best to chew and swallow it, Sir."

"I guess so," Josiah said, in a way very impressed with Leigh and her integrity on the heels of such poor judgment. "Get a good night's sleep, slave."

"Yes, Master," she said. "May ... may I kiss you?"

"Yes, you may," Josiah said, and Leigh stepped into his arms for a tender and lingering kiss.

"Thank you, Sir," she said. "Goodnight."

"Jesus, that whip will keep me on my best behavior," Molly said when Josiah entered. "I'm so sorry I've been such an awful person, Master. I ... I promise I'll make you proud of me."

"And if I decided to take Leigh on long-term?" Josiah asked.

"Sir, I like Leigh," Molly said. "I was angry when she moved for my suspension, but ... she was right. And I won't do anything to influence how she votes at the practice on whether to exclude me. This is assuming you'll permit me to keep working, Master. You might have other ideas, as far as I know. But I'm fond of her, and God knows she has all kinds of guts coming here like she did with that confession and surrender. Even if her online dom sent her here, it was gutsy as fuck. I've ... Master, I've discovered I'm bisexual, and even now I fantasize, when the punishments are over, about sleeping with her. It was all I could do not to cum when you had me eating your seed out of Lucretia. God, that was hot."

"So you have no regrets?" Josiah asked.

"I regret the behavior that's seeing me punished, but I think ... I think I need it, and I know I deserve it," Molly said. "Even when you horsewhipped me – Christ, how that hurt! – even then, I felt … I felt a strange sort of peace, that I'm where I belong. So in a way, I think it's good that I did the things I did, so that I put myself right where I am. I wonder if I wasn't being passive-aggressive, even, doing what I did so you'd find out and do this to me, but at the same time concealing it fully from you so there was no chance you'd learn what I'd been doing."

"Okay," Josiah said.

"Master, I've been with you for a long time," Molly said. "Not right now, because I know I have to prove myself, but we both know I'm in this for the long haul. Would you consider branding me sometime, to mark me forever yours?"

"Like a cow or something?" Josiah asked, surprised.

"Yes, just like that," Molly said. "Your animal, Sir."

"We can put that on a shelf for now, but perhaps down the line, yes," Josiah said.

"Thank you, Master," Molly said. "By the way, I was too weak to show it, but it turned me on watching you fuck Lucretia and then Leigh. Especially Leigh. I'll be sure to choose bigger butt plugs in the future, Sir."

"I think she's liable to be walking funny tomorrow, but then, so will you," Josiah remarked.

"Was it wrong that I wanted to giggle when she came and that plug shot out of her like a rocket?" Molly asked, grinning.

"It was darkly amusing," Josiah snorted, and then chuckled.

"I guess this bigger one in me will make it easier to take the buggery tomorrow," Molly ventured. "But … Sir, I really need to use the toilet."

"I'll get more lube for you," Josiah said. "Go on to the bathroom."

"Thank you, Master," Molly said, and went into the bathroom. He heard her yelp as she removed the plug, and heard the loud sounds of her being completely unladylike on the hopper, and chuckled to himself. He found more lubricant and waited for Molly to come out of the bathroom after what seemed an inordinate amount of time with the water running.

"I took the liberty of washing it, Master," she said sheepishly when she came back into the bedroom. "I guess I should have picked up enema kits. I'll do that once I'm allowed off the grounds, Sir. But here." She handed him the big plug.

"Over my lap like a naughty girl about to get spanked," Josiah ordered. Molly grinned and obeyed.

"Am I to be spanked, Master?" she asked.

"You'd only enjoy that, and there will be precious little pleasure for you these next two weeks," Josiah said. "Honestly, your punishment and training will probably take longer than that two week span. It's kind of like basic in the military. You will learn to reject yourself in favor of your obedience. It has to be that way, Molly."

"I know, Master," Molly said, opening her thighs a bit when he touched the groove of her buttocks.

"Take a deep breath," Josiah ordered, and Molly obeyed, gusting it out when he drove the plug fully into her. "There. Now you need to get some sleep. I have to return Darla to her life tomorrow, assuming the roads are open, and you and Leigh have a busy day ahead of you."

"Thank you, Master," Molly said. "Sir, you've always been a considerate lover, but … I hope not tomorrow or for these two weeks coming. I … I need to feel used, like property, Sir."

"I'll use you as hard as I did Leigh," Josiah promised. "Now get some sleep."

Josiah walked into Lucretia's room last, and she looked up at him in surprise, and then smiled. "I like that," she said.

"What?" Josiah asked.

"That you walk in without knocking or warning," Lucretia said. "It's another way of making me feel enslaved, that denial of even basic privacy, Sir. It reminds me I'm your captive and not a guest."

"I gather you have no regrets," Josiah remarked.

"I … I need what you offer, Sir," Lucretia said. "Not necessarily a full-time thing, but more than just the twice-a-year thing I've done all this while. Look, I know we're only acquainted, but I like to think our reputations precede us, Sir."

"They do, I guess," Josiah said. "Yours is a good one, at least."

"So is yours, believe me," Lucretia offered, and fell silent for a long moment, visibly thinking while Josiah waited her out.

"I was born in England and lived there until I was thirteen, when my dad got transferred here in his job," Lucretia said. "Lucretia is my scene name. I'm plain old Sarah Louise Barton. I got US citizenship when I was in college. I went to college mostly on scholarship, and then into the WNBA. I made it four seasons before I had to retire. Fortunately, I took good advice and didn't live the party lifestyle there. I just drove a pretty basic car and lived in a pretty basic apartment and saved one hell of a lot of money, or what seemed to me like one hell of a lot of money. So when my knee went south on me, I had a nice nest-egg for myself. It wasn't near enough to live out my life on it – women's pro sports don't pay like men's pro sports – but it was invested well and I had a degree in business rather than Applied Basket weaving or some other useless bullshit. But I'm getting ahead of myself here."

"I'm listening," Josiah said.

"The slavery thing isn't such a big deal in the UK, or wasn't to my family, at least," she said. "I knew there'd been slavery here in the States forever ago, but it wasn't a part of me or my own British ethos, so I could look at it with more … detachment, I suppose … than natural-born Americans do. So I got here and sometimes would see a movie with this slave or that, or perhaps prisoners or sailors getting lashed, and the sheer power of it … it moved me. I swear, this sounds fucked up, but one of the sexiest scenes I saw in a movie was in *Roots*, where they horsewhipped him into submission, kept lashing that man until he broke and took the name Toby. It moved me, Master. I fantasized about being the slave and about being the master. But I can tell you after seeing that, I went to my room and it was the first time I ever masturbated. I came … Christ, I don't even know how many times … but I was sore in my pussy for four days that followed, and even the soreness was exciting to me.

"Anyway, I know this is a really circular stream of consciousness I'm dropping on you, but it's all part of me," she continued. "So I retired from basketball but I'd come to love that lifestyle of I had to be at practices and games, but otherwise could do what I wanted when I wanted, so I knew I wasn't going to do well in Corporate America. I couldn't see myself in a skirt-and-jacket suit every day working my ass off a hundred hours weekly for The Man and not having a life of my own, so I thought about my options and realized I could be a professional dominatrix. Other than my clients – I have a smattering of regulars, one who sees me every Tuesday from 2:00 until 3:30, for instance – my life is my own. Leigh had become pretty much of a frequent flyer these last three years. Christ, I think the longest I went without giving her a session was six weeks. More often it was two or three weeks, sometimes a month. Blake shoveled one hell of a lot of money at me. I have Tony, and the passion is there, but my need to submit, at least from time to time, has been growing stronger, and those sessions with the other dominatrix just aren't doing it. Again, no passion."

"That makes sense," Josiah said, fascinated. "Leigh made similar remarks, that she deeply respects you as a person, and your skills, but at the end of the day it's fee-for-service and without passion or a personal touch."

"But while I can be slave for a weekend or several days, I couldn't do it continually, I don't think," Lucretia said. "It's just not me. But I've been around this a long time, Josiah, and you know we all tend to make our own rules as we go in this. So here's what I ask of you. Let me come to you when I need a weekend or just a session, but also … I want you sometimes to just summon me, and when you do, unless there is a good reason to the contrary, I have no choice but to drop everything and rush to your summons. Not daily or even weekly, but maybe every four or six weeks, no rhyme or reason, just summon me and I must come directly to you. And when I'm here, I am your slave. No rights, no limits, no recourse, you have full and complete right to do with me as you please. Now, there will be blackout dates or times, like my Tuesday client, and I fly to England for two weeks every spring to visit my parents, so I'd be unavailable, and sometimes there are the unavoidable out-of-town times."

"Those would be 'good reasons to the contrary,'" Josiah said, using air quotes with his fingers.

"I suppose so, Master," she said.

"What of Tony?" Josiah asked.

"I gather you're not bisexual," Lucretia said.

"No, I'm not," Josiah replied. "I've punished males out here before, but again, it's just business, no passion."

"I'm sure there's always work to be done out here," Lucretia said. "He's strong as an ox. Hell, if you have nothing else, he can bench press that old truck out there or something. I think you could hitch a plow to that big fucker and he'd move forty acres of dirt in a day." She grinned, and then they both laughed.

"Are you sure?" Josiah asked.

"Master, when you took Leigh up her ass – I'm a virgin there, by the way – I envied her," Lucretia said. "I don't question anymore what makes me tick, but right now, this is what's making me tick. And I think it's long-term. I've had greater need for a long time now, but I can't jet off to Memphis every time I feel the urge, Sir, and those urges are growing more into a constant than an occasional thing, and growing stronger or ... maybe deeper. And even if I could zip off to Memphis at will, that would rely on her availability. And even if she was fully available, again, the passion is lacking. It's a job to her, like painting a house or heating a pizza in the oven."

"So be it," Josiah said. "Be sure I have all of your contact information before you go back to your life tomorrow."

"Thank you, Master," Lucretia said. "Look, if you still have the energy after you bugger Molly, my ass is yours when I'm on this estate, Sir. You just order me on all fours and take me, Master."

"All fours right now," Josiah ordered, and Lucretia obeyed. And then Josiah found a large plug, lubricated it, and thrust it into her bottom. She yelped and bit her forearm to stifle it. "There, in case I do feel like buggering you, it'll loosen you some."

"Thank you, Master," Lucretia said. "I think this is going to be the start of something beautiful."

"Was being horsewhipped as sexy as you thought?" he asked.

"It hurt horribly, but … yes, it was," Lucretia admitted. "With my dominatrix friend in Memphis, I feel whipped. With you, I feel owned, and even as much as that whipping hurt, I felt safe, Master. I needed it. And I hated it but I beg you to do it to me from time to time, even if you feel like you have to trump up an excuse, Sir."

"I'll keep that in mind," Josiah said. "Get some sleep. I'm worn out and tomorrow promises to be a big day."

"I need to leave by 4:00, Sir," Lucretia said. "But other than Tuesday's session, right now my entire calendar is clear for the week."

"Then I'm likely to summon you, but probably not until Wednesday or Thursday," Josiah said. "I suspect I'll have my hands full with Molly and Leigh, breaking them."

"Perhaps I can be the exemplar, but I ask you not to have me top anyone here, unless you're eyes-on supervising," Lucretia said. "I want to be purely enslaved here. I'll even make that plain to Tony, that here he answers only to you, Sir. And I'll enforce that at home. If he's trouble here, you do with him what you will, but when I get him home, he's in trouble with me too."

"Perhaps I need to cook up a reason to lash him too," Josiah ventured.

"I think that would be wise," Lucretia confirmed.

"Okay, bedtime," Josiah said. They kissed and Josiah trudged down to his truck and drove to the main house, where he showered and fell into a deep sleep, and knew nothing until sunrise the following morning.

FOUR SLAVES

SEVENTEEN

"Get in the van," Josiah said to Darla.

"Yes, Sir," Darla said, and obeyed. Josiah buckled her in place and closed up the van, then drove off to the warehouse, considering his sudden influx of slaves and how to handle them. They were all intelligent people and as much as he would like it to be like military boot camp, the fact was that he would have to tailor how he handled each of them as individuals.

He arrived to the warehouse in the driving rain and took a moment to feel sorry for Darla, who was in for even more misery, but he'd subjected four slaves on his estate to similar misery during the night. He helped her from the van and told her to dress herself. And then he told her to get into his car. From there, he drove her to an IHOP and parked the car.

"Your master's final instructions were that you are to walk home from here," he said. "It's about ten miles from this spot, which he designated. He specified that you are not to accept rides or hail a taxi, but to walk home."

"I guess I'd best start walking, then," Darla said. "I guess he'll send me back to you soon to complete what was planned, Sir. I … this might sound fucked up, but I'm grateful, Sir. I hated a lot of it, but I'm grateful. Thank God I didn't wear a white t-shirt, huh? She flashed a sardonic grin and Josiah chuckled. "I'll see you again soon, if I had to bet." She got out of the car and began walking through puddles and hard rain. Josiah decided he was safer in something other than his car, and returned to the warehouse, where he got into a 4x4 Suburban and drove back to the farm, and then to the cabin. He'd checked in on the slaves and found Tony in the kitchen and the women eating ravenously, and knew that's where he would find them now. He doubted anyone wanted to tromp through the mud and hard rain to get anywhere, and hoped Darla got home safely.

"Tony, put Leigh on the post," Josiah ordered, and Leigh trembled as Tony led her to the post, and then cuffed her in place. Despite all the discipline the big man got from Lucretia and his stated dislike of being here, Josiah couldn't help noticing that his penis was twitching toward erection as he bound the pretty physician to the post, rubbing his growing member against her lower back, and decided that was a good excuse for lashing the man later.

"Thirty lashes," Josiah said, although he doubted this knowledge had left Leigh's mind for even a second of the hours since she'd seen Lucretia and Molly undone by this whip. He lashed Leigh's back, and was rewarded with a loud screech of agony as she fought her bonds in sudden panic, and watched as the welt grew on her back, and then lashed her again while she howled and sobbed. The eighth lash, the first that opened her skin, was likewise the one to break her, Josiah easily saw, as Leigh groaned and slumped some in her bonds, but otherwise made no outcry and stopped fighting the post and cuffs, simply enduring as the harsh whipping continued. A few minutes later, eight wounds bleeding slightly, the horsewhipping was done. Leigh was broken and Josiah made a bet with himself that she wouldn't be much of a problem, moving forward.

"Remove her from the post, Tony," he ordered, and Josiah noted that Tony again pressed his member against her lower back as he undid her cuffs, and surely didn't miss the man's erection when he was done. Neither, he noted, did Lucretia miss his response.

"Molly, you know what's about to happen, yes?" Josiah asked.

"Yes, Master," Molly said, and assumed the position. Josiah removed the plug from her, grasped her hips hard in his hands, and thrust hard into her bottom. Molly gasped and yelped, but Josiah held her firm, plundering her bottom as he grew closer and closer to his eruption, finally blasting his seed into her bottom as she trembled, and then came. Josiah remained inside her for a long moment further.

"Oh, God," Molly sighed. "Thank you, Master."

"You came," Josiah remarked.

"I will have to be punished, Master," Molly agreed. "God, I … it was amazing, Sir."

Josiah drew his member from her bottom, and then stood, and was surprised to find Lucretia on her knees before him. She washed his member and patted it dry, and then, as if to prove she'd done a good job, sucked him into her mouth for a moment.

"I hope Master is satisfied," she said.

"I am," Josiah affirmed.

"Master, thank you for lashing me," Leigh said.

"You're welcome, Leigh," Josiah returned. "There will be plenty more for you, but I think you broke on the post."

"Master, if you'd ordered, I'd have sucked you clean a moment ago," Leigh said. "I swear, you own me for as long as you'll have me, Sir."

"That brings me to my next order of business," Josiah said. "Tony, your sister slaves aren't here for your gratification. You grew erect and pressed your dick all over Leigh before and after her whipping."

"Master, it wasn't —"

"Save it," Josiah interrupted. "Thirty lashes. Offer your hands to the cuffs."

"Fuck you," Tony snapped. "Won't happen."

"Tony, you will obey and accept, or we're done," Lucretia said. "And by that, I mean you can walk to the house, clothe yourself, and walk to your apartment, and I won't speak with you again. We're done."

"Mistress, I —" Tony began.

"That's your choice," Lucretia said. "You can accept this new evolution, or be gone."

"I just can't … I can't," Tony said.

"Get out of here," Lucretia snapped. "Go to the big house, get dressed, and leave. It's a natural male reaction to grow aroused at a very attractive naked female. I understand that, and I'm sure so do Leigh and Molly. They're maybe even flattered they have this effect on you. So your arousal isn't the offense. But touching her with it – and I saw it too – isn't acceptable or excusable. She's not your fuck doll, as sexy as Leigh is. So you can take your whipping from Master, or you're persona non grata with me from here on in. I love you, but we both need what happens here, and I won't let you fuck this up for me."

"And you just upped the ante to forty lashes," Josiah chimed in. He remained calm, but knew himself well enough to know anger was brewing inside him. "And I agree with Lucretia. If you leave here in dishonor, there's no way back in. That's a one-way door out of here, Tony."

"Master, I would ask for a few minutes alone with Tony to explain all the ramifications to him," Lucretia asked. "And if he refuses his whipping, I will endure it in his place."

"So will I," Leigh added in a grim tone. "After all, I'm apparently the one who turned him on."

"And me," Molly said. "I guess I'm the one who lit this fuse yesterday."

"Fifty for me, please, if he refuses, Master," Lucretia said, and Josiah saw Tony's eyes widen and his jaw drop. "Tony, into your room. We're going to talk, boy."

"Yes, Mistress," Tony said, and went toward the room designated for him.

"Molly, bend over the sofa," Josiah ordered. "I may as well cane you for your stolen cum while those two discuss what's about to happen. Leigh, go upstairs and choose a cane for your sister."

"Yes, Master," Leigh said as Molly positioned herself.

"Thank you for this, Josiah," Molly said. "I've needed this for years now, maybe my whole life, and didn't have the lady-balls to admit it."

"I think you're right," Josiah said.

"I hope when I've earned your esteem, my asshole is a regular visit for your pecker," Molly said. "Jesus, that was intense."

"Bet on it," Josiah said. "Bet on it."

Leigh returned with a cane, a twin of one that Josiah had used on Lucretia the night before. "Thirty lashes," Josiah said. "Leigh, circle in front of her and be prepared to hold her in place if she tries to evade ..."

FOUR SLAVES

EIGHTEEN

"Master will hold me responsible for you since I brought you to his estate," Lucretia said to Tony. "Look, it's time I told you that my trips to Memphis weren't to see a client. They were because I was the client. Sometimes I need a hard session, but ... I need more than Wanda is able to do for me, or to me, in Memphis. As it is, if you go out there, he'll lay forty lashes on you, and I might as well tell you now you'll get at least that from me at home. And if you take those forty lashes, I will probably get at least twenty out there, and you know what, Tony? I deserve at least that for my shame in bringing you here. I'm ashamed of you, Tony. For the first time, I'm not disappointed with you or mad at you ... I'm ashamed of you."

"Mistress, I love you, but I'm not queer," Tony objected.

"Neither is Josiah," Lucretia said. "I don't think he'd do a sexual act with you for all the tea in China, Tony. A whipping isn't sex. It's punishment and discipline, and you damn well deserve it. Leigh isn't a sex toy for you. Yeah, she's hot as hell ... Jesus, I didn't think I was particularly bi, and I'd fuck her in ways the Kama Sutra didn't imagine ... but she was to be whipped, not for you to rub your dick all over her."

"I'm sorry, Mistress," Tony said.

"Look, in time, Master might allow you dalliances with me, or with Leigh or Molly, but right now the order of the day is discipline and punishment, and God knows you and I deserve it. So do I get fifty lashes out there, or do you get forty and I get twenty, Tony?"

102

"I just … even setting the gay thing aside, I don't like the son of a bitch," Tony said. "And I don't want him to be part of my life, part of our life, Mistress."

"Since when do your wants matter?" Lucretia returned. "Turn around, hands behind your back."

"Why?"

"Because the last time you see me in this life is going to be me suffering a fifty-lash horsewhipping, a nigger slave, on that post, and then Master is going to exile you forever, and you'll already be exiled forever from me. And I don't want you interfering before he decides I deserve a hundred for bringing you here and not just fifty. Now, turn around!"

"Because I love you, I'll take the lashes from him, but after that, if you want him in your life, I'm out of here, Lucretia," Tony said.

"You need to understand something," Lucretia said. "I'll be under his authority from now on. If he summons me and there's not a client, I will rush straight over here to serve him. It won't be daily, but probably monthly, and I don't care if your dick is in my mouth, I'll spit it out, get dressed, and make a beeline here."

"Then I'll save you from the worse whipping, but after that, send me away," Tony said. "I despise that jackass, and I won't put up with this."

"Tony, as Josiah said, that's a one-way door," Lucretia returned. "If you leave under those circumstances, there is no returning, now or ever."

"I love you and this breaks my heart, but I can't serve under a man," Tony said.

"So be it," Lucretia replied, swiping tears from her eyes.

"Get lost. There's no point in you being whipped if it won't correct you, Tony."

"Mistress —" Tony began.

"Just Lucretia," Lucretia returned. "You're exiled and an unperson to me. Start walking to the big house."

"Mistress —" he repeated.

Lucretia slapped his face, hard, and then slapped underhand into his scrotum. "I told you, I'm done with you, Anthony," she said. "Get your ass to the house, get dressed, and start walking to your apartment."

"We can work this out," Tony insisted.

"A mistress and slave relationship is on the mistress' terms," Lucretia said. "You gave up negotiation four years ago, Anthony. And you just gave up take-backs as well. You crossed that line I told you couldn't be crossed. We're done, Mr. Doyle. Get out of here." Lucretia valiantly struggled to hold her emotions in check, and succeeded in maintaining her cold perspective, and Tony fled the room, and rushed to the post, offering his hands to the cuffs.

"Master, please don't whip him," Lucretia said. "I have released him and exiled him."

"I see," Josiah said. "Tony, your former mistress likely told you to walk to the main house, get dressed, and leave my grounds. I suggest you do so immediately."

"Goddammit, just whip me and get it over with, asshole," Tony snarled.

"It doesn't work that way," Josiah said. "I regret that you weren't the slave you presented yourself as being."

"Whip me and you'll see my devotion to my mistress," Tony said.

"It's too late for that," Josiah replied. "Leigh, secure Lucretia to the post for fifty lashes. Those lashes will commence once Tony is exiled from the estate."

At this, Tony lost his temper, and bellowed a sound of rage and charged at Josiah. Josiah easily side-stepped, and drove a hard punch into Tony's ear and staggered the man. Tony slowly recovered and made another, even more clumsy, charge at Josiah, and wound up gasping and choking on the floor after a pulled karate chop from Josiah hit him in the throat and staggered him.

"Son, I know you're used to being the big guy and beating people to a pulp, but big doesn't mean shit here," Josiah said. "I can keep kicking your ass, or you can just get lost. Your choice."

"You're a despicable asshole," Tony snarled. "But Lucretia wants to pick you over what we built together, then fuck her. She deserves you, asshole. I'm out of here. I'll wait on the porch, and when Leigh brings me my clothes, I'm gone. Fuck all of you. Especially you, Lucretia!"

"Master, I beg you for more lashes still for bringing Tony here, and for his disruptions of your mastery," Lucretia said. "I'm responsible for him and deserve it."

"Bind her to the post, Molly," Josiah ordered.

"Yes, Master," Molly said. Lucretia approached the post and docilely offered her wrists to the cuffs.

"Tony, you have no more business here," Josiah said. "Get lost."

Tony bellowed his rage and charged at Josiah, who easily sidestepped him and tripped the big man, who went sprawling in an untidy heap. His head crashed into the wall, dazing him. He was struggling to rise when Leigh rushed to him and grasped him in an odd way at his neck, and he screamed out.

"If I do this hard enough for long enough, I could permanently paralyze that arm," she said smoothly. "Now, you put your hands behind your back or I swear to God I'll fuck you up forever, Tony."

"I'd suggest you do what she says," Molly piped up. "That's pretty much a Vulcan death pinch she has on you, Tony. And if she fucks you up or kills you, I think the rest of us will all swear we were in Chicago taking in a White Sox game or something."

Tony obeyed, and Molly cuffed his hands, and then cuffed his ankles, and then Leigh released him. Josiah smirked, and remembered years ago being worried about Molly and suggesting she take self-defense classes. She showed him that move and he remembered being in pain for three days that followed.

"On your feet, Tony," Josiah said.

"Sixty, please, Master," Lucretia said, weeping. "I can't believe I brought this to your door."

"Please don't do this, Lucretia," Tony said.

"Tony, you had your chance," Lucretia told him. "You know about honor and I've always had clear expectations of you."

"Two hundred," Tony said. "I'll take two hundred lashes in her place."

"It doesn't work that way, Tony," Lucretia said. "Releasing a slave, as I've done with you, is a 'death penalty' punishment. It would make no sense to whip someone who cannot be forgiven. You're ..." she sobbed. "You ... you ... you're dead to me, Tony. Just ... please leave so Master can punish me."

Tony sobbed too, and Josiah felt his heart break a bit for both of them, but he knew Lucretia was right. Some things were beyond the pale. He also knew he wasn't about to lay sixty lashes into Lucretia's back, but understood the calculus of the matter, that Tony needed to think so.

"Molly, remain here with Lucretia," Josiah ordered. "Leigh, you and I will get Tony back into his clothes and then remove him from the property."

Tony was heartbroken, too emotionally shattered even for anger, as he quietly dressed and went out to the Suburban. Leigh put on another scrub suit to wear while on the drive. Josiah drove him to a gas station five miles from the farm. "Do you want me to call a taxi for you?" he asked Tony.

"I think I need to walk," Tony said, and got out of the Suburban and began marching down the road. Josiah shrugged and headed back toward the cabin.

"I feel sorry for him," Leigh said.

"So do I, but if he no longer fits Lucretia's needs, then the best she can do is send him away instead of whipping a dead horse," Josiah said.

"I hope you find me suitable," Leigh ventured.

"Thus far," Josiah said.

"Are you really going to lay sixty lashes on Lucretia?" she asked.

"Tony seems to think so, but no," Josiah said. "She'll be whipped, and soundly, but sixty would be too harsh for something she didn't do. Yeah, she's responsible for his behavior up to the

107

point that she cut him loose, but … here's the thing, though, Leigh. She needs to be whipped, because she needs the catharsis it'll afford her. It forces her to cry, to scream, to open the gates for her grief."

"I … I guess I hadn't thought about that," Leigh admitted. "She loves him, so this has to be killing her inside."

"She does, and it is," Josiah confirmed.

"Will you love me like that?" Leigh asked.

"Probably I will," Josiah said. "You're not a client here, honey."

"Honey," Leigh echoed. "Thank you, Master. I like that. I'm sorry I'm in trouble, but at the same time, I'm not at all sorry. I know this sounds premature, but I feel like I came home yesterday, in a way. That whipping was awful, and I know it's far from my last, but … I loved it too, because it also meant I was worth the effort and time that you're giving me, Master. And it's … comforting, I guess, that it brings me closer to Molly. I've always been fond of her but for her bitchy temper at the office, if that makes sense at all. Do I sound crazy?"

"Probably, but we're all mad here," Josiah said, and grinned.

"Anyway, I could see being yours for the long haul, beyond this coming week," Leigh said. "I don't think it's Stockholm Syndrome."

"Not this soon, I should hope," Josiah said. "Besides, you willingly entered captivity here. And I'm not holding you against your will. If you backed out right now and asked me to take you to your car so you could go back to your life, you'd be free to go. But it's like with Tony there. You would never be welcomed back, for any reason."

"You're going to have to throw me out of here and make me

go back to work, maybe dragged behind that nasty old truck of yours," Leigh chuckled. "Thank God that's mostly banker's hours, though. I hope I'm welcome to return here."

"Ask me in a week," Josiah decided. He stopped the Suburban and looked her in the eye, and then kissed her and growled his desire. "I hope you know my dick will be in your ass again before this day is done, slave."

Leigh shivered and groped her new master. "Hurt me," she begged. "I don't think I've ever felt more ... *alive* ... than I've felt here, Master. I'm even looking forward to pulling one of those buggies for you, Sir."

"The rickshaws," Josiah said. "There is a race here in two weekends that maybe you should come and see."

"A race?" Leigh asked.

"This one is male slaves," Josiah told her. "It'll be a whole bunch of them, a dozen teams in all, all pulling rickshaws with their owners riding. There will be three heats of four teams, master and slave, and then the winners of each heat will race for all the marbles. We weigh them all and make them the same weight. And they race hard. This one is four laps. Each team puts up an entry fee – this one was five hundred per team – and winner take all."

"Wow," Leigh said. "Will I be racing?"

"Not in this one," Josiah said. "But if you have the speed and drive, perhaps in the future. But realistically, probably not. You're trim and fit, but the really long-legged ones are the competition. Tall ones simply run faster. It's a heated competition. The slaves are whipped furiously by their owners to spur them onward, and I've seen serious punishments handed down to those who underperformed. A year ago, one girl placed dead last by a whole lap. She went straight to the whipping post and suffered fifty of the horsewhip for embarrassing her owner."

"Christ," Leigh gasped. "Would that happen to me?"

"If I race I want to win, but … no," Josiah said. "I mean, if I think you're intentionally lagging behind or not giving your best, yeah, I'll punish you for it. But I personally thought fifty was excessive." He left out that he was so thoroughly disgusted by the matter, that he struck the owner in question, a man named Royal Suggs, from further invitations to race here again. He remembered hearing a year or so ago that Royal was arrested in a fraud scheme, but never followed up on what came of it.

"I wonder if you shouldn't do that to me, at least once, so I know the helplessness of it, Master," Leigh said. "Fifty, maybe even a hundred, where I know unquestionably that I'm nothing but property here."

"I'll keep that in mind, but I think, again, you're biting off what you really can't chew, Leigh," Josiah said. "Get out of your clothes, slave."

Leigh contorted herself but stripped naked in the Suburban, and Josiah grew harder seeing the marks still fresh on the creamy skin of her back. "Get out of the car and walk to the back," he ordered. She obeyed and he met her at the back of the Suburban, and opened the rear. "Bend over. I'm going to beat your ass before we go to the cabin."

"Yes, Master," Leigh said, and smiled a bit as she assumed the position. Josiah noted she didn't ask why he was whipping her, and guessed it was good enough for her that he simply chose to whip her. He unbuckled his belt, took his position, and lashed the belt hard into her upper thighs. Leigh yelped and almost stood, but seemed to think better of it, and kept her belly and breasts pressed hard to the carpet. Josiah kept whipping her, focusing more on her thighs than her rump, although after fifty strokes he had pretty thoroughly painted the slave red.

"What are you?" he snarled.

"A slave to be punished, Master," she gasped, trying not to sob. "Thank you, Sir. I deserve far worse."

The rain was finally lightening some, but still coming down. "Walk to the cabin, slave," Josiah ordered. "Be glad I'm not hitching you to the car and making you pull it."

NINETEEN

"Remove Lucretia from the post," Josiah ordered Molly a few minutes later in the cabin. "Go wait on the porch. Leigh will be along shortly. I made her walk. You will remain on the porch until I summon you."

"Yes, Master," Molly said. She hurriedly uncuffed Lucretia and then went outside.

Josiah sat on the middle of the sofa after removing his clothes, which were soaked. "Come to me, Lucretia," he ordered. "Straddle my lap, facing me."

Lucretia did so. "Am I to ride Master's erection?" she asked.

"If you like," Josiah said. "But I want to talk with you about you, and about what you need."

Josiah groaned pleasurably as she slid down onto him, seating his erection fully into her vagina. "Somehow it's better like this, Master," she said. "Sir, I ... I asked for sixty lashes for how Tony behaved, and I ... I think I deserve at least that. I know it's going to hurt. I know I'll probably bleed. But I think it also will help me to cry Tony out of my system, or at least start that process. I guess it was an enormous mistake bringing him here, but things unfolded differently than I could have predicted, and ... I think we're growing in different directions. But I'm hurting in my heart, Sir, and I think I need ... with your permission, I would ask to cancel my appointments this week – there are only three – and remain confined here, enslaved here, keep me busy and hurting, please. I think now more than ever I need time away from my life, time to be enslaved, used, pushed, time … I guess time to slowly process Tony and compartmentalize that situation, Master. By the way, God, you feel good inside me, but I think I need to be buggered right after you beat me, Sir."

Josiah cradled her face in his hands, pulled her to him, and kissed her gently and lovingly. "I'll do it, Lucretia, but … you need to understand you might well be scarred."

"I know, Master, and I'm good with that if it happens," Lucretia said. "Some people get tattoos to mark major life events. Some college fraternities even brand people. I remember seeing a Greek letter, maybe omega, branded onto the upper arms of football players. Probably it was some sort of a college fraternity thing. Maybe scars will remind me forever that once upon a time, Tony was a very important part of my life. And from here on in, I think you're going to be maybe even a defining element of my life."

"Go bring Molly and Leigh in here, please," Josiah said.

"Yes, Master," Lucretia said, sighing as she rose and slid off of his erection.

"Leigh, Molly, Lucretia has reiterated her request for sixty lashes," Josiah said. "I have decided to accommodate her wish, but I have also decided to be safe about it. The key to the Suburban is in my pants pocket. What I want you two to do is go to the barn and get medical equipment to monitor Lucretia before and throughout the whipping, and IV supplies if she bleeds too much. I also want you girls to go to the house and bring me back three sets of dry clothes. I will sleep in bed with one of you three tonight, drawn by lottery. Lucretia has also asked to remain here all week to be worked and enslaved, and I have agreed to that. However, she has appointments she needs to cancel, so bring her phone."

"It's in my car," Lucretia said. "Plugged in to the charger."

"We'll return soon, Master," Molly promised. She dug his keys from his pocket and she and Leigh were gone.

"Master, please be angry with me," Lucretia begged. "Hate me, even. I think you know I'm full of pain inside and I need to get it outside, like lancing a boil, I guess. The harsher you are, the kinder you're being right now."

"Suck your juices off me, bitch," Josiah snarled. In an instant, Lucretia was on her knees and swallowed him down, frantically cleaning her juices from him, until Josiah pushed her away. She looked at him and gasped when he slapped her face, hard. "You talk a lot, but until tomorrow morning, you are not to speak unless bidden to do so. Is this understood?"

Lucretia opened her mouth as though to speak, but shut it, nodded, and looked down at the floor. Her lower lip was trembling, and Josiah knew it was all part of the process, even though he hated feeling cruel. But at least it had a beneficial purpose, he told himself, even as he admitted this was a self-serving philosophy. She looked up at him a moment later, and he saw gratitude on her face, and then she looked down at the floor again

Molly and Leigh returned a few minutes later. Molly backed the Suburban up to the porch and they unloaded the medical supplies, and then a suitcase with clothing for their master.

"Girls, I want you to give Lucretia a fresh physical examination," Josiah ordered. "She is restricted from speaking until tomorrow morning. If she speaks, you will report it to me for her to be punished. If she speaks and you don't report it to me, you and Lucretia will receive double punishment. So if you have questions for her, restrict your questions to those she can answer by nodding or shaking her head."

"Yes, Sir," Molly said. "Does Master have a specific concern about her health?"

"No, only that this is a vigorous whipping she's about to receive, and I want to be assured she won't be endangered," Josiah answered.

"Sir, we brought her phone, but if she's under order of silence, how will she be able to cancel her week's appointments?" Leigh asked.

"Goddammit, I forgot that, didn't I?" Josiah said, annoyed with himself.

"Pardon my saying so, but you're at least human," Leigh grinned.

"Smartass," Josiah chuckled. "Lucretia, how many calls do you need to make?" Lucretia held up four fingers, and Josiah nodded. "Very well. You may call your clients to cancel, and then your order of silence will resume."

Leigh handed Lucretia her phone, and Lucretia looked at her reminders, and began making calls. The final call was to a man named Mark. "Mark, I'm going to be unavailable for … until a week from Monday," she said. "I need you to adjust the website to reflect that, so nobody makes an appointment I can't keep."

"Of course, Mistress Lucretia," Mark said over the speakerphone. "Uh, can we take it out in trade rather than me billing you, Ma'am?"

"An hour?" Lucretia asked.

"Ninety minutes would be better," Mark sighed.

"Fair enough," Lucretia told him. "When?"

"What about a week from Monday, starting 10:00 in the morning?" Mark asked. "It'll start my week off on a good foot."

"Book it," Lucretia ordered. "I'll see you then, Mark, and God help you if you're so much as thirty seconds late, boy."

"God ... yes, Mistress," Mark said in a trembling tone. "I need you, Ma'am."

"Mark, I really need to go," Lucretia said. "Get on the update immediately, please. I'll look in an hour, and if it's done, I'll give you two hours next Monday."

"Consider it done, Mistress," Mark said, sounding excited. Lucretia hung up the phone and handed it to Leigh.

"Should I check your site in an hour, then?" Leigh asked, and Lucretia nodded.

"Two hours ... I think Mark likes you," Leigh said, and again, Lucretia nodded.

"Okay, let's get you checked out," Molly interjected. She did the examination and wrote down the information.

"Master, her blood pressure and pulse are a bit elevated, but nothing surprising or alarming under the circumstances," Molly reported a bit later. "Her ECG shows sinus rhythm at a rate of 106, but there are no anomalies. Lung sounds are clear as can be, pupils respond equally to light. As Leigh said last night, if everyone was as healthy as this bitch, we'd both have to sell toothbrushes door-to-door."

"Put her on the post, but keep the blood pressure cuff and ECG on her for constant monitoring," Josiah ordered. "The next fifteen minutes are going to be hell on earth for this slave. I'll bugger her immediately afterward."

"Come with us, Lucretia," Leigh ordered, and Lucretia followed her new sisters to the post, where she was tightly bound. Josiah could hear the beeping of the ECG speeding up, and understood.

"Can the volume be turned down on the heart monitor?" he asked.

"Not on this model, Master," Molly said. "I'm sorry, Sir."

"Can't be helped," Josiah said. "Very well. Lucretia, you will be horsewhipped now. Your sentence is sixty lashes to your naked back, and you have stated your understanding that bleeding or even scarring is possible. You consent to this?" Lucretia nodded her head, and her body hitched a bit as she choked back a sob. "I will pause at thirty lashes and seek advice from your sisters as to whether this can proceed to the end." Again, Lucretia nodded her head. "Molly and Leigh, you are to offer her no encouragement. Lucretia is being punished, and a girl on the post isn't to be comforted but hurt." Molly nodded quickly. Leigh's eyes widened, and she nodded a bit more slowly.

Josiah slashed the whip into Lucretia's broad and muscular back, and she yelped. He lashed again and again, and on the fourth lash she screamed and fought her bonds, already breaking and losing her resolve. Josiah continued the whipping, lashing her without mercy. At thirty strokes, six of the wounds were bleeding, but nothing was deep. Josiah looked expectantly at Leigh and Molly.

"Master, her numbers are all rising, but she can take the remainder, in my opinion," Molly said in a grim tone.

"Agreed, Master," Leigh echoed, and the whipping continued. To Lucretia's credit, she remained upright and conscious throughout the beating, although very vocal. By forty lashes she was just continually sobbing, and Josiah knew it was from her heart, not the physical pain. His heart ached for her, but he knew he was doing what she needed, and continued the lashing. She lost control of her bladder with six lashes remaining, but still remained conscious. And finally the sixtieth lash was laid into her, and it looked like about a third of the welts were bloody as he coiled the whip.

"Treat the wounds if they need treatment," he ordered.

"This is going to burn like fire," Molly said to Lucretia, and then applied a coagulant stick of some sort to the welts, stanching the bleeding as Lucretia screamed anew. It took a few minutes to finish the job. "Master, I think two of the wounds might scar, but we'll need to monitor them," she said.

"Remove her from the post," Josiah ordered. "Lucretia, once off the post, you will get on all fours to be buggered, and then you're going to clean up your mess from the floor." Lucretia nodded with a pained moan as Leigh helped her from the post.

She went to all fours, offering her ass high, and Josiah ordered Molly to remove Lucretia's plug. Leigh, unbidden, knelt and sucked Josiah to complete hardness, and then lubricated his erection. And then he knelt behind the pain-addled slave, and plundered her bottom. She grunted, but pushed back to meet his thrusts, taking all of him into her even as she silently wept. Josiah fucked her hard, relentless. The plug had considerably loosened her, and he was able to last a while inside her, but finally arched his back and erupted deeply into her as he groaned and shuddered at the very powerful climax. He could tell Lucretia was highly aroused and correctly guessed she was fighting back a climax, teetering on the brink before she finally got herself under control and reeled back from cumming. Josiah was ornery enough to put a girl under an order not to cum and then making her cum, but Lucretia had been through the wringer, and enough was enough. In truth, he thought it was more than enough, but he sensed that he should follow her lead and accord her requests in this, until he got a better handle on her needs and what made her tick. He withdrew from her and Molly knelt and cleaned his member, and sucked at it after, to prove she'd cleaned him well.

"Lucretia, there are cleaning supplies in the laundry room closet," Josiah ordered. "Get a mop and bucket and clean up the mess you made."

Lucretia turned and knelt, and made the sign-language sign of "thank you," and then got to her feet and slowly made her way to the laundry room, almost totally spent from her use. She returned a moment later, and mopped up her puddle, and then took the bucket out on the porch to pour it out. She took mop and bucket back to the laundry room closet and then returned to the living room and knelt again before her master, waiting further instruction.

"Lucretia, you may go to your room for ..." he consulted the clock "... two hours, and then there'll be work for you to do. Go."

Lucretia went up the stairs and closed the door, and Josiah heard the sounds of her crying for a while.

"That poor woman," Molly said. "Master, she cried a lot about Tony while you were taking him away, Sir. It's going to take her time to get over this, no matter how tough she tries to behave. I hated seeing her whipped that savagely, but ... I think it was what she needed, Master."

"I concur," Josiah said. "You two build a lunch for us. Heavy on the protein, because you'll all need it."

"Master, with your permission, I can go catch some fish," Molly suggested. "They're usually hungry on the heels of rain. If not, I know there are steaks in the freezer in the big house I can thaw. I think we only have microwave dinners and eggs and bacon in the fridge here, Sir."

"A fish fry sounds good," Josiah agreed. "And fries and hush puppies. Maybe a salad to go with it. I know we bought a bunch of salad fixings Friday."

"That sounds wonderful, Master," Molly grinned. "I'll swap the Suburban for the truck. Shall I take Leigh with me, Sir?"

"Yeah, she needs to do her part," Josiah decided.

"Let's go, Leigh," Molly said.

The physicians first swapped the Suburban for the farm truck – Molly didn't want to get fish stink in the Suburban – and then drove to the barn, where they rounded up tackle, and then to the pond, where they quickly caught a small mess of eight bass.

"That seems like too much," Leigh said.

"Oh, it is," Molly agreed. "But Master loves cold fried fish from the fridge, so he'll snarf the leftovers around midnight. Disgusting, I know, but there's no accounting for taste. He's a good man, but I think they all have bachelor habits here and there in their lives. He likes cold leftover pizza too, which also grosses me out. Anyway, let's fillet these fish and get moving. I don't know about you, but I'm halfway starved here, and I expect we're going to be pulling him about in a rickshaw this afternoon, and we'll want fuel for that."

"How hard is it to pull that rickshaw?" Leigh wanted to know.

"Your guess is as good as mine," Molly said. "Leigh, you're more experienced at slavery than I am. Until now, he's spanked me a few times, even paddled me, but nothing harsh, just foreplay. My ass was virginal until he plundered me this morning. I'm a newbie."

"What brought this on?" Leigh asked.

"Friday," Molly said. "Well, that was the final straw for me, anyway, when I realized I was out of control. I've also been fucking around on him, and confessed that to him. I ... I think he'll go easier on me while you're here, but the week after next is terrifying."

"I doubt he'll break any spousal abuse laws," Leigh offered.

"Wouldn't matter," Molly said. "Josiah is a clever lawyer. The law doesn't mean jackshit on this farm."

"How's that?" Leigh asked.

"I'm probably talking out of school here, and will have to confess this to him, but you deserve to know, Leigh," Molly decided at length. "Master obtained this property several years ago. A client of his went bankrupt and needed fast cash, and sold it to him for far less than it was worth. Master just felt sorry for him, I think, and figured he would re-sell the place, until it occurred to him how he could use this property. But what it is that we do isn't entirely in line with the law. Sometimes the cops overlook the S&M people, but sometimes they get puritanical and treat us like we're running whorehouses and abuse."

"I know Lucretia has to be very cautious," Leigh remarked. "Sir Blake wanted her to bugger me with a strap-on, but she said she couldn't do that because it would cross the line into prostitution."

"Yeah," Molly said. "So Master leased the property to a diplomat from some African country for 99 years, and then the diplomat put it under diplomatic immunity. Legally, we're on the soil of Sierra Leone or Liberia or Malawi ... but Master secretly sublet it from the diplomat and here we are. But we're immune to American law here. Master could manufacture a hundred tons of cocaine out here and nobody could do anything about it."

"Clever," Leigh said. "So if he wanted to assemble a firing squad and execute us, the law wouldn't come into play."

"I don't think he'd go that far, but … yeah, he'd be immune," Molly said. "I … I asked him to brand me like a cow, when he talked to me last night."

"Jesus," Leigh said. "Scary … but … God, that sounds sexy, permanently marked as property."

"I think he'll do it eventually," Molly said. "Maybe to you too, if you and he meld well. I … Leigh, I like you, and I always have. I don't resent you for Friday. I … I hope you become permanent, is what I'm saying. I hope you make him love you and need you, even if it means I'm low girl on the totem pole. God, when we kissed, if he'd allowed, I'd have fucked you a hundred different ways to Sunday."

"It turned me on too, in case you didn't notice," Leigh said, and snorted. "Jesus, you're both so sexy. Throw Lucretia into the mix and it's a thousand different wet dreams all at once."

"It's a safe bet that once we're not being punished, he'll be okay with us sleeping together," Molly said. "But we should always do our best to ensure his balls are emptied, and he's a horny one. I went to Chicago for that CE six months ago. Three days I was gone, and he decided to show me how horny he was. He put the Kleenex on my nightstand. In three days there were twelve of them. Twelve."

"Kleenex?" Leigh asked.

"I wasn't around to suck him off, so he jacked off instead," Molly said bluntly.

"Jesus," Leigh said.

"Sometimes I think it's a shame I can't have babies, but I

think if I could he'd have turned me into a baby factory like that dimwit clan in Arkansas or Missouri or wherever on TV," Molly said, and grinned. "I think now that I've entirely surrendered, he's going to be very interested in my ass for a while to come. For some reason it's always turned him on. I think because, at least ostensibly, we shouldn't orgasm from it, although I think the sexual overtones make it happen anyway, and it's hurtful and even humiliating. I guess in a way, it's like he's saying, tacitly, that my pussy isn't worth it to him. Turns out, I have a huge humiliation trigger inside me. The last two days have been news to me, Leigh."

"I knew it about myself already," Leigh said. "Do we need to take the skin off these fish, or the scales, or leave them as-is, by the way?"

"Take the skin off," Molly said. "We'll fry these. If he was grilling them, we'd leave skin and scales so they'd hold up on the grill better."

"Take the skin off," Leigh said. "About what's going to happen to all three of us all week."

"We deserve it," Molly pointed out.

"Yeah, we do," Leigh agreed. "I couldn't help it as Lucretia was getting that whipping, thinking I deserved at least that for how I've been with Sir Blake for so long, realizing how much he's tolerated from me on the altar of loving me."

Molly was silent for a long moment. "Look, I guess I need to say this too, Leigh. I'm suspended from the practice for two weeks, and then back a week on probation, and then the partners all decide whether I am to be fired. I'm going to love you just the same no matter how that decision goes. So please … don't let our time here influence how you vote on whether I'm fired. Vote on whether or not I'm an asset to the practice. If I'm a liability, fire me. Master will punish me harshly, but … in a way I want and need that. I'm tempted to seduce you out here just so you'll tattle and I'll get whipped for it, but that's foolish. He'll beat me harshly for the next two weeks. God knows he's about to run all three of us ragged on his rickshaw."

"I got a glimpse of it, but I don't know how it works," Leigh remarked.

"You are to run flat out, fast as you can," Molly said. "Master lashes the slave to spur her onward. Usually, he sets a goal and times it, and if the slave is too slow, she's put on the post and given extra lashes."

"Jesus, I'm glad I stay in shape," Leigh said.

"I wish I had," Molly told her. "Oh, I'm only about twenty pounds overweight and I think for my age I'm in decent shape, but I don't run or exercise all that much. I'm sure he'll beat me bloody after my run. I'll do my best, but … I'm … I won't do well at it and I know that."

"I'll tell you a secret," Leigh said. "I hope I do well enough that he races me in an event. Something about being reduced to an animal … God, I don't know what it is, but it turns me on in a huge way."

"Run like hell, then," Molly said.

"I worry about Lucretia," Leigh remarked.

"Yeah, her knee is bad, but I don't think Master notices what we do," Molly said.

"I never offered to look at the knee, but I'm going to suggest she makes an appointment with us," Leigh told her. "Maybe there's something we can do for it. You have an impressive setup out here, but there are no x-rays or MRI units, and why diagnose what you can't treat out here? I noticed you have casting supplies, though."

"So far, thank God, they've been unnecessary, but ... I figure if someone breaks a leg running a rickshaw or breaks a bone in some other misadventure, I'd rather not be here with only a spool of duct tape and a broken-off board for a splint, right? I've seen a hundred sprains and scrapes, and you can imagine how many various whip marks."

"That makes sense," Leigh said.

"Okay, let's go to the big house, wash our hands, and round up fries and the salad stuff," Molly said. "I'm half-starved and the sooner we're back to the cabin, the sooner we're eating."

After Leigh and Molly left, Josiah had a cup of coffee and then went up the stairs to see Lucretia. Again, he walked into the room without knocking and found her in bed, on her belly, but awake.

"How're you doing?" he asked.

"Master, that was the worst pain I've ever known," Lucretia said. "Worse than when my knee blew out, even. But ... I wanted or needed even more, maybe a hundred instead of sixty, or maybe even the two hundred that Tony offered to take in my place. But ... it was a start. I'm where I need to be, Master. Something in me has changed, or one need has intensified. It took every scrap of my self-control not to cum when you were taking my ass. Good Lord, that was intense. I hope it's not the only time."

"It won't be," Josiah promised her. "Asses are tighter and don't make babies."

In spite of herself, Lucretia actually giggled at this remark. "Jesus, it hurts to laugh, but that's hysterical," she managed to say.

"Master, I guess I'm about to be whipped all over again for speaking when you put me on a silence order, but ... Sir, I'm grateful. I've needed this for a long time. I wonder how well I'll do as a dominatrix after this, but I don't even care. I need this. I need you, sir. I'm ... I keep coming back to I'm where I need to be, Sir. And thank you for this. I know Molly and Leigh are sexier than I am, but I need you, Sir."

"Oh, you're plenty sexy, trust me," Josiah said, being honest. "But this isn't a contest. You'll get my dick as much as Leigh and Molly will."

"I love it in my ass, apparently," Lucretia said. "That surprised me. I had no idea. God, that was amazing, Sir. I loved it. It took all I had not to cum all over the place. Maybe I should have done it so you would have lashed me more. It's helping, the suffering, the absolute robbery of control, being enslaved, Sir."

"Perhaps after you deal with Mark you'll need more time here?" Josiah asked.

"Master, I think ... I'm trying to make sense of this ... I think maybe once I've done my session with Mark – I owe him that – I might need to close up shop in that business and just be a slave from here on in. But that's an enormous decision. I would beg Master to give me a month or freedom or maybe even six weeks to let me make a clear-headed decision as to what I should do, moving forward. But I could see being your field slave here, Sir, and being entirely satisfied with that life, Sir. You ... you opened a door inside me, Master. I think that might lead me to being entirely a slave."

"Is that what you want?" Josiah asked.

"Master, if you offered right now to put a collar on me and own me for life, I'd accept," Lucretia answered. "I think a week from now that would still be my answer. I honestly think a month out, that will remain my answer. I … I like being a dominatrix, but that's not the same as saying it's really me. I like driving fast, and even race a car I have out at the track sometimes, but I don't want to be Danica Patrick. I keep coming back to those movies I saw as a kid, and envying the slaves more than the masters, if that makes sense."

"It does," Josiah said. "Come give me a kiss, and then I'm going to whip you for talking, Lucretia."

She rose from the bed, and the two kissed deeply and passionately, Josiah's nails raking across Lucretia's wounds as she groaned but intensified her kiss, showing her submission and need for what he was doing to her., and then the kiss broke.

"Thirty of the cane," Josiah said.

"Please, more, Master," Lucretia growled. "I would beg for the greater of fifty or until I bleed, Sir."

"Lucretia …" Josiah began, and then paused. "I guess you know what you're asking me to do, don't you?"

"I've made them bleed before, Master," she said. "I know the consequences. I know I could scar from this, Sir. Should I shut up now?"

"Yes," Josiah said. "Bend over the edge of the bed, elbows on the bed, palms flat, elbows on the bed, legs straight, no bending at the knees. Fifty or until bleeding."

Lucretia rose from the bed and kissed Josiah again, and then positioned herself as ordered while he picked up her cane and positioned himself to lash her. Lucretia sighed, and then arched her back to present her rump for the cane, and Josiah began lashing her, lashing her severely without mercy. She hissed at several of the strokes, but endured, finally yelping at thirty-three lashes, and crying openly at forty. Finally, Josiah laid in the fiftieth stroke, but her tough skin held firm throughout.

"No blood," he remarked. "I shall lash slave in ten-stroke increments until it bleeds. But I will focus the lashes to slave's upper thighs and lower rump, to split the skin."

Lucretia moaned, but offered no verbalization of the matter, and Josiah begin lashing her anew, all ten lashes into the "sit-spot" where buttocks and thigh meet. Lucretia grunted through the lashes, but held her tongue. Still, there was no bleeding, and Josiah noted that Lucretia's skin was notably tough, and laid ten more lashes into the hapless slave while she cried, but held her place. "Ten more," Josiah decreed, and resumed the caning, focusing the lashes all inside a two-inch band where buttocks meet thighs. Ten more lashes finally opened the skin as a weakened Lucretia slumped onto the bed, gasping and groaning.

Josiah wiped her cane clean and used another coagulant stick to stanch the bleeding, and Lucretia let loose a fresh howl at the burning on her raw flesh. "You may recover," Josiah said. Lucretia knelt before him and kissed his hand, and then pointed to her lips with a questioning look, and Josiah nodded. She rose and they kissed, and he grew more erect at the sound of her moaning in mingled suffering and desire.

"You're going to get one hell of a lot of buggering this week, slave," Josiah said, and Lucretia smiled as she groped him, and then signed a thank you to him. "Okay, we're running rickshaws later, slave. Once Molly and Leigh return and make some food for us, we're all going out there and I'm going to run you three ladies very hard. You should rest here until you're called down for our meal. The table only has hard wooden chairs, but perhaps you'll agree they're good for fresh-caned asses, so slaves are reminded anew of misbehavior's consequences."

Lucretia nodded, and Josiah kissed her again. "Rest," he ordered, and went back down the stairs. A moment later, Leigh and Molly arrived and busied themselves in the kitchen.

"We'll be eating in about another twenty minutes, Master," Molly announced a bit later.

"Excellent," Josiah said. "I'm hungry as hell, and I can't imagine you slaves are less so."

"Can ... can we talk, Master?" Molly asked.

"Sure," Josiah said, and went out onto the porch with Molly.

"Master, I know I'm in for hell but ... Sir, I want you to know I've never felt happier than I do right now, and ... thank you, Sir."

"You're welcome," Josiah said.

"I ... Master, for what it's worth, I hope Leigh proves a good fit and you keep her long-term," Molly said. "Probably Lucretia as well. I don't know her as well as I know Leigh, obviously, but ... she draws me in a way, Master. I think we're going to have a happy family once you've broken us all, Sir."

"I hope so," Josiah said, and kissed Molly. "Bend over that chair. I want your palms flat on the seat and legs straight."

"Did I speak out of turn, Master?" Molly asked as she obeyed.

"Not at all," Josiah assured her. "But this term for you is one of punishment, when and where I wish to do it, and there will be a good amount of me asserting myself on all three of you. I guess you noticed Leigh's ass and thighs, yes?"

"She said you went over her with your belt, Master," Molly

129

confirmed.

"I did," Josiah said as he loosened his belt and drew it through its loops. He began whipping Molly, much as he had Leigh, laying in fifty strokes while the woman sobbed in pain. Her ass was a bright red mess when he was done.

"Thank you, Master," Molly groaned.

"Put my belt back on me, slave," Josiah ordered.

Molly took the belt, knelt and began threading the belt through the loops. "God, I love you, Master," she said, and buckled his belt.

"I love you too," Josiah said. "Let's eat."

Josiah raved about the lunch, devouring fish and fries and salad, and washing it all down with about a quart of iced tea. He noticed the slaves were all eating heartily as well, and smirked at how gingerly all three were sitting on their chairs.

"You made a wonderful meal," he told them.

"Thank you, Master," Leigh said, and blushed. "I'm glad you enjoy it. That was the first time I ever caught fish. It's … interesting, Master. I find it really satisfying to have done the entire process from catching and cleaning through cooking and eating."

"I agree," Josiah said.

"Master loves doing that out here," Molly remarked. "And he's a whiz at cooking up fish all kinds of ways. He really hides his light under a bushel."

"As long as he keeps a strong hand on us," Leigh said, and smiled. Josiah noticed the silent Lucretia nodding and smiling at that remark.

"Let's go to the track," Josiah ordered.

TWENTY

Unfortunately, it soon became apparent that rickshaw runs would be impossible, probably for several days, after the rains had entirely saturated the track. Even petite Leigh sunk halfway to her knees in the muddy track, to her consternation and Josiah's laughter as Molly and Lucretia struggled to get her out of the mud.

"Okay, that's a wash, no pun intended," Josiah said. "Molly, there's a trailer of wood in the second barn. You three fire up the log splitter and start splitting it for firewood. That should keep you busy for several hours. Is there water in the refrigerator out there?"

"I threw four cases in it a month ago and we haven't been out there since, Master, so I'm sure there is, Sir," Molly said.

"I'll be back in a few hours," Josiah told them. He got in the Suburban and drove back to the house, and there, turned on the TV to see what was going on. He was worn out already and the day was only half done. Apparently some moron stepped out in front of a moving train going sixty miles per hour, according to Local 22 News. Police were still trying to identify the remains. Beautiful weather was forecast for the coming week, with nice winds to help things dry out. The Russians were still being warlike and turbulent, and the Middle East remained at the brink of a thousand years' war with the whole world, including themselves. Several teams won and lost sporting events, and some moron in Kentucky went to the police to complain that he had been shorted on crystal meth he'd purchased. Just then, Lucretia's phone rang, and Josiah glanced at it, curious, and recognized the number as that of the local sheriff's department.

Curious, he answered the call.

"I'm trying to reach Lucretia St. Cyr," a male voice said, sounding official.

"This is her telephone but she's unavailable at the moment," Josiah said. "May I ask who's calling?"

"I am Sergeant Michael Vickers of the Sheriff's Department," the man said.

"I am her attorney," Josiah hedged. "Is my client in some sort of trouble, Sergeant?"

"No, Sir," Vickers said. "Shit, no offense, but I hate dealing with lawyers. Occupational hazard, huh? Okay, you're her attorney, so here's what's going on ... who are you, by the way? Your name, Sir?"

"Josiah Bailey."

"Okay," Vickers said. "Sir, a man was found dead today. His ID is Anthony Doyle, and a next-of-kin card lists Ms. St. Cyr. I suppose I need her to positively ID his remains and to handle the official stuff that comes with a death."

"Jesus H. Christ," Josiah said, disturbed. "What happened?"

"Sir, he stepped in front of a train," Vickers said. "It was a suicide."

"And you want her to identify ... what?" Josiah asked. "He's bound to be so much ground meat and splatter after a train got him." Josiah had been a prosecutor as a young lawyer, and had seen many gruesome photos in that job.

"Sir, the head is intact," Vickers said. "What we've done is photographed that ... it's not as gruesome as it sounds. But we'd ask her to identify the photograph as Mr. Doyle, if it is indeed him and not a man running around with stolen ID."

"Where will she need to do this, Sergeant?" Josiah asked.

"The county morgue," Vickers said.

"Okay, let me contact her and … is this a good number to call you back?" Josiah asked.

"Let me give you my cell number," Vickers said. He rattled off the number and Josiah wrote it down.

"I'll call you back within the hour, Sergeant," Josiah said, and ended the call, then sighed and rubbed his face. He went out to the Suburban and drove to the barn, where he found three slaves sweated but a lot of work done, by the look of the split logs.

"All of you, get in the car," he said. The slaves looked curious, but not particularly worried, and all three got into the Suburban. Josiah drove back to the big house and had them all come inside.

"Master, you look really upset," Molly said. "What happened, Sir?"

"All of you, sit on the sofa there," Josiah said, and the slaves sat. Fortunately, Lucretia was in the middle. Josiah sat on the coffee table and looked at Lucretia. "There's no easy way of saying this, Lucretia. The sheriff's department phoned your cell phone a while ago. I took the call since I thought it might be important. A sergeant there … he says Tony killed himself."

"Oh, God!" Lucretia howled, and then burst into sobs as Molly and Leigh hugged her from either side.

"I'm very sorry, Lucretia," Josiah said. "I know that doesn't come close to helping. I'm afraid you need to shower and get dressed. There's paperwork that needs to be handled there. I'll be with you to ensure you're protected and to offer my advice, legal and personal.

"We'll all go," Molly said. "We're family now. Come on, Lucretia, let's get you showered and ready to go."

"I need to climb into a suit so I look the part," Josiah said. "I don't think there will be problems. The sergeant made it sound as though this is all going to be pretty straightforward."

"I … Jesus, I killed him," Lucretia said.

"No," Josiah said with just a bit of steel in his tone. "Tony killed himself. He had choices and this was his choice to make, Lucretia."

"There's an issue I need to discuss with you," Lucretia said. "I told you Lucretia is not my name. I think Tony suspected a name like Lucretia St. Cyr wasn't my real name, but I don't think he ever knew what my name is."

"The officer asked for Lucretia St. Cyr," Josiah remarked. "I need to ask you … were there legal matters in which you and Tony were entangled?"

"None," Lucretia said. "His official address was a condo, a one-bedroom place about five miles from my house. I own that under a corporation, as well as my house, and another house where I ply my trade. I don't have clients come to my home. But to pass all the sniff tests, Tony had a job, employed as a secretary with my company, and paid rent on the condominium. I never let him get too close to me. He lived in the condo, and only slept at my place once or twice weekly. We didn't own anything together. He listed me as his next of kin because there was nobody else. His father was killed by the police when he was four years old, trying to rob a corner liquor store. A local minister got involved in his life and kept him on the straight and narrow. He even lived with the minister when Tony's mother got into cocaine in a big way. He found out in his junior year of college that she OD'd and died. The preacher who raised him was old. He and his wife both passed. Tony had two brothers and a sister, but hadn't seen them since he was about ten years old. I was all he had, Sir."

"Tragic," Josiah remarked.

"So ... how do I sign him out?" Lucretia asked.

"As Sarah Louise Barton," Josiah answered simply. "Lucretia, you know that anything you need from this family is yours for the asking."

"Thank you, Master," Lucretia said. "I'll need to arrange for cremation. I was all he had, so there's no point to a memorial service. May I go clean up? Christ, all I have to wear is what I wore over here the other day."

"If you want, we'll run by your house and you can change there if you want," Josiah said. "But the slacks and blouse you wore here will —"

"It's a very sheer blouse, Master," she interrupted. "I ... it'll put whip marks on display. I'm not ashamed of them, but they're nobody else's business, just the same."

"Then we'll run by your house and let you change," Josiah said.

"In that case, I may as well shower there, Sir," Lucretia said.

"Let's shower here," Leigh suggested. "Master, what happened? I mean, how did he do it?"

"He stepped in front of a train," Josiah said, and Lucretia howled anew. Josiah knew there was no way Lucretia could be protected from this knowledge, but still hated himself for bringing her this news.

"Molly, I'm sure, saw as much terrible stuff in her internship and residency as I did," Leigh said. "We'll be right there with you, Lucretia. Let's go get cleaned up, sweetie."

The women went up the stairs, supportive of Lucretia, and Josiah went to his bedroom, showered quickly, and dressed in an expensive suit, sensing it would be best if he looked the part. He went down the stairs and called Sergeant Vickers.

"Sergeant, this is Josiah Bailey," he said. "I'll bring my client to the morgue in about two hours. It took some time to track her down."

"I'll be there," Vickers promised. "Thank you, Mr. Bailey."

Twenty minutes later, the women were downstairs. Molly was in jeans and a polo shirt, Leigh in the pantsuit she'd worn when she arrived recently, and Lucretia in her slacks and blouse, which were fairly wrinkled. Leigh's attire was in little better shape than Lucretia's, and Josiah made a mental note to have both women bring a few changes of clothes here. While he loved having them naked, sometimes proper clothing was indeed a necessity. He and Molly both had plenty of clothes here already.

"You ride up front so you can navigate," Josiah said to Lucretia. Twenty minutes later they were at her house, a nice 3-bedroom place in a middle-class neighborhood, nothing ostentatious or fancy. It was anonymous, which allowed Lucretia to live more or less unnoticed.

"Please come in," Lucretia said, and the three followed her into her house. Josiah admired some of the art on her walls, which included a piece that he was pretty certain was a genuine Picasso. A few minutes later, Lucretia returned to the living room, dressed down in jeans and a Kelly green silk blouse.

"Leigh, I have a few clothes that might fit you, if you want to change too," Lucretia said. "That pantsuit looks like you've lived in it a week."

"Hit by a wrinkle-bomb," Leigh agreed. "I ... yes, I'd like to look a bit more presentable."

A few minutes later, Leigh was attired in tan slacks and a red polo shirt. "Jesus, I'm Jake from State Farm," she quipped, and Josiah snorted at her joke. And then they left the house and were on the road to the morgue.

TWENTY-ONE

"Sergeant, for reasons that aren't anything to do with this matter of Mr. Doyle's passing, my client operates her business interests under a pseudonym," Josiah said to Sergeant Vickers when they met at the morgue. "She's a very private lady. Mr. Doyle was an employee of hers, but didn't know her legal name. She operates as Lucretia St. Cyr in her business interests, but her name is Sarah Barton."

"I see," Vickers said, looking closely at Lucretia. "Sir, this looks like an open-and-shut suicide, so it's ... I don't think the name of the next-of-kin is going to be at issue here. Who are these other two women?"

"One is Dr. Molly Bailey, MD. The other is Dr. Leigh Murphy, MD," Josiah said.

"Bailey," Vickers echoed. "Your wife? Sister?"

"My wife," Josiah confirmed. "She and Leigh work in the same medical practice and offered to come along in case things were too upsetting to my client."

"That might prove to have been a good decision," Vickers said, and turned his attention to Lucretia. "Ms. St. Cyr, this isn't quite as dramatic as what they do on television, but I do need you to tell me whether or not the man in question is indeed Anthony Doyle. What we've done is we've shot a photograph of him. If you can identify the photograph as him, then that's all we need. If you are ... uncertain ... we have other photos that we might need you to

139

review."

"Was there a tattoo of a Greek letter on the upper left arm?" Lucretia asked, pointing to her own upper arm to illustrate.

"Yes, there was, Ma'am. I looked it up, the letter epsilon," Vickers said in a gentle voice. "And what looks like a surgical scar on the right knee."

"Show me your photograph," Lucretia said.

"Please be seated," Vickers said. He opened a laptop and typed on it a moment, and then brought up a photograph.

"Oh, dear God," Lucretia moaned, and broke into braying sobs, inconsolable, as Molly and Leigh flocked to her and held her."

"Sergeant Vickers, I would have been the last one here to have seen Mr. Doyle alive," Josiah said. "I can positively identify the photograph as that of Mr. Anthony Doyle."

"How is it that you saw him last?" Vickers asked.

"He and Lucretia were our houseguests over the weekend," Josiah said. "I have a getaway property in this area. Mr. Doyle asked for a ride to the gas station, the Chevron out on 73. He and my client were … dating … and things came to an end with them this morning. I offered to pay cab fare for him, but he told me he'd rather walk. I figured he was just going to go up the road to Mabel's and hook a ride from there."

"Did he indicate any suicidal ideations?" Vickers asked.

"He was upset by the breakup, but beyond that, no," Josiah said, making a mental note to suggest to Lucretia that her website be taken down for a week or two until this all died down. She didn't need uncomfortable light shining on her.

"Ms. St. Cyr, as part of the routine investigation, we came across your website," Vickers remarked. *Shit,* Josiah thought. "Was the nature of your relationship with Mr. Doyle rooted in sadomasochism?"

"The nature of our relationship was that I loved him," Lucretia said. "Not because of what we did or didn't do in and out of bed, but because I loved him, Sergeant."

"Ma'am, I'm too old and I've been in this job too long to get all that cracked about what anyone does in their own homes," Vickers said. "He was a big man, looked like he could've ripped hundred-year-old oaks right up out of the ground, so I don't think he was unwilling in whatever you two were doing. But the news was all over this story out there, and the Freedom of Information Act means we're going to have to release his name to the press, the sorry bastards. They don't care about your grief, but I do. Not because I'm a cop but because I'm a fellow human being. Now, your lawyer can give you better advice than I can, but sooner or later one of those bastards is going to dig up this angle and try to make a story where there really is none. The good thing is, those dummies mostly have the attention span of goldfish. Maybe the hairspray kills off the brain cells over time, I don't know." He snorted, not with particular amusement. "You'll probably be happier if you can lay low for a week or two and stay off their radar until something else shiny gets their attention."

"Mr. Bailey, can you phone Mark Litton? He's in my phone book here. Please tell him what happened, and ask him to take down the site altogether until further notice," Lucretia asked.

"Sure," Josiah said, and found Mark in her phone book, and dialed the number, stepping off for quiet and privacy.

"Hello, Mistress," Mark said into the phone, sounding excited.

"Mark, my name is Josiah Bailey. I'm Lucretia's attorney," Josiah introduced himself.

"Oops," Mark said, sounding sheepish. "What can I do for you, Mr. …. Bailey, you said?"

"Bailey," Josiah confirmed. "Mark, I don't know if you know Lucretia's guy Tony —"

"I know him," Mark said. "What's up?"

"Mark, Tony killed himself today," Josiah said. "It was … pretty spectacular."

"Jesus, I'm so sorry," Mark said, and sounded sincere.

"There is concern that the news will learn of Lucretia's business and shine too much uncomfortable light on it —"

"I understand, Sir," Mark said. "I'll take the page down right now. One moment, please … and … it's … gone. Please ask her to let me know when she wants it to come back online, Sir. And tell her I understand if she needs to postpone a meeting we had scheduled a week from tomorrow."

"Will do," Josiah promised. "Thank you for your help here."

"Please tell her I'm very sorry," Mark said. "How is she taking it?"

"She's heartbroken," Josiah said. "She loved Tony."

"He was a good guy," Mark said. "I liked him."

"She'll be in touch," Josiah promised, and hung up.

"Ma'am, I think our business here is done," Vickers said. "I'm sorry for your loss. I know you have a lot to do in all of this. If you'll let the people here at the medical examiner know who is to retrieve his remains, they'll handle it from here."

"Jackson & Steinberg," Lucretia said. "I'll go directly there and make the arrangements."

"Yes, Ma'am," Vickers said. "I'll tell them."

Minutes later, they were back in the Suburban. Lucretia looked shell-shocked, still. "Master, will you take me to Jackson & Steinberg, so I can make arrangements, please?" she asked.

"Sure," Josiah said. "That's over on Boudreaux Road, right?"

"Yes, Master," Lucretia said.

Twenty minutes later, Josiah parked at the funeral home, and thirty minutes after that, Lucretia (who'd asked to go in alone) walked out and got back into the Suburban. Uncertain what else to do, Josiah drove back to the farm, and to the cabin. He'd been gently holding Lucretia's hand for most of the trip.

"You know you're welcome to remain here as long as you need," Josiah said to her.

"Master ... God, I need you like I never would have guessed," Lucretia said. "Thank you."

"Master, I think Lucretia needs you in her bed tonight," Molly said.

"She does," Leigh agreed.

"Yeah, I think that's best," Josiah said. "Leigh and Molly, you're dismissed for the night. I'm taking Lucretia to the main house with me."

Leigh and Molly exited the Suburban and Josiah returned

with Lucretia to the main house. "Master, I think right now I need you to make love to me," Lucretia said. "But … tomorrow … I need you to rape me and beat me like you hate me. Make me scream, make me bleed, make me sob Tony out of my system so I can let that poor tortured soul to rest. I feel … I don't even know how to feel. I killed a man today, Master."

Josiah grasped her hair and glared into her eyes. "You're *not* to blame for Tony," he said, calmly but with plenty of steel in his tone. "The only person who killed Tony was Tony. Now, I think under ordinary circumstances I would have liked the man, but he freely chose how he was going to behave here, and he freely chose how to kill himself. You didn't do that. I didn't do that. Leigh and Molly certainly didn't do that. It was all on Tony. I know you're hurting because you love him, but don't take on guilt you don't deserve."

"Thank you, Master," Lucretia whispered. "If only my heart would listen to my mind. Please … make love to me, Master."

Upstairs, Josiah undressed Lucretia and then shed his own clothes. He nibbled at her neck while she moaned, and then kissed and nibbled a trail down her body, teasing and building her need, while she shook and begged. He found his way to her womanly parts, and right as his fingers touched her clitoris, she arched her back and cried out with an intense orgasm, riding it through its crest before she fell onto the bed, gasping and weeping. But Josiah wasn't done. He slid two fingers into her, twisting and thrusting, while his tongue darted at her clitoris. In moments, she was quivering anew, her breath coming in short hitches, when she suddenly exploded into another, even more intense, climax, screaming with this one and gasping, panting and begging him to let her breathe.

"Jesus … Christ … where did you learn that?" she breathed.

"Cub Scouts, for a merit badge," Josiah said. "And then I ate a Brownie and that's why I was banned for life."

"Ass!" she exclaimed, and giggled in spite of herself. "You're as bad as those *American Pie* movies." Her tone changed to an eerily accurate impression of Allison Hannigan. "There was this one time ... at Band Camp ..."

Josiah chuckled and kissed a trail up her body while she began quivering anew, and then slid his erection into her. She growled her own passion and wrapped her long legs around him as he slid in and out, and they kissed deeply.

"Can I go cowgirl, please?" she begged. In a moment, she was riding him reverse cowgirl, and Josiah's eyes fixed on her welts, which looked so sexy on her lovely brown skin. She stopped and shuddered her way through another orgasm and then rode him hard until he grasped her hips and erupted his own seed deeply into her.

"Jesus ... I've been with some skilled men in the sack, but you ... holy crap," she managed to say as she slid up his body and curled up into his arms. "Thank you, Master. I needed this. I know this might sound a bit fucked up, but ... I'm starting to love you, Sir. Please be vicious with me tomorrow. I'm going to need that."

"How vicious are you begging me to be?" Josiah asked.

"I want what you've done so far to seem like a kiss from my kindly old grandma back in Kent," Lucretia said. "I ... please, Master. It's not the first time for me. I need it."

"How do you mean?"

"A cousin of mine had a surprise heart attack about ten years ago," Lucretia said. "She was 22 years old, picture of perfect health, and keeled over dead without warning. Two hours after her funeral I was on a plane to Memphis, and I spent the entire next day having the shit beaten out of me. She caned me, strapped me, slapped my face, used birches on my belly and breasts. I was marked everywhere from shoulders to knees, front, back and even my sides, but it let me pour out the grief. I loved Martina very much and was crushed when she died like that. She'd have graduated from college in another two months, already had a career lined up … and gone."

"I'm sorry," Josiah said.

"It's okay," Lucretia assured him. "But it's how I need to get through grief, Master. I think I've needed this evolution a long time, Sir. Right about now – and I know I may feel different by the cold light of dawn – but right about now I'd be pleased if you captured me and never let me leave, Master."

"We'll see how you feel in a week," Josiah promised.

TWENTY-TWO

Josiah was surprised when he snapped awake at 5:45, a good two hours before he usually woke on his own. Lucretia was sound asleep beside him. He quietly dressed and left a note on the nightstand that he would return shortly, and did a mental inventory of the cabin's kitchen, and loaded eggs, bacon, and other provisions into the Suburban – which he noted was now in desperate need of a wash – and then drove to the cabin, where he found Leigh and Molly in the kitchen on their first cups of coffee. This wasn't a surprise. Medical school and her residency had made an early riser of Molly her entire life since, and she seldom slept beyond 6:15.

"Good morning," Josiah greeted them.

"Good morning, Master," Leigh said with a smile. "Coffee, Sir?"

"That sounds good," Josiah said. "Black, please. Molly, I brought some groceries over. Get them from the Suburban, please."

"Of course, Master," Molly said, and stepped out.

"Here's your coffee," Leigh said, handing him a hot mug of rich black brew. "How's Lucretia?"

"Last night helped, I think," Josiah said. "That's what I wanted to discuss with you and Molly this morning."

"We're all ears, Master," Molly said. "God, if I have it and she needs it to get through this, consider it hers for the taking, Sir."

147

"She asked me last night to be her lover, and I was, but she asked me to be cruel to her today, to beat her harshly, fuck her ass harshly – she used the word 'rape' – and to work her hard. She seems to think the catharsis will help her come to terms with Tony's suicide."

"She's probably right," Leigh shivered. "It'll also make her feel totally helpless in her enslavement, immersed. I hope you pick the occasional times to do that to me, Master, just be a hateful bastard to me to put me in my place, make me feel lower than snake shit, as my old man used to say. It scares me but ... Master, it also turns me on in a big way, feeling utterly in your thrall, helpless, hopeless ... it's powerful stuff. All I can tell you is that physical wounds heal, Sir. If they help lance some emotional boil she's suddenly developed, then so much the better. If she wants to be a slave – and I think that goes for all three of us – she should be treated as a slave at times, to make that point that here, in your presence, she's only property, and you have the prerogative of treating property as you please."

"Master, I think Leigh is right," Molly said. "It scares the shit out of me, but ... I deserve to be nothing more than a slave after how long I mistreated you and our marriage."

"Perhaps you'll get one day monthly of it," Josiah said to Molly.

"I ... Master, I hope you decide to keep me and do the same," Leigh chimed in.

"It's unanimous, Master," Lucretia announced, surprising them all. "I woke when I heard you leaving, Sir, and decided a slave should walk and not be chauffeured about like a movie star."

"You're right in time to prepare breakfast," Josiah said. "Get on it!"

"Yes, Master," Lucretia said, and strode into the kitchen while Josiah, Leigh, and Molly went into the living room with their coffee. Josiah finished his coffee and Molly refilled his mug.

"Master, sisters, breakfast is ready," Lucretia announced as Josiah was finishing his second coffee.

Prepared to be overly critical of breakfast, Josiah found such to be unnecessary. Breakfast was horrible. The sunny-side-up eggs were either still half-raw or burnt. Ditto for the bacon. The toast was all burnt. The only things she didn't manage to fuck up were the orange juice and jam for the toast, but all she needed to do where was open the jug of juice and the lid from the jar of strawberry jam. And the jam was a moot point because the toast was near to being ashes.

Josiah carefully concealed his amusement at the mortified look on Lucretia's face. "Slave apologizes, Master," she said. "I never learned to cook, Sir. If it wasn't for my microwave I wouldn't have survived a year out of college."

"This is unacceptable, Lucretia," Josiah said. "Go wait on the porch. You'll be horsewhipped out by the track. You'd best get accustomed to that post, because I just might lash you at a big assembly just for interim entertainment."

"Should slave walk there?" Lucretia asked in a timid tone.

"Yes," Josiah decided. "Get going while Molly actually puts edible food on this table. Dismissed to the track."

"Yes, Master," Lucretia said. She pushed back from the table and exited the cabin for the long walk to the track. The morning air was pleasant, especially with the breeze.

"I don't know what to think about that breakfast," Molly said. "I don't think she fucked it up intentionally so much as she really isn't all that domestic. Not at all a house slave, Master. What's going to happen to her?"

"She'll be horsewhipped and buggered, and then she'll be put to work doing a full detail on the Suburban," Josiah said. "I'll be fair, but if she's as bad at car washing as she is in the kitchen – Christ, we're lucky this cabin didn't burn to the ground – there'll be another horsewhipping and she'll have to re-wash the Suburban. Molly, can you be trusted off the estate if I send you out for groceries and the like? We didn't anticipate two weeks of meals for four out here."

"I'll return from the store as fast as I can, Master," Molly promised. "May I cook breakfast, Master?"

"If there's enough," Josiah said.

"It'll be a bit light but … yes, Sir, there's enough," Molly said after inspecting the fridge. "If Master feels like firing up the grill with some of that wood we split, I can pick up steaks for us, Sir."

"That'll make for a good supper," Josiah agreed. "I'll tell you what … why don't I light up the big pit too and you pick up enough that I can cook a range of stuff we can refrigerate and reheat for the next two or three days? I like cooking on the pit and it gives me something to do."

"Yes, Master," Molly said. She began breakfast and a list for the grocery store. Josiah was always amused because he couldn't decipher her physician handwriting even with a pistol aimed at his head. But if she could read it, that was good enough, he figured.

Take Two of their breakfast proved far to be the more successful, and the three ate a hearty breakfast. Josiah phoned his secretary and told her cancel his appointments for the coming two weeks.

"That shouldn't be a big problem," his secretary said after a long moment of looking through his calendar. "Have a nice vacation, boss."

"Thanks," Josiah said. "If something blows up, hit me up, but … only if you or a junior associate can't put out the fire."

"Gotcha covered," she promised. They hung up and a moment later, Josiah's phone rang again.

"Sir Josiah, it's … it's Darla," Darla said.

"Hello, Darla," Josiah returned.

"Sir, because I didn't complete our … our business this weekend, I —" she began.

"It would be better to discuss this in person," Josiah said. "Do you know where Mabel's Diner is?"

"I've heard of it, Sir," Darla said. "I'm sure I can find it."

"Ten o'clock," Josiah said, and ended the call. He put the whip in the Suburban along with cuffs, and drove out to the track, parking the big vehicle in the barn. He would drive the farm truck to meet Darla, he decided.

"Put Lucretia on the post," he ordered.

In a moment, Lucretia was bound for her whipping. "Ten lashes for you fucking up breakfast," Josiah decreed. "After that, you will be buggered and then you're going to be detailing the Suburban, and when I inspect it, it had better look showroom new, slave."

"Yes, Mas —" Lucretia began, but it turned into a screech when the whip lashed across her back. Josiah continued whipping Lucretia, showing her no mercy at all, until the tenth lash found her.

"Take her off the post and put her face-down-ass-up," Josiah ordered the other slaves. He pulled his pants off and got a tube of lube from his back pocket, and thrust hard into her, his hips colliding against her ass as she grunted. She'd loosened a bit, and it was a pleasurable fuck, at least for Josiah, and then he came hard into his slave's ass. Leigh came to him with a bucket of soapy water and rags, and cleaned his penis completely, and then patted it dry.

"Get busy washing and detailing that Suburban, slave," Josiah ordered. "When I return, if it's not perfectly done, you can count on many more lashes."

"Yes, Sir, Master," Lucretia moaned. She struggled to her feet, and began blubbering as she stomped off to the barn, seemingly angry. Josiah drove the truck back to the big house, and then showered, got into slacks and a dress shirt, and drove to Mabel's to meet Darla.

TWENTY-THREE

"Are you hungry?" Josiah greeted Darla.

"No, Sir," Darla said.

"I'm going to order a Coke to go," Josiah said. "You want something? I figure we can talk in the truck with more privacy."

"A Coke sounds good," Darla said. Josiah ordered two large Cokes to go, and paid for them, and a moment later they were on the road in the rattletrap truck.

"Why are you driving this beater?" Darla asked.

"I own a range of vehicles but only can drive one at a time," Josiah said. "Because of all the mud and rain, when I dropped you off yesterday, I decided to drive the Suburban – it's a 4x4 and good in mud – back to the property. But it's a nice one, all the options and so forth. Since the rain is done, I'm having it detailed. Besides, I like this old truck."

"Yes, Sir," Darla said. "Sir, because I failed this session with you, I have to do either three more sessions or one week of punishment with you. The punishments are harsher. I'm even to be horsewhipped."

"Sounds like you really got Tim peeved with you," Josiah ventured.

"He's not happy with me, Sir," Darla admitted. "Sir, I ... I'm available to you seven days a week. I could even come now and remain until next Monday. Master has deployed to … somewhere in the Middle East. I am to have photographic, preferably video, proof that I was properly punished, Sir. I can tell you that you can even use me … well … sexually, Sir. Even if I pick up a scar or two, that's acceptable as well. I could be at your warehouse … I can drive straight there from the diner, Sir."

"There's more to this than meets the eye, isn't there?" Josiah asked.

"There is," Darla said. "I … I'd rather not go into that. But I seriously fucked up, Sir. I think right now if it didn't cost nine tons of money I'd be serving you on that ranch until he returns from over there."

"How long will he be gone?" Josiah asked.

"Who the hell knows?" Darla returned, sounding bitter. "I love him but you don't know how bad I wish he'd retire and go civilian. But … Sir, my vagina belongs to him, but my mouth can pleasure you, and … and my bottom, Sir."

"You understand your sexual favors don't give you a better rate," Josiah said.

"Nor should they," Darla returned. She reached into her purse and pulled out a thick bank envelope, and put it on the seat between them. "I think that amount should be sufficient for what has to happen to me."

"I want you to understand something," Josiah said. "You saw other slaves out there because it couldn't be avoided … things got a bit crazy over the weekend. But they're not clients."

"Even that man?" Darla asked, surprised.

"No … he won't be returning," Josiah said. "But they're all on the farm for the coming week or two, perhaps further. You would have to serve with them, and you would be made to sign a non-disclosure agreement. Do you know what that is, Darla?"

"A contract that says I can never talk about what happened out there, Sir," Darla said. "If I do, I can be sued and you can take me for ... well ... whatever the court decides."

"Close enough," Josiah said.

"Sir, I ... I'd never mention what happened to me over the weekend, or what might happen to me, moving forward," Darla said. "I guess if Tim wasn't gone you could deal with him on this, but he's ... I don't know when I'll get to talk with him. I'm sure you can imagine, considering what he does, that communication with him is nearly impossible."

Josiah held up a finger to silence her, and picked up his phone. He first dialed Molly's cell, but got no answer, which didn't surprise him. And then he phoned the big house and Molly answered. He explained to her what was going on with Darla.

"I'll have her sign an NDA, but considering the three of you, I figured I should seek your counsel before bringing her out and throwing her into the mix," he concluded.

"Sir, slaves have no rights," Molly said. "Besides, four of us will do more work than three, Master."

"You're about to head to the store?" Josiah asked

"Yes, Sir," Molly said. "I'll get provisions for seven rather than for five. I figure four of us are liable to eat like six, since you're working us harder. Heavy on the proteins, Sir."

"Have an NDA on the kitchen table in the cabin," Josiah ordered. "I'll be there with Darla in about an hour."

"Yes, Master," Molly said, and Josiah hung up, took a long

drink of his Coke, and eyed the nervous young woman beside him. "When we get to Mabel's, you will get into your car and follow me. If you lose me, you have my cell number."

"Yes, Sir," Darla said, and shivered a bit. Josiah drove straight to Mabel's, and Darla got into her car, an older Honda Accord, and followed him. He led her to the office where he'd initially met her, an office he rented strictly for conducting business with his special clients, and therefore empty except when he and Molly were meeting clients. He had her park her car and get into the truck, and fashioned a blindfold for her from an old necktie that was in the glove compartment.

"I'm making any number of exceptions in your case, Darla," he said as he piloted the beat-up old truck to the warehouse. "But it's going to go harder for you. I have three slaves on the grounds for a period of training, and I'm very hard on them. I don't have time to handle them and something entirely separate and apart for you, so you're going to work alongside them, and be punished the same as they are when you step out of line. For a variety of reasons, all of them are banned from orgasms, and I want you to understand if you have an orgasm without my permission, I will punish you vigorously for it. One was horsewhipped right after breakfast this morning and is liable to be horsewhipped again as soon as we return."

"Sir, I ... I have to beg you to horsewhip me, vigorously as you say, today and right before I'm returned to my life, and at least once in between," Darla said. "Christ, I'm scared to death now that this is happening."

"You should be," Josiah said. "And since your master has given his permission, you can count on being buggered several times this week. Do you know what buggery is?"

"Fucking me in my ass, Sir," Darla said. "I hear that hurts bad."

"I think it will," Josiah confirmed. "I think my slaves are growing to like it. What did you do that he wants me to go so hard on you, Darla?"

"I'm not at liberty to say, Sir," Darla answered.

"When we get to the warehouse, you know the drill," Josiah said. "But in case you might need to directly depart the estate, I'll bring your clothing along. But you are to be naked as birth at all times unless I grant you clothing."

"I ... Sir, I deserve this and more," Darla said. "The truth is, I couldn't survive what I really deserve. I know I'm going to cry a lot this week. But ... please go hard on me so I can show Tim how devoted I am to us."

"Sounds to me like you really screwed the pooch," Josiah ventured.

"Bad," Darla confirmed. "I screwed the pooch really bad."

"Will he forgive you?" Josiah asked.

"I pray he does," Darla said.

TWENTY-FOUR

"Lucretia, this is unacceptable," Josiah snapped. She had done a decent job of washing the Suburban, but the drips of water hadn't been wiped well and there were specks and streaks all over it. "Get your ass to the whipping post."

"Yes, Master," Lucretia whispered, and did as bidden. Leigh had seen the Suburban a few minutes before Josiah arrived and knew there was going to be another horsewhipping for the woman. She had almost told Lucretia she should redo the job, but she knew Lucretia wasn't blind or lazy, and knew the poor woman needed this harshness. Leigh felt badly for her over Tony's suicide, and knew if it was someone she loved, she would probably be out here begging Josiah for the very same thing. Lucretia offered her wrists to the post and Leigh deftly cuffed her.

"I deserve it, Master," Lucretia said. "I ... I'm sorry, Sir."

"You're about to be very sorry," Josiah said. "Twenty lashes. And then you're going to crawl back to the Suburban. By 'crawl' I mean your nipples are to drag the ground. And then you're going to wash it so clean you can eat from it. I don't want to see a single streak or speckle on that car. Jesus, you're a shit slave. Molly, bring me the whip!"

Molly handed Josiah the coiled whip and led Darla aside, whispering to her that there would be plenty lashes intended for her, and she didn't want to be in the whip's way to get lashes not meant for her. Darla, wide-eyed, nodded. She wept silently as Josiah began lashing Lucretia. Lucretia took the first several in silence, trembling and gasping, and even grunting. But the thirteenth lash, the first to open her skin, shattered Lucretia's considerable resolve, and she shrieked to the skies above, howling agony that was in no small part from her heart. Darla began sobbing in sympathy for Lucretia and terror for herself as Josiah continued the lashing, until the twentieth stroke was laid into her back. Lucretia slid down the post and howled anew as more coagulant was applied to her three open wounds, and then Leigh removed her cuffs and Lucretia weakly crawled toward the barn, keeping her nipples in the dirt as she sobbed.

Darla was surprised to see Josiah wiping his own tears, and wondered after that.

"Darla, that was Lucretia, the one I just whipped," Josiah said. "You know Molly, and this other slave is Leigh, who is about to put you on the whipping post for your own breaking-in. You'll get twenty, just like Lucretia did, and when she's done washing the Suburban – I'm getting horny again – I'm going to bugger her again, and then get some food cooking."

"Master, when you called about Darla, I had Leigh start the fire in the pit while I went for provisions," Molly said.

"Good," Josiah remarked. "Leigh, put Darla on the post. I'll go get some things on the pit and return shortly."

"No," Darla begged. "Please ... no."

"Your twenty lashes just became twenty-three," Josiah said. "How far do you want to push this? Walk up to the post and offer your wrists to Leigh."

"Oh, God," Darla whispered. She stayed rooted to her spot. Molly opened her mouth to speak, but shut it at a warning glance from Josiah.

"Twenty-seven," Josiah said. "Start walking or it goes to thirty-five."

Darla sobbed but started half-staggering to the post, her knees trembling as though her legs had lost most of their strength. But she was afraid and stopped halfway, and Josiah's patience slipped. "Leigh and Molly, force her to the post. She just bought forty lashes."

Darla really didn't offer resistance, and Josiah knew she simply didn't have the nerve to approach the post this first time, not after seeing Lucretia so easily undone. He knew she would be a broken girl after this, and knew the next day he would have to push on that, treat her like he was treating Lucretia this day. He drove toward the cabin and smelled the smoke from the pit, which was already making him hungry. He went into the cabin and found an array of meat, including five large steaks and baking potatoes wrapped in foil, as well as sausages, two fryers, and a pork loin, all things that could be easily reheated later. He put the potatoes and meat, except for the steaks, on the far end of the pit and then returned to the track.

TWENTY-FIVE

"Are you insane?" Molly asked Darla once she was bound to the post.

"I'm scared," Darla said, barely above a whisper. "I knew I was going to be whipped, but right then it became real and I ... how bad is it going to be?"

"Bad," Leigh answered. She turned so that Darla could get a long look at the welts decorating her back. "He'll break you, Darla. He's breaking us. But you should be grateful. He's ... we all came to him freely and with open eyes. I don't feel sorry for you, Darla, and I doubt Molly does or Lucretia will. We're all grownups. You phoned Master today. You came a good long way to meet him. You stated your sentence to him, or at least the outline of it. You drove your car to park it somewhere, and could have turned for home at any second on that drive, missy. Now, I was on that post yesterday. You saw the marks Master put on me with that whip, and you certainly saw Lucretia broken with far less than you just bought, and you're starting to realize the depths of humiliation that are waiting for you for however long you're here. I was scared and I know you're scared. But don't think for one second that I feel sorry for you. I don't even feel sorry for myself. I deserve what I'm getting, and I know it. I saw some of what happened to you here, and I bet you deserve it as well."

"I do," Darla admitted, resigned. "God, I hate myself."

"I hate myself too for what I've done," Leigh admitted. She surprised herself and Darla by kissing the girl. "Look, unless Master has other directions regarding you, we're going to treat you as our sister, like the three of us are being trained to do. But Master expects us to tattle on one another for misbehaving, so don't ask us to keep secrets from him."

"Should I call him Master too?" Darla asked.

"No," Molly answered instantly. "Your master is Tim, not Josiah. Most masters would see that as a worse betrayal than fucking around, to be his but call another man Master."

"I … I understand," Darla said. "He's coming back." Leigh and Molly looked in the distance and saw Josiah returning in the cargo truck.

"I'll see if he wants us to go fetch the truck later," Molly said.

"Lucretia, come out here to witness punishment," Josiah ordered. Lucretia, busily polishing a fender of the Suburban, instantly set her things aside and came out to the whipping post.

"She's really beautiful, Master," Lucretia said softly to Josiah. "Army wife?"

"He's a lieutenant colonel on deployment," Josiah said, not surprised Lucretia picked up on that. She was certain to have had any number of military personnel and dependents among her own clientele.

"What did she do?" Lucretia asked.

"She won't say," Josiah said. "She's not my slave, but a client. I ordinarily wouldn't do this, but I like her husband – he seems like a good guy – and I gather she really fucked up if he's paying the freight to send her here for an entire week. And I basically like Darla. She … I think she just has a lot of growing up to do."

"Married to a lieutenant colonel who is probably old enough to be her father," Lucretia said. "I would guess he needs her to grow up quickly before any antics of hers upset his career."

"Bingo," Josiah said. "So she told me he wants her horsewhipped, and that I can have her orally or anally at will, and otherwise work her like a slave. I decided to go against my policy of keeping clients out of my life since I don't have time to keep shifting hers to her and then to the rest of you and back to her. So she'll be trained and lashed with the rest of you."

"She's a haughty one," Lucretia said. "I can see that from here. Even on the post, she's posed as best she can, still not a hair out of place. She's used to men kissing her feet."

"Probably," Josiah agreed. "I need to break her of that. But it's hard to do, knowing that out in the world, men will worship her. She's in her twenties, toned and beautiful, a magazine model."

"You have your work cut out for you, Master," Lucretia said. "Do you want to hear something funny, Sir?"

"Sure," Josiah said.

"She'll learn in time what a burden that is," Lucretia said. "She hasn't figured out yet that men who see only her beauty don't really give a damn about the human being under the skin of that golden girl. They only care about trying to seduce her. From what I understand from Molly, we need to feel special since we're the first women, Leigh and me, that you've fucked outside your marriage. She tells me you get horny a lot with clients and she's always been on hand to blow you or otherwise soothe your urges, but that she's never seen you fuck a client or anyone else but her until she surrendered to you."

"That sums it up," Josiah said. "But obviously the last few days have seen huge shifts in the landscape around these parts."

"Obviously, Master," she said. "What's about to happen to her now, Sir?"

"Forty of the horsewhip," Josiah answered.

"Jesus, she has to be scared out of her mind after she saw what happened to me," Lucretia said. "Nice touch, by the way. I don't know if I was ever so humiliated as to be whipped in front of a kid ... well, she's very young, I know she's a woman ... but a kid I don't know. Is she even 21 yet?"

"25, actually, a college grad," Josiah said.

"Well, it reduced me, Master. I realized when you made me crawl to the barn to polish your car right this time that if the Pope had descended bodily from Heaven in a cloud of heavenly glory with fairy glitter and unicorn farts, you'd have entertained him with my whipping as well, and ... something inside me swelled, Master. You own me now, Sir. Say the word and I'll close my business tomorrow, you can brand me like livestock, and I'll stay on this farm the rest of my life."

"That's not going to save you from more lashes and buggery again, Lucretia," Josiah pointed out.

"I ... I deserve and need it, Master," Lucretia said.

"Molly and Leigh suggested I do the same to them, maybe once monthly," Josiah said. "Just pick a day and break them again."

"It ... Master, it would be good for me too," Lucretia said. "I'm not exaggerating, Sir. Say the word and I'm yours on this farm permanently."

"I'm not ruling it out," Josiah said. "But that's a speedy

decision. Let's get through this coming week first."

"Will this client be your bed bitch tonight and your whipping child tomorrow?" Lucretia asked. "Christ, I hope the Suburban is up to your standards."

"You'd better hope so," Josiah said. "Let's go whip this girl."

"Darla, state your sentence," Josiah ordered.

"Sir, I am to be horsewhipped forty lashes, and am to serve a week as a slave here, with your other slaves," Darla said. "If Sir wishes, I may be buggered or made to give oral pleasures … to you or anyone here … for that week. I am to be worked hard and I am to be strictly obedient in all ways. In short, I am here to be punished, and the only limitation is that my vagina is reserved to my … to Tim."

"Forty lashes will begin now," Josiah said. "Molly, Leigh, do you think she should be monitored, or no?"

"Sir, I would like the right to halt the lashing when she loses consciousness to evaluate her then," Leigh said. "Molly tells me she examined this one just a few nights ago."

"Granted," Josiah said after a moment. "Darla, if you have anything to say, any final statement to utter, this is your chance."

"Oh, God, this is about to happen," she moaned. "God help me get through this. God —" her prayer ended in a pained scream as Josiah laid the first lash across her back. She fought her bonds, seeming to try to climb up and over the post, but she was going nowhere. Josiah laid in seven more strokes, harsh ones, and Darla ran out of air to cry or howl, and finally slumped in her bonds.

Four more lashes found one of the welts bleeding, and Leigh

called a halt. She checked Darla out and woke her. "Master's feelings get hurt when you fall asleep during a whipping, like he thinks you're bored with it," Leigh said cheerily, and then scowled at Darla. "Wake up and take it like you know you deserve it!"

Darla seemed to flinch at the harsh words, but stood, trying to prepare herself for the remainder of the onslaught. She sobbed as the whipping resumed at Leigh's nod, out of voice to scream after twenty lashes, when Josiah paused again at Leigh's sign. She studied the wounds a moment. "These shouldn't scar, Master," she said. I'm sorry, and continue, please."

"Please stop!" Darla begged. "Please! I'll leave. I'll go away, Sir. Please don't —" Again, Josiah halted her oratory with the whip, and was rewarded with a pained groan from the beautiful slave. He kept lashing her, keeping a count in his head and realizing he should have had Molly or Lucretia do the count. Too late for that, he realized, and continued the whipping until Darla fainted again on the thirty-third stroke and Leigh halted the beating again, and once again revived Darla, who was beyond anything but the pain. Josiah laid in the final seven lashes, and Molly and Leigh treated the wounds with coagulant, making her groan pitiably. They then looked at Josiah for orders.

"Take her from the post," he said. "She can stand or kneel or drive her tits in the dirt. No, throw her in the van and we'll go have lunch. I'm hungry."

At the cabin, Josiah grilled the steaks, all medium-rare without asking how people liked their steaks. He wasn't going to be a short-order cook. He looked into the smoker and saw things were coming along nicely, and ordered Leigh to throw four more chunks of wood into the fire, and then snagged the steaks and potatoes and went into the house.

Darla moaned when asked if she was hungry, and Josiah looked questioningly at Molly. "She's fine, medically, just weakened from the pain, Master," Molly reported. "She'll come around. To be fair, it was her first time for the horsewhip – I know it was the first time for the rest of us as well – but forty is a pretty stern sentence."

"You think I went overboard?" Josiah asked.

"In truth, if anything, underboard, if that's a word," Molly said. "She didn't obey you and needed a consequence. In your shoes, I might have given her fifty or maybe even sixty. She's laying there on the floor and she knows there's food. If she doesn't want to eat, then let her go hungry. I did get some photos but no idea where to send them or what to do with them, Sir."

"Put them on a flash drive, I guess," Josiah said. "I'm sure she can figure out a way to get them to Tim." He ate heartily, and so did the other slaves. Toward the end of the meal, Darla crawled up to her hands and knees.

"May ... may I eat, Sir?" she asked.

"It's a big table," Josiah said. "Your plate is in there with a steak on it, and there's baked potatoes and salad. Tea or water if you're thirsty."

"Thank you, Sir," Darla said. She slowly rose to her feet and went into the kitchen, and brought her plate to the table, using both hands. She then got a glass of water from the tap and carried it to the table, again using both hands, and sat to eat. Josiah didn't express his amusement, but noted that she didn't so much eat as attack her plate, devouring almost all the 16-ounce steak and most of the potato. She'd passed on the salad, and didn't touch the water until she'd nudged her plate a couple inches away, and then slammed it down, and went to the sink to refill it, returned to the table, and drank most of that. But she seemed more revived for having eaten and drank some water.

"So now you know what it is to be horsewhipped," Josiah said. "I'm going to break you in hard tomorrow, Darla, like I've done with Lucretia today. Lucretia, I'm going to inspect the Suburban. You can all stay here and girl talk. I'll let you know whether it passed my inspection when I return. God help you if it doesn't, slave."

"I deserve it, Master," Lucretia said.

Josiah rose, went to the van, and drove out to the barn. He parked the van and went through the Suburban with a fine-tooth comb. There was a slight scuff on the rear bumper that he had picked up in a parking lot when some moron backed into the Suburban a week after he'd gotten the thing, and he'd just been too busy to get it re-painted. He made a mental note to have one of the girls take it to the body shop for paint, and resolved to get the truck back to the farm rather than driving the big cargo van. He liked using the van with clients so they had no idea where they were here, and were disoriented and less likely to try to escape and cause him a lot of trouble. But otherwise, it was enormous and a pain in the ass to drive on the farm, and pretty useless for anything but transporting clients, as it was configured.

The Suburban was in good shape, and he was pleased with the effort Lucretia had put forth on Round II of the work assignment. He decided to put Lucretia and Darla on hard physical labor, sawing a downed tree into firewood lengths. He decided to leave the cargo van where it was, and got back into the Suburban. Sometimes he needed the behemoth SUV for legal clientele and needed it to look the part. He'd briefly considered an Escalade, but didn't like that much ostentation. Besides, too many criminal types seemed to gravitate to those. If he was going to dump that kind of money into a pimpmobile, he'd just get another big Mercedes or 7-series BMW. Or a Bentley, he considered with amusement.

FOUR SLAVES

He'd been turning something over in his mind, something that really didn't add up, and decided to place a phone call.

TWENTY-SIX

"I guess we all need to get to know one another," Lucretia said to Darla. "I'm Lucretia St. Cyr. You know Molly already, and this is Leigh Murphy."

"How did you come to be here, Lucretia?" Darla asked. "All of you. I mean, I know Molly is married to Sir, but you … I'm about to stick my foot in my mouth here … most of the submissives I see are like me, regular ordinary everyday people … you three have a certain … I'm trying to put my finger on it. Self-confidence? Polish? Education? I mean, I graduated college but I know I'm nowhere near as sophisticated as you three."

"Thank you for saying that," Lucretia said. "I'm … I've done a lot of traveling and —"

"Our stories all sort of interconnect with one another," Molly interrupted.

"True," Lucretia agreed.

"Why don't I begin, and then Leigh can tell her part, and then you, Lucretia?" Molly suggested. "That way we're not telling a story backwards or out of order."

"That makes sense," Leigh agreed.

"It does," Lucretia said, gesturing to Molly. "Lead on, Doc Molly."

"Okay, this all brewed up this past weekend around what was

happening with you, Darla," Molly began. "Let me back up a smidgen. I got in hot water at my job and suspended for two weeks. I go back for a week for evaluation and at the end of that week, there will be a vote on whether to fire me."

"Jesus, I thought doctors were self-employed," Darla said, surprised.

"It's ... Jesus, I hate saying it's complicated, but it is," Molly said. "It's a big practice with several physicians in partnership, and yes, I'm one of the partners and shareholders, but it was foreseen that for one reason or another some would depart, sometimes for retirement or relocation, etcetera. But it's in the contract that if 60% of the shares vote to do so, a partner can be removed unwillingly from the practice, which simply buys out that partner's share. In my case it's about seven percent of the partnership, so it's somewhat of a golden parachute, I guess."

"I see," Darla said.

"I deserved it," Molly admitted. "But it triggered a rockslide inside me. I hid a lot of wrongs from Jos ... from Master ... and ... you know, you can get away with a lot of bullshit when your husband loves and trusts you, and I shattered that trust in a thousand ways and he never guessed, because he loves me. But ... I made a full confession and surrendered fully to him. I also told him I could no longer require his sexual loyalty to me and he has the unquestioned right to put his dick wherever he wants, to include my ass, which I'd denied him for years."

"And mine too, I guess," Darla said, shivering a bit. "How big is he?"

"Considerable," Lucretia said. "He's not hung like a porn star or something, but above average, from all the dicks I've seen, and God knows I've seen hundreds of hard dicks in my life."

"How's that?" Darla asked.

"We're getting to that, but unless Molly has more, I think this is where Leigh comes into our tale," Lucretia said.

"Go on, Leigh," Molly said.

"I found out by accident that Josiah and Molly are into kink," Leigh began. "I saw them at a dungeon club meeting, but they didn't see me. I suppose I should have approached them there, said hi, and seen what happened, but I was scared about being direct. I'm … I can also be bad about snooping on things that are none of my business, so I hired a PI to look into them and found out about this place. And I started spying on them, and even saw you out here Saturday. I had … have … I think 'had,' past tense … I had a dom online who helped keep my shit together, but I never met him in person. He sent me to … to a dominatrix, when I had to be punished for this or that, which was far too often, frankly. He was growing tired of me not behaving, and this time he told me my punishment was to be different, and sent me here to confess to Josiah and give him blanket consent to punish me as he saw fit to do. So I came and confessed, while Molly was here in the cabin, totally in the dark about me – she and I are physicians in the same practice, so you know, by the way – and gave him my dom's number to call. They spoke by phone and my dom sent Josiah an array of material, including photos of me after whippings, and one video of me getting it rough from the dominatrix pretty recently. I also told him I had the entire coming week off, for vacation, and am at his disposal, so here I am."

"This is where I come in," Lucretia said. "In my outside life I am a professional dominatrix, the one who lashed Leigh on Blake's behalf whenever she misbehaved. Blake called me and asked me to come meet with Josiah and perhaps reinforce continuity to Leigh. He'd probably shit his pants if he knew what's gone on since." Lucretia snorted ruefully. "So I put on my dominatrix hat and went too far with Josiah, and realized I deserved … what I'm getting. It's a long and complicated story, but I have deep slave tendencies I'm discovering as we speak, Darla. I had been going now and then to a dominatrix I know a long way from here, a few times yearly, for a lengthy tune-up, but I was coming to see it wasn't enough. Something inside me, something that was there since I was a kid and saw a slave horsewhipped in a movie, was growing enormous inside me."

"Must have been a powerful movie," Darla said.

"*Roots*," Lucretia told her. "Did you ever see it?"

"I did," Darla said. "In college there was a class about the facts and myths of slavery here, and watching the miniseries was part of it."

"Do you remember that scene where he escaped and was captured, and they hung him up by his wrists and horsewhipped him until he broke, and said his name was Toby?" Lucretia asked.

"It was a climactic part of the show," Darla agreed. "Besides, I thought that guy LeVar Burton … something about him was sexy as hell to me."

"Yeah, me too," Lucretia agreed. "I fantasized about being the one whipping him, and about being him, doomed to the lash. That power exchange, the power to own a human being so utterly that you take his name away from him … God, I masturbated a thousand times over the idea, of slavery, whippings … anyway, I think at this juncture of my life, I need to be slave."

"How is that going to fit in with you being a dominatrix?" Darla asked, looking intrigued.

"That's a good question," Lucretia said. "You're smarter than I would have thought. The answer is, I honestly don't know. I mean, there is a difference between what you are and what you do, and I think four of us here could tell you that. What Molly and Leigh do is heal the wounded – they run a sports medicine clinic – and what Josiah does is tend to peoples' legalities while what I do is to punish people or fulfill fantasies for them. What I am is a slave, I'm growing certain. I would say the same applies to Leigh and Molly. What Josiah is, is a master, our master, irrespective of how he earns his living."

"I hadn't thought about that," Darla said. "What I am is an Army wife. He doesn't want me to work since his career has to come first. So I manage my inheritance as a day trader."

"Explain that, please?" Lucretia asked.

"When my grandparents were alive – all four of them were well-off, not rich, but well-off – anyway, they set up trust funds for me," Darla said. "They amount to a tidy sum of money. Anyway, the way they were set up is the funds would be used to pay for my education and then would be handed off to me either when I graduated college, married, or had my first child. So a few days after I graduated college, a lawyer met with me and had me sign a stack of papers, and suddenly I was on top of nearly a million dollars. I got my degree in finance and even have a stockbroker license, believe it or not, and I started managing the money myself. About sixty percent of it is in long-term bonds and stuff that mature in twenty to thirty years. Thirty percent is in relatively stable and boring shit in the stock market that takes up little attention. But the final ten percent, I decided to see what I could make happen with it in higher risk stuff. In three years, I've run that hundred grand up to a hundred sixty, and I'd about decided to pull more from the stock market to manage. By extrapolation, had I managed the whole thing that way, I'd have made six hundred grand, one hell of a lot more than the Army pays my husband … but you can lose your shirt too easily there. There was one day, on that fund, that I lost twenty thousand alone, for instance. So it's not for the faint of heart. If I don't get stupid with it, I could be a wealthy woman at forty."

"Jesus, I wish my stockbroker did as well," Lucretia chuckled.

TWENTY-SEVEN

Josiah parked at the cabin and sighed, and then walked up the steps and inside. "Darla, I'm going to say this in front of the other three, and seek their input," he said. "Something didn't add up in what you were telling me and how fast you were sent back here, so I took the chance and called Tim. Lo and behold, he answered the phone. He allowed that his deployment has been advanced and he leaves in a week for the Middle East – apparently the man he's replacing suffered a devastating stroke and isn't expected to live – but Tim told me he found out you'd had a one-night-stand a month ago with a captain from photos that were sent to him, probably from the captain's wife, and he told you yesterday he was filing for divorce and you're out of his life once and for all. True?"

"God," Darla wept. "May I ... may I tell my side of this?"

"It sure won't make your situation worse," Josiah said.

"May I have an hour to prepare my presentation?" Darla asked.

"You ... yes, you may," Josiah said. "Remain here. The rest of you, come with me."

"Holy shit, I was starting to like her too," Leigh said.

"She's a likeable woman," Josiah allowed. "And one thing my law career has taught me is she's probably about to tell me one hell of a story in an hour."

"Yes, Sir," Leigh said.

"Okay, when we get to the big house, here's what I want to see happen," Josiah said. "Lucretia, the job you did on the Suburban was very good, but you probably noticed the scuff on the back bumper."

"Master, I swear to God, that was already there," Lucretia said nervously.

"It was," Josiah said, and chuckled. "Some jackass hit it while it was parked one day right after I bought the thing. Anyway, Leigh and Molly, I want you to drive the Suburban to the warehouse and get the farm truck. And then take the Suburban to the Chevy dealer so they can repaint it. And then come home in the farm truck."

"Yes, Master," Molly said. "Let's get dressed, Leigh."

"While you're at it, run by Leigh's place and get clothes for her, three or four changes, and shoes, including work shoes or boots. If she doesn't have those, run by the Red Wing store and get her some."

"We'll need to go to the Red Wing store," Leigh said.

"Okay, get dressed and get gone," Josiah said. "I want you both here when Darla makes her pitch, so come to the house."

"Of course, Master," Molly replied, and she and Leigh went to the bedroom to get dressed.

"You're going to keep her?" Lucretia asked.

"Darla? We'll see what her side of this is," Josiah hedged.

"I like that about you," Lucretia said. "I guess that's the lawyerly side of you, that wants the whole story before rendering a decision."

"Thanks, I think," Josiah said.

"It was meant as a compliment, Master," Lucretia told him. "What would Master have me do now, Sir?"

"Your master is growing aroused again, slave," Josiah said.

"Slave will be honored to offer her ass to him," Lucretia moaned, and immediately positioned herself face-down-ass-up, and in a moment, she grunted as he plundered into her, thrusting and grinding, stopping when he got close to his cum to get back under control, and wanting her to remember this one for a long time. He thrust again, stopped again, and heard Lucretia cry out in frustration, and then began thrusting for real, needing to cum, and heard Lucretia scream out as she came, her ass ruthlessly squeezing his erection and milking him of all his seed before she collapsed, spent, to the floor.

"God, that is so sexy," Leigh breathed.

"Yours is coming one day this week, slave," Josiah said, and Leigh squeaked just a bit. "I'm afraid our Lucretia came this time so it's another visit to the post for her. You girls hurry home."

"Yes, Master," Leigh said, and she and Molly were gone. Josiah decided to let Lucretia rest, and went upstairs to shower. As he was drying off from the shower his phone rang and he answered.

"Josiah, this is Tim again," Tim said. "What does she have to say for herself?"

"She asked for an hour to prepare her side of the story," Josiah said. "I decided to give her that."

"God, I'd love to hear that," Tim snorted.

"Do you know where Mabel's is?" Josiah asked.

"Yeah, of course," Tim said. Mabel's Tables, even as remote

as it was, had become somewhat of a landmark diner for the region. The food and service were good, and the utterly mismatched and tacky décor just made the place quirky and fun.

"Can you meet me there in twenty minutes?" Josiah asked.

"Yeah, sure," Tim said.

"From there, if you want, I'll take you to her," Josiah said. "I'll be in a black Infiniti sedan. It's Molly's car. Just get in and we'll talk, and if you still want to come to confront her, you can."

"See you then," Tim said, and hung up. Josiah dressed and found Lucretia kneeling in the living room.

"I know I have to be whipped for that cum, Master," she said.

"Yes, but later," Josiah told her. "If your sisters get back before I do, have them wait for me. I'm going to ask you a question here, and you're going to be answering for all three of you. I'm bringing Darla's husband back here with me for this little presentation she's giving. Should you three remain naked for it, or clothed?"

"Naked, Master," Lucretia said. "This is so humiliating, but it … it … having to display my enslavement before someone I don't know is … it moves me. He's certain to see the whip-marks and already knows you're a master, so it shouldn't surprise him."

"Very well," Josiah said. "Have Molly and Leigh strip naked as well and we'll all go together to the cabin."

"I … thank you, Master," Lucretia said. "I think I love being denied clothing, denied the opportunity to hide anything from anyone here."

"Tell them if any of you try to cover anything with your

hands, it will be punished," Josiah decided. He agreed with Lucretia's thinking and knew it would similarly benefit Molly and Leigh, although he was certain Molly would hate it, and wondered how Leigh would be with it. *Doesn't matter*, he considered. *They're slaves, and answer to me and not themselves, not this week, and maybe never again.*

"Okay, a lot has happened the last several days," Josiah began when Tim got into the car. "Jesus, this is only Monday?"

"It's been eventful," Tim allowed. "Josiah, what did she tell you?"

"What she told me initially was that you'd been deployed, she'd done something else wrong she wasn't at liberty to discuss, and that she was to be spending more time on my farm. She said you'd put her vagina off-limits but that she could be made to give anal or oral sex, and to be horsewhipped at least three times."

"Horsewhipped?" Tim asked, sounding shocked.

"Horsewhipped," Josiah confirmed. "She had forty lashes earlier today. She also told me you were sent to the Middle East on an emergency deployment but would want to see photographs or videos of her marks."

"I told her yesterday when I got those photos of her with Captain Jackson that we're done," Tim said. "Before she got home, I took her things to a residential hotel a couple miles from the base. I confronted her with the pictures and told her we're done. In fact, I'll tell her today that I'm meeting with the lawyers to begin divorce proceedings. That's tomorrow at 0900. I did get the deployment notice and won't be here long. But I already notified the housing officer and they're packing my items for storage and will quarter another officer in there once I'm gone."

180

"No chance you two could reconcile?" Josiah asked.

"Has your dick been inside her?" Tim asked.

"No, it hasn't," Josiah said.

"I wonder what's her angle on this," Tim said.

"Maybe … I'm guessing here because we haven't spoken further on it … but maybe she wants to show you a penance done in hopes of forgiveness, or at least redemption," Josiah said.

"How many lashes did she get today?" Tim asked.

"Forty," Josiah said.

"Jesus H. Christ," Tim breathed. "And she took that and wants to stay?"

"She does," Josiah confirmed. "If my guess is correct, I would contend she's sincere."

"She's also pissing in the wind," Tim said. "But maybe what you're doing will make her a better slave for someone else on down the line. Let's go see what she has to say."

"So you know, I have three slaves out there, all naked as birth, and so is Darla," Josiah said. "You'll definitely see her marks unless she heals mighty fast."

"I'll keep that in mind," Tim said. "I don't think she could say or do anything that'd put our marriage right again, Josiah. At least I'm not being a prick. She has money and can live well, no bills."

"She paid me a thick envelope of money for her time on my place," Josiah said.

"Then it was her money, not mine," Tim told him. "I paid

for a month of that hotel for her to let her get her shit together and gave her five hundred bucks seed money since it usually takes her a good week to get a disbursement from her account. But that's all I gave her."

"Interesting," Josiah said. "It feeds into my idea that she's trying to offer you her penance."

TWENTY-EIGHT

Tim got into the passenger seat of the farm truck, and Josiah's girls got into the bed for the ride to the cabin. Josiah noted Molly's dubious and displeased look, and saw that Lucretia and Leigh seemed uncomfortable being naked around Tim, but he sensed it was the right thing as he drove to the cabin to hear what Darla had to say.

Darla gasped as Tim followed Josiah into the cabin. "Tim, please ... please forgive me, Master," she begged.

"I'm here to hear what you have to say," Tim told her. "Your side of this should be interesting."

"Yes, Master," Darla said.

"Don't ever call me that again," Tim told her in a chilly tone. "Present your side."

"Y ... Yes, Sir," Darla said.

"Sir Josiah, I told you a lie, actually several lies, but I'm trying desperately to save my marriage," Darla said. "I hope you'll hear me out, and I'll even make an offer here. If Tim can't forgive me, can't give me the chance to earn my way back to him, you can lay claim to me and do with me as you will."

"For how long?" Josiah asked, surprised.

"The rest of my life," Darla said. "I don't deserve freedom or happiness unless Tim wants me back."

183

"Present your case," Josiah said.

"Tim, I am guilty," Darla began. "I could tell you I was high as hell and drunk too that night Marvin and I slept together, and that would be the truth, but it's no excuse. I knew I was doing wrong. I think the weekend taught me, too late, that it's high time I grew from a headstrong child into a woman, an honorable woman. But I can't get back what Marvin and I did, and I know I deserve punishment, far more than I've had to this point. But this is what happened to me just today." She turned her back and gave Tim a long moment to see her wounds from the horsewhip.

"So you're doing some kind of penance or act of contrition out here?" Tim asked.

"I think of myself more as a prisoner, Sir," Darla said. "Sentenced to this penal servitude until I can earn my parole back home to you."

"Who sentenced you?" Tim asked. "It wasn't me. I suppose, following this penal trope, that I exiled you."

"I rendered a vague sentence, permitting Sir Josiah to do with me as he will, Sir," Darla answered. "I wanted ... my plan was to spend a lot of time out here while you were deployed, to get thousands of lashes over the coming year, to be worked, broken, humiliated and shown how to be your slave, and then present it all to you, all the videos and photographs, and hope you would know I mean it, hope that you would see an altogether different woman, one worthy of you, on your return."

"Lying to Josiah all the while to make up for a lie to me," Tim observed.

"I ... yes, Sir, you're right, and that was and is dishonorable, and separate and apart from what you might decide, Sir Josiah may well exercise his prerogative to ban me for life from here, and I deserve that too. But if he does, Tim … I swear to you I'll find someone to break me, to beat and punish me until you return and I try to win you back."

"Win me back," Tim echoed. "You make me sound like a kewpie doll at the county fair. Throw the baseball at the milk bottles. Knock 'em over and win a Lieutenant Colonel fresh back from the Middle East!"

"Tim, I know you're angry with me, even hurting from what I did, and I deserve your anger," Darla said, and swiped at her tears. "But I can't believe you loved me enough to send me here Friday and stopped loving me by Sunday."

"Yeah, I love you, but I don't trust you, and you've betrayed me and have become a threat to my career," Tim said. "I'd guess Jackson's wife is going to enter those photographs into evidence at their divorce. If it gets into court and becomes official record, he'll be court-martialed and dishonorably discharged. But I'll get a lousy efficiency report indicating my family issues are too much a distraction in an intelligence officer's life, and I'll be forced to resign. I kept telling you the stakes were high for me and you needed to be a proper Army wife. I should've kicked you to the curb six months ago, Darla." He snorted. "Hell, I should've never married you. Josiah, she's yours if you want her. If she wants to make a pitch to me when I get back, I guess she can, but … I think this marriage is dead and just needs to be buried. Darla, I am meeting the lawyer tomorrow to begin divorce proceedings. We don't have children and there's little common property between us, so it should go through slick and easy in six or eight months. Please just sign the divorce papers when you get them. If Josiah is unwilling to be your attorney, I'm sure he can send you to one."

"Sir Josiah?" Darla asked.

"You know where the cell in the barn is," Josiah said. "Go

there and lock yourself in. We'll discuss you and decide whether you have any place here at all. Dismissed."

"Tim …. Please?" Darla begged.

"Get lost," Tim said. "We're done, Darla. I don't wish you a bad life, but I want you to remain out of my life."

Darla staggered out to the porch and loosed great braying sobs as she stumbled toward the jail in the barn.

"Jesus," Leigh breathed.

"Tim, do you want a drink?" Josiah asked.

"No, I just want to go and pick up my life again," Tim said.

"I'll take you to your car," Josiah told him. "You three discuss what you think of this matter and we'll talk when I get back."

Tim sat woodenly in the truck as they drove back to Mabel's, saying nothing the entire drive. Josiah tried drawing him out but Tim just stared at some point a thousand miles beyond the truck's window, and Josiah sensed he might have inherited another slave, if he decided to keep her. For his part, he figured Darla was desperate to keep Tim, whom she obviously loved, and was willing to go to enormous and hellish measures to do that. But he knew military minds, and most officers, once a decision was made, wouldn't go back on that decision for love nor money. In truth, he felt sorry for both of them, but he couldn't impact that.

At Mabel's, Tim got out of the truck and into his car and left without a word, and Josiah returned to the farm.

TWENTY-NINE

"Master, we all like Darla, is what we keep coming back to," Molly said on Josiah's return. "I can hardly look on her and suggest banishment after how many dicks I sucked without you knowing about it while you're keeping and punishing me."

"I ... Sir, isn't that the essence of punishment here, to address the wrongs a slave has done?" Leigh interjected. "We're all here for our wrongdoings. I've seen that stubborn look before like that asshole husband of hers has, and I think the marriage is doomed, but she deserves redemption in her own eyes, at least. I'm not saying that's your obligation. She made her own bed, so to speak, but ... I hope you hold on to her. Besides, a lot of work needs doing around here and she is another set of hands, so it's not like you can't keep her busy."

"She's not the first person I've seen doing what she tried to do," Lucretia said. "I've had an easy half-dozen clients, four men and two women, come to me for beatings – one even brought his wife to witness it and screamed like a bitch all the way through it – to offer a tribute and gain forgiveness for a damaged marriage. I know for a fact that it saved two of those marriages. One was a woman who'd done similarly to Darla, got caught in an affair. She brought her own video camera and tripod, made a long and flowery apology, and then I put her on a St. Andrew cross and horsewhipped her front and back, a solid hundred lashes in all. She sent me an e-mail the next day that her husband wept when he saw it and forgave her. That was two years ago. About three months ago she e-mailed me a birth announcement. They have a daughter and are happy as hell with each other. Another, a man … he fucked up and pissed his wife off. He went on a business trip to Vegas, got drunk, and lost about eight grand gambling. I horsewhipped him too, very much like you're doing to us, and she forgave him. Apparently he turned submissive. She sent me an e-mail six or so months ago with a video of her caning him, and said things are great in their marriage. But I know military minds, and I don't think he's going to relent. Even so, I agree with Leigh. I hope you keep her and try to lead her out of the darkness. But I think her conscience is going to require about how you're treating me today. She should probably be beaten again today, in fact, Master. Maybe before or after you punish my orgasm."

"So take her in hand tomorrow and treat her like I did you today?" Josiah asked. He was surprised when all three slaves nodded.

"Assuming she still wishes to do this, yes, Sir," Molly said. "Besides, this sounds selfish, but … Master, seeing you bugger Leigh and Lucretia has really turned me on. Being buggered by you even turned me on, as much as it hurt. Darla's a virgin to this and I'd imagine we three are all going to be wishing you'd let us masturbate when you use her for your cum dump all day tomorrow. Let's face facts here, Master. She's stone beautiful, a living magazine model. As much as I fear it, I'm … Master, I'm looking forward to my day like you gave Lucretia … are giving Lucretia, maybe I should say … today."

"Let's go to the barn," Josiah said. "Lucretia, after we speak with Darla, you have another twenty strokes coming. And then I have work for you all this afternoon. I'll be by to pick you up for supper, of course."

"I … Master, I really needed today," Lucretia said. "I know I've been more work for you, but … I'm grateful, Sir. I've had clients express gratitude before, but never really understood it in its entirety. I never felt grateful after a tune-up in Memphis. It was just a business transaction. But this … this is from my heart, your heart

... all our hearts, and it means more to me than I know how to say. Thank you, Master."

"Come here," Josiah commanded, and Lucretia approached him. He kissed her very tenderly, resting his hands at the flares of her hips. "I want you all to know I do care about you. It might not feel like it when you're being lashed or buggered, or made to blow me, but I treasure all three of you slaves."

"I love you, Master," Leigh blurted. "I know it's too soon and I can't expect you to love me back, but I love you and I hope someday soon you love me too." She blushed bright red at the completion of her heart's confession and Josiah kissed her as well.

"I think Leigh spoke for Lucretia too," Molly offered. "And I hope someday I'm worth your love as well. I know right now I'm not, not until I'm cleansed and scourged, but I ... Master, I love you and I'll live out my life regretting the woman I was until this weekend."

"I think I could easily love you all," Josiah allowed, and then harrumphed. "Get your asses into the bed of the truck now."

THIRTY

Darla stood nervously, almost at attention, in the cell, when the truck pulled in. The slaves all discharged out of the bed of the truck, and all of them took formalized kneeling positions behind the truck, eyes cast downward. Josiah realized they must have come up with this idea on their own, maybe on the ride over here. He was surprised, and in a way, touched at their display of submission in this manner. He pulled up a plastic chair and opened the cell to let Darla out. Surprising him, she took her cue from the others, and knelt similarly.

"Tim seems unwilling to change his mind," Josiah said simply. "I've known enough military men to know he's unlikely ever to change his mind, and that if this penance is to regain his esteem, it's a doomed effort, Darla. With that in mind, I cannot in good conscience hold you here against that possibility, so if you wish, I can bring you your clothes and return you to your life."

"There is no life, Sir Josiah," Darla said. "Sir, please ... Keep me here? Work me, lash me, punish me ... not for the sake of my marriage but the sake ... Jesus, I can't believe I'm saying this ... for the sake of my soul, Sir. I'll pay whatever it takes for you to keep me here at least until Tim returns."

"Do you have any idea what Lucretia and Leigh are paying me?" Josiah asked.

"No, Sir Josiah," Darla said.

"They're paying me devotion and obedience, not dollars and

cents," Josiah said. "My work as a beadle is predicated on lashing other peoples' slaves and submissives, not free people or my own slaves."

"So I have to leave," Darla said.

"I didn't say that, young lady," Josiah returned. "Silence until I'm done. Understood?" Darla nodded, smart enough to know not to answer verbally.

"I'm going to return the money you paid me earlier, Darla, and I won't accept a penny for your service here," Josiah continued. "In exchange, you will serve here with your heart. You will be punished severely, to be sure, and I will work you hard. Lucretia might've given you a glimpse into her day today, but maybe she didn't. Lucretia?"

"I didn't, Master, but if you wish, I can," Lucretia said.

"Yes, do so," Josiah ordered.

"Darla, I don't think we have a term for it, but today for me was ... I guess you'd call it Hell Day," Lucretia said. "Master has been extra harsh on me today, even unfair, working me hard and whipping me severely. He's buggered me a few times and I'd guess is likely to do so once more today. We're lucky – pardon me saying this, Master – but we're lucky he's a horny old goat." Leigh and Molly both burst into giggles at this remark, and Josiah snorted and then laughed, and he was heartened to see Darla struggling not to grin at this remark.

"Anyway," Lucretia continued. "He's made up reasons to beat me today. You saw one of the horsewhippings and there's about to be another for me. But he's right. This isn't commerce but mutual respect and affection, Darla. Perhaps tomorrow should be your Hell Day. He has promised Leigh and Molly the same, to break and humiliate us, and make us know we're slaves here. Hell, he even makes us ride in the back of that nasty old truck to make the point that we're animals here, and I know you figured out from our girl talk that we're reveling in it."

"So … so I can … I can stay, Sir Josiah?" Darla asked.

"As long as you agree to accept that I am the law here, I am the master here, and I will do with you as I please," Josiah said.

"May … Sir, I … right now I need to feel owned, without rights," Darla said. "May I call you Master?"

Josiah shot a glance at Leigh, who looked up, and nodded with a tear leaking from her eye. He saw Molly nodding too.

"You may," Josiah said.

"Thank you … Master," Darla said. "Sir, the limit about my pussy was from me, not from Tim. I'm your slave now and can deny you nothing." She chuckled. "I think I need a horny old goat, Master."

"Come to me," Josiah said, and Darla knee-walked to him and looked expectantly at him. He took her face in his hands and kissed her as he had done with his other slaves, a kiss of passion and affection, as she moaned. His nose picked up the aroma of desire from her.

"Thank you, Master," Darla said when the kiss broke.

"Often, I will pick a night to sleep with a slave in her bed," Josiah said. "I will announce that at bedtime. But your sisters suggested – and I agree – that tomorrow should be your Hell Day."

"Jesus … they're … Master, they're right," Darla said.

"I treat my slaves equally," Josiah said. "I expect you to all be sisters who love one another, but your ultimate loyalty —"

"Is to you, as it should be, Master," Darla said. "Sister Leigh explained as much to me while I was waiting for my whipping earlier."

"Good," Josiah said. "Escort Lucretia to the post for her whipping, Darla, and bind her to the post."

"As Master wishes," Darla said. "Lucretia, come with me, please?"

"Yes, Sister," Lucretia said. Surprising everyone, she remained on hands and knees, crawling behind Darla with her nipples dragging, abasing herself before her entire family. At the post, she stood and offered her wrists, and Darla cuffed her in place.

"Jesus, she's really setting the bar for us, isn't she?" Molly said.

"Let's crawl too," Leigh suggested. "Humbling is good for us, Molly."

Josiah shrugged and Molly nodded, and they crawled as Lucretia had done. It was more of a struggle for Leigh, who had far smaller breasts than Molly or Lucretia, but she did it, and Josiah didn't miss the aroused flush in her chest nor the erect nipples she had when she knelt up near the post to witness Lucretia's whipping.

Lucretia again screamed her way through her lashing, writhing and even fighting her bonds through several strokes, before just enduring it, moaning and utterly broken. She howled anew as coagulant was rubbed into her wounds, and then Josiah considered one more evil idea. He went into the barn and got a collar and a leash and attached them to Lucretia. "Leigh, walk her back to the cabin," he ordered. "Lucretia is to crawl like the animal she is. If her nipples come off the ground, lash her with this strap, and hard, at your discretion. If the nipples lose contact three times, report her to me and she will be caned. She is to crawl up the steps and keep her nipples on the floor in the cabin as well."

"Oh … wow," Leigh breathed, seemingly unaware she'd spoken. "Yes, Master. Let's go, Lucretia."

"Yes, Sister," Lucretia said.

"God," Darla breathed.

"Something?" Josiah asked Darla.

"Sir, that's … really sexy to me," Darla breathed.

"Molly, another collar and leash for Darla," Josiah ordered. "Get a strap for disciplining her. Same orders."

"Yes, Master," Molly said. "God, I think I envy Darla and Lucretia, Sir."

"Oh, I think you'll all take crawls," Josiah said, pleased he had learned from Lucretia.

"God, I'm so horny right now I think you could blow in my ear and make me cum," Molly breathed. She dashed toward the barn and returned with collar and leash, and led Darla away. They'd barely made it thirty feet when Molly lashed Darla a half-dozen strokes with the heavy strap she had chosen. Darla yelped and they began crawling anew. Further away, Josiah saw Leigh giving Lucretia a lengthy whipping with the strap. Josiah counted twenty strokes and then Lucretia began crawling again.

Josiah smiled, knowing that things like this would help bond his girls to one another. But each girl would have to leash, walk, and strap the other three sisters, he would have to ensure. He was growing horny again, and decided Lucretia needed one more buggering, something to make Darla fretful about her fate to begin at sunrise.

He watched for another long moment and then got into the truck and drove to the cabin. Unfortunately for Darla and Molly, he hit a puddle and splashed them in mud. He hadn't seen the puddle, which was covered with fallen leaves and twigs, and was torn between feeling bad about it and amused at it as he looked in the mirror and saw Molly laying the strap furiously into Darla, who cried out loudly enough for Josiah to hear it over the loud engine of the truck. He arrived to the cabin to see Lucretia weeping and gasping as she struggled to crawl up the stairs, but admired her devotion as she kept her nipples pressed to the rugged wood. Her left knee was bleeding a bit and he figured her palms were equally worn, but she made it up the stairs, across the porch, and into the cabin , and then remained on hands and knees.

"Her nipples only came off the ground once, Master," Leigh reported. "Sir, she picked up a splinter from the steps, though. Permission to remove it, Sir?"

"Kneel up, Lucretia," Josiah ordered. He saw the splinter, jagged and perhaps an inch long, jutting from her left aureole. "Granted, Leigh."

"Take a deep breath, Lucretia," Leigh said, and Lucretia obeyed, and yelped a bit as the splinter came out of sensitive flesh.

"Thank you, Sister and Master," Lucretia said.

"Welcome, slave," Josiah returned.

In a moment, the door opened and Molly called into the cabin. "Master, should we hose off out here, or come in?" she asked.

"I'll hose you down," Josiah said. "Stand to attention out there." Darla and Molly, both dripping in mud, stood uncertainly and more or less at military attention.

"Here, 'at attention' means stand with your feet spread half-again shoulder's width, with your fingers laced behind your head and elbows extended," Josiah ordered. "That way, you're exposing yourselves to me, in case I need to whip you or torture you somehow."

"Yes, Master," the slaves said, and both assumed the position of attention. Josiah got the hose and sprayed them down while they yelped not in pain but at the cold stream, but he got them cleaned off well enough to come into the house.

"Hands and knees, Darla," he ordered. "Molly walk her in." He went and stood on the porch while Darla crawled, taking care to keep her nipples on the ground, and just as clumsy on the steps as the far taller Lucretia. Finally, she was on the porch, panting a bit, and through the door, where she knelt beside her darker sister.

"You'll all be walking one another thus from time to time," Josiah said. "Consider it bonding, knowing you will obey my orders when I tell you to exert my authority on a sister."

"God ... yes, Master," Leigh moaned. Josiah didn't miss the trickle escaping her vagina to roll hypnotically down her thigh.

"Molly, how many times did Darla's nipples come off the ground?" Josiah asked.

"Three times, Master," Molly said. "I whipped her six lashes the first time and twelve the second. The third time – it's why we were slower getting back, she got twenty."

"What's about to happen to you, Darla?" Josiah asked.

"The ... Master, I am to be caned for my disobedience," Darla said.

"Bend over the back of the sofa," Josiah ordered her. "Lucretia, go choose a cane for your sister's lashing."

Lucretia went up the stairs without a word, and returned a moment later with a long and thin rattan rod, and Josiah nodded his approval as he accepted it. "Darla, I think twelve lashes should suffice, for now," Josiah said. "But you'd best be on your best behavior for tomorrow. In a moment, I'm going to bugger Lucretia again, and tomorrow is your day, by the way. But we'll get to that in a moment."

"Y ... y ... yes, Master," Darla said, and Josiah flicked the cane into her rump. She was still heavily decorated from her weekend, and cried out as the rattan left its welt on her, but held her place, seemingly knowing better than to rise up or evade. Josiah lashed again, and Darla yelped again, simply stretching her legs out behind her and on her tiptoes. Josiah recognized the simple self-bondage that would make it more difficult for her to rise up. It also presented her thighs for the cane, and he nodded approvingly, then slashed the cane into her upper thighs. She cried out, beginning to sob, and Josiah kept to the lash, knowing this poor girl was in for a rough new reality, no matter her stated understanding of what was coming her way. Finally, a dozen lashes were laid into her, and Josiah set the cane aside.

"Slave ... slave thanks her Master," Darla choked out.

"Recover," Josiah ordered, and Darla clumsily stood, noting Molly and Leigh in the at-attention position Josiah had required outdoors, and hustling beside them, and likewise standing at attention. Lucretia, he saw approvingly, was already face-down and ass-up, ready for yet another buggering from her "horny old goat," and chuckled his approval of her. Obviously, he realized, she loved what he was doing to her, and he took her hips in his hands and thrust into her once again while looking up to see Darla gaping. He could feel Lucretia pushing back to meet his thrusts into her, and heard her grunting as he plundered her loosening ass, finally erupting into her again as she moaned and visibly fought off an orgasm, finally succeeding as she breathed easier.

"Thank you for your use of me, Master," Lucretia said.

"You're welcome," Josiah said as he saw Leigh whisper something to Darla and then Darla darting off to the bathroom, returning quickly with water and rags. She knelt before him and thoroughly washed his penis, and, as coached by Leigh, sucked it into her mouth to prove she'd been thorough, before patting it dry. Josiah liked this ritual and decided someone would be designated to that task the next day after his buggery of Darla.

"God, that's going to hurt being inside me," she whispered. "I hope I don't disappoint Master tomorrow."

"Why don't you slaves all gather round and discuss anal use?" Josiah suggested. "Which of you wishes to get Darla a plug and insert it into her?"

"I will, Master," Molly smiled, and went up the stairs, choosing a large plug for her sister, one that made Darla's eyes widen.

"Darla, position yourself as Lucretia did," Josiah ordered. "This will loosen you and make it go easier on you tomorrow, but it's going to hurt going into you, especially how Molly is about to insert it."

Darla took the ordered position and Molly lubricated the plug, and then squirted a bit of the lube into Darla's rectum. She worked the tip of it into Darla's bottom and then, as she had done with Leigh, placed the foot of the plug over her own pelvic bone, grasped Darla's hips, and thrust hard into her, seating the plug fully into the girl and holding her in place, forcing her to accept it. Darla sobbed as she was plundered, fucked by this woman, in front of everyone, but didn't object or fight.

"Darla, we all get this from one another from time to time,"

Leigh said. "I … Master wants us to bond with one another, and to our duty, and when we do these things to each other at his orders, and have them done to us, it helps establish his mastery and our sisterhood. Saturday night, while you were in your cage, he had Molly and me do this with one another, sent each of us to choose a plug. I chose a bigger one and Molly a smaller one, and then he made us each insert our choices into the other. So I got a more comfortable plug while she got one a bit more painful. But it made his later use of us … Molly had an easier time with it for my choice, and you may not believe me, but she showed you a kindness just now."

"I … yes, I see how endowed Master is," Darla agreed. "Thank you, Master, and thank you Sister Molly."

"You're welcome," Molly said.

"Okay, teach Darla what you ladies know and have learned about being taken anally," Josiah ordered, and then countermanded himself. "Let's talk about it over supper, actually. Leigh?"

"I'll go reheat some things," Leigh promised, and went toward the kitchen.

"Darla, go make a glass of iced tea for me," Josiah commanded. "There should be a pitcher of it in the fridge in there."

"Sugar and lemon, Master?" Darla asked.

"Just plain, please," Josiah said.

"As Master wishes," Darla promised, and walked a bit bowlegged into the kitchen.

"She'll learn to be more graceful wearing a plug," Lucretia chuckled. "Molly, did you know that Leigh has had to wear one overnight and all day to work on some occasions?"

Molly gaped, shocked at this news. "No, I didn't," she said. "Jesus, I can't imagine."

"You'll do more than imagine the first day you're back to your job," Josiah promised, and Molly shivered. Darla came in with the tea and handed it to Josiah.

"Master, this plug feels like it's trying to force out," Darla said. "May I sit on one of the hard chairs to help hold it in, Sir?"

"Yes, you may," Josiah said, and Molly slapped her own head like she was in one of those old V8 commercials. "What is it, Molly?"

"I went off today on errands and completely forgot to hit the medical supply for enema kits," Molly said in obvious annoyance with herself.

"Enemas?" Darla asked.

"To clean us out for Master before he uses us," Molly said. "Although I expect he'll have other nefarious plans for us."

"Oh, God," Darla moaned as she sat on the chair, hissing as her well-whipped flesh pressed into the hard wood. "Master likes humiliation a lot, doesn't he?"

"He seems to thrive on it, on controlling us," Molly acknowledged. "But it's good for us, Darla. Besides, Leigh and I are physicians, so we're good at monitoring slaves' health, honey. Remember the physical I gave you?"

"I do," Darla said, and blushed.

"I'm not going to readily suggest that Master put anyone to unnecessary risk," Molly said. "And I'm sure neither will Leigh."

"Darla, I'm older than you other three," Lucretia contributed.

"Master wanted to be certain I could take this, and had them give me a complete physical and kept me on a heart monitor and monitored my blood pressure all through that first horsewhipping, while you were locked up in the barn the other night."

"Will I be monitored like that?" Darla asked.

"Only if we see a risk factor," Leigh said from the kitchen. "But you look disgustingly healthy."

"Who was the big man that was with you all?" Darla asked. "He looked like a lumberjack."

"His name was Tony," Lucretia said simply, shooting Josiah a glance. "He won't be coming back."

"He looked dangerous," Darla said. "Like he could eat one of us for a snack if you forgot to feed him."

"May I … uh … may I be excused, Master?" Lucretia asked.

"Yes, dismissed," Josiah said. "I'll be up later."

Lucretia started up the stairs and then stopped dead four steps up, then turned and looked at Darla. "Tony … Tony was my slave out in the world until yesterday, Darla. He couldn't face this, me being enslaved, and I released him and dismissed him. He was a good man, a gentle man, and I loved him. He killed himself shortly after leaving here yesterday. I know you didn't know that, couldn't have known, but that's what happened, Darla." And then, exhibiting obvious self-control, Lucretia turned precisely on the stairs and marched up to her assigned room, closing the door gently behind her.

"Oh God, I'm so sorry," Darla said. "I didn't know."

"There was no way you could know," Josiah said. "It was a shocker to us all, Darla."

"May I go up and apologize to her?"

"Yes, you may, but if she sends you away, just come right back down here," Josiah said.

"Lucretia, how do I say I'm sorry?" Darla asked a moment later.

"Come sit beside me here," Lucretia said, and Darla sat, albeit gingerly.   In spite of herself, Lucretia smirked.   "You'll grow accustomed to the plug soon.   I think Leigh is probably the best about us at taking them.   She might have advice to offer."

"Thank you," Darla said.   "Lucretia —"

"You were right," Lucretia said, cutting her off.   "Tony was a huge man and if you didn't know him, he looked dangerous.   The cop we met yesterday said he looked like he could rip oak trees right up out of the ground, and he was right.   Tony always wanted to play pro football, and played in college but wasn't quite enough to make the NFL draft.   He envied that I got to go to the big show when I was younger."

"The big show?" Darla asked.

"I played pro basketball in the WNBA," Lucretia said.   "I wasn't a standout or a star, but played, until my knee went flooey on me."

"Wow, that's impressive," Darla said.   "My father was always wild about sports, and was nuts for Duke basketball and Dolphins football."

"I like watching once in a while, but mostly made a clean break when I left the league," Lucretia said.   "Darla, I appreciate you coming up here.   It shows character, strong character, on your part.

But you didn't know the story there. We weren't introduced and Tony ... well, he was gone before you returned."

"Thank you," Darla said, still seeming ashamed of herself. She was surprised when Lucretia grabbed her hair and gently tugged, tilting her face up, and surprised again when the woman gently kissed her.

"Let's go back downstairs," Lucretia said. "You need to learn assplug from Leigh, and how to be a good assfuck from me, so Master is pleased with you." She paused a moment. "Master was kind and gentle to me last night, because I begged him for it. He's an amazing man at making love to the whole woman. I begged him for today too, Darla. I'm healing from Tony, and being worked hard and whipped hard was good for me to help put it into more perspective. If I seemed bitchy when I stormed off, I'm sorry. I ... I can't forgive you because there's nothing to forgive, though, okay?"

"I can see how submissives and slaves love you," Darla said. "Jesus, I didn't think I was bi until you just kissed me, but now ... well ... wow."

Lucretia smiled and then chuckled. "Let's get our asses downstairs before they pick up more stripes, honey," she said. "I've had enough lashes to last me a while."

"I ... you got it bad today," Darla observed.

"And you will tomorrow," Lucretia said. "And Leigh and Molly will soon follow."

"The enema thing scares me," Darla said. "I've never had one."

"Don't be scared of what you can't control," Lucretia advised. "I've never had one either, nor given one, but I'd bet our mad doctors down there have, and I'm sure if they determine Master needs instruction, they'll instruct him, and one way or another, we're slaves, honey. It's not like we have the choice. I don't even want the choice. I need this, and I think so do you, or you wouldn't have come back here."

"You're right," Darla said. "I guess in my own way I'm grieving too, but losing Tim was my own fault. I'm a fucking slut and … he deserves better. But maybe … no, I can't fool myself into thinking he'll take me back, even. I just hope Master Josiah will keep me. I need to … well … to belong, you know?"

"You're smoking hot," Lucretia said. "I think he'll hang onto you."

"I … I hope not just because he thinks I'm attractive or a good fuck," Darla said. "That's what got me in trouble in the first place. You know, there's times I wonder if I shouldn't gain forty pounds and ask him to horsewhip the pretty off my face."

"Sit back down," Lucretia said, and sat beside Darla. "Master is a sexy and sexual man. But look at Molly. She's pretty in a plain folk kind of way, but hardly anyone's idea of a magazine model. He adores her, Darla. God knows after what she confessed, one hell of a lot of men in his position would've sent her packing and nobody would have blamed him if he'd done just that. But he loves her. Look at me. I'm a black woman in my forties, and if he got jungle fever, there are far lovelier specimens than me, but here I am."

"Bullshit," Darla said. "Jesus Christ, you're exotic, even stunning. In your forties? Really? I figured you were just maybe thirty. I'm not shitting you, Lucretia. You're … God, if he told me to fuck you right now, not even sure whether I'm bi, I'd do it in a heartbeat."

"Don't be surprised if he does exactly that with all of us, the same as making us walk each other," Lucretia said. "He fucked me hard Saturday night, felt like he pushed a quart of his spunk into me, and made Molly eat it all out of me while Leigh sucked him clean."

"Jesus, keep telling me these kinds of stories and I'm going to cream your bed here," Darla said.

Lucretia chuckled, seeing a flush in Darla's neck and chest that told her the woman was indeed moving into a high state of rut. "Master uses sex and sexuality ... well ... masterfully," Lucretia said. "He's learned a few things from me – I think I might be the first professional dominatrix he's ever really gotten to know, and in some ways I'm like an instructional laboratory to him. Just remember from here on in, you're a slave. You don't get to say no. And I think you won't want to say no."

"Because I'll be punished," Darla asked.

"No, but you will be punished for defiance," Lucretia said. "I understand you earned double your original sentence for that earlier today."

"That was harsh," Darla said. "I ... he was right, though."

"Yes he was," Lucretia agreed. "But no, you'll obey him because, like me, you'll find yourself enthralled with him, even falling for him, and would rather die than to disappoint him. Already, I don't think there's anything I would refuse him, Darla. Look, you're probably just now figuring something out about life and yourself, but I'm going to spell it out in Dick-and-Jane terms. You are downright beautiful, Darla. You're athletic, have a stunning body, and like Helen of Troy, a face that could launch a thousand ships. And for that, you've probably always gotten your way from men, and probably a hell of a lot of women, trying to gain your favors, preferably in bed."

"I ... yeah ... I came to realize that I'm a user of people," Darla said. "I'm ashamed of that. I think I even reeled Tim in with my big tits and washboard abs. There was a band long ago … something named after birds … Hawks, maybe, or Vultures or Kestrels … shit, I can't remember …"

"The Eagles," Lucretia said. "Pretty girls learning young how to smile and open all doors."

"Yes, that one!" Darla exclaimed. "All about how you can get away with all kinds of shit, but your lies show up in your eyes. I think that's why Tim didn't even ask me if the picture was a Photoshop job or something. I think he just knew."

"Then he's smarter than the average bear," Lucretia said. "Honestly, even smarter than our master. Molly could have fooled him for years."

"I guess love is the difference," Darla said. "I … I've been thinking of Tim all day. He loved me after his own fashion, I think, but he's Army all the way. He's a West Pointer, like his father and his grandfather and great-grandfather before him. His great-grandfather retired as a two-star general. His grandfather was a one-star when he died of a heart attack. His father retired with three stars, and Tim is determined to wear four stars before he's done. I think he'd love to be chairman of the JCS before he retires, and when he saw those photos, he saw me as … well … as a hindrance. And anything that poses any threat at all to his career is to be burned to the ground. He doesn't love me like he loves his career."

"Darla, I know you love him," Lucretia said after a moment of visible thought. "I know you feel like a crumb for fucking around on him, and you even should. It was wrong for you to do that, no matter what excuses you might've tried to make. But from my chair, honestly, he did you both a favor by throwing you out."

"I've been circling that conclusion too," Darla said. "I still feel guilty. I feel like shit, and I know I deserve what's going to happen to me here, even knowing I won't get Tim back. But today has been momentous. I could easily see being Josiah's for the long haul."

"Join the club, sweetheart," Lucretia said. "Let's get downstairs."

"Assplugs are good," Leigh said as they all sat to eat. "I've used them a lot, often on my own, but often at Blake's orders for discipline. If I could teach you anything with them, it's to use them often to accustom yourself to them, and to learn the right amount of lube, and the right sizes of them." She laughed. "The other night, Molly's choice that wound up in me was smallish, and ... well, I came. I came hard, and that plug shot out of me like a rocket. I guess I should be glad my ass was aimed at the floor or I'd be getting ready to do time for manslaughter."

"Jesus!" Darla exclaimed, and then giggled at the imagery.

"Yeah, laugh, bitch," Leigh grinned. "I got buggered and beaten for that one." And then she laughed too, and Molly chuckled.

"Master, you've enjoyed us all anally," Molly said. "Who's the best for you, and why?"

"Good question," Josiah said. "Lucretia is the answer. She ... because, I think, of her professional experience, she understands from the dominant's point of view, for one thing, why I do what I do. But from the ... I guess the mechanical standpoint, she positions herself well for it, but most importantly, she pushes back to take full impalement. She gives herself to it, and makes it better on me. Of the three of you, so far she's been the best anal partner, but I hope you all become as good."

"Please don't get good at it, or he'll get bored with me,"

Lucretia said, grinning.

"Not a chance, slave," Josiah said. "I'm keeping your ass."

"Master, I hope this is just insecurity, but … please indulge me," Lucretia said, suddenly serious. "My ass, my black ass, my beautiful ass, my exotic ass?"

"Your ass," Josiah said, looking into her eyes. "Lucretia, I don't give a damn about anything but my slaves, and your race isn't an issue to me. You asked for today, and for that matter, for last night. Do you need work? Yeah, you do. Breakfast this morning was a good illustration of that. Do you really think for even a second that I'm only into you because you're black and I'm white and can pretend it's 1830 again?"

"No, Master, but … I hope you …Jesus, I fucked this up," Lucretia said.

"Master, can I add to this talk?" Darla asked.

"Darla, you're equal to all my other slaves," Josiah said. "I endeavor mostly to treat you all the same, although I now some things have to be individually tailored. I don't think Leigh could fit well into Lucretia's wardrobe, nor vice versa, for instance. Chime in, slave."

"Master … Lucretia is exotic and lovely, and as a black woman, I think she's probably even more a minority in the S&M community than in the general culture," Darla began. "We had a talk upstairs about being … attractive … and I think maybe it opened some insecurities with her, Sir."

Lucretia nodded, and wept, and Josiah's heart broke a little bit for her. "Lucretia, I own you because you're you," Josiah said. "I don't see your race, your 'black ass' as you put it, as a merit or a demerit. I don't give a shit. I … okay, I'll just say it and bare my heart here … I love you. I love you for you, not your skin, not your height. I love your heart. I admit I love your mind and your insight. Your intelligence and wit are the greater appeal to me than your height or skin tone. You're not my nigger, Lucretia. You're my slave, and … yes … I love you. And Leigh, before you get insecure over there, I love you too, damn it."

"I love you, Master," Lucretia said. "Please, spank me, horsewhip me, rape my ass for a month, but please forgive me, Sir." And then she broke down into huge sobs and Josiah held her tightly while she cried it out of her soul. Finally, she hitched a few times and the storm passed. "I'm so sorry, Master," she said.

"Lucretia, you don't owe me an apology," Josiah said. "Sometimes I forget that even beautiful women – and you walk in that company – have insecurities. No punishment for this, at least, this time. But learn to believe in me, in our family, please."

"Th … thank you, Master," Lucretia managed to say. "I … God, I sound like a fucking idiot."

"No," Josiah said. "You sound like a fucking human." He kissed Lucretia, a loving exchange.

"I love you, Master, and … if it's what you want, I'm your nigger, even, Sir."

"Just my slave, my woman," Josiah re-asserted.

"I've made an ass of myself," Lucretia said. "May I be dismissed?"

"I'll look in on you before I go to bed," Josiah said. "But if you wish to go, you're dismissed."

"Thank you, Master, I'm sorry," Lucretia said, and fled to her assigned room.

"Leigh, go wait in the bed of the truck," Josiah decided. "You'll be my bedmate tonight. Molly, give Darla a room and go to your own room, please."

"Yes, of course, Master," Molly said. "Come with me, Darla."

THIRTY-ONE

"I'm sorry, Master," Lucretia said when Josiah walked into her room. "I made an ass of myself, and cast our sincerity into doubt. I know I deserve even more lashes, and I'll take them without pretending I don't deserve them. I dishonored you, and you didn't deserve my stupid insecurities."

Josiah didn't answer her at first, but sat at the edge of the bed. "Lie over my lap," he ordered. Lucretia looked at him in surprise, but did as ordered, and cooed as Josiah caressed her rump. "This ass belongs to who, again?" he asked.

"To you, Master," Lucretia said. "Get a knife and carve it off me, if you wish, because it's yours to do with however you please, Sir."

"I'm pleased just to fondle it for now, mine," Josiah said. "Lucretia, 'I love you' isn't a cheap phrase with me. I'm slow to say it, and don't say it as often as I should, probably, but I do love you. Get that into your head, honey. Because it's true."

"Master ... please force me to quit my business and just be yours," Lucretia begged. "I swear, if I never lay a lash again that you don't have me lay, I'm okay with that, Sir."

"That's a possibility," Josiah said. "But ... I think at the very least, you owe Mark his session with you. I guess you do better with your own minion in your dungeon?"

"I do, Master," Lucretia acknowledged.

"Take Leigh with you," Josiah ordered. "She knows your dungeon and how you are, and would probably serve well under you. If she messes up, report it to me and I'll deal with her here."

"My heart won't be in it," Lucretia said as Josiah continued caressing her welted rump.

"How often do you think I have real passion in lawyering?" Josiah asked. "It's a job. It's income. But … if it was ever a passion, it surely isn't anymore. 'Yes, Mr. Davis, your real estate contract is straight-up and nothing indicates a rip-off.' Or, 'Ms. Johnson, you can file for divorce, but if he contests it, you and he will both wind up broke on attorney fees. By the way, it'll cost you ten grand for my representation if it stays out of court. If it goes to court, grab hold of your hat and ass, Ma'am, because I'll get your half of the marriage in legal fees, and his lawyer will get the other half and you'll both be panhandling on opposite corners of 3rd and Main. Are you sure you want to do this?' Or, 'No, Mr. Hollis, it sounds totally eccentric, but the hard reality is that you really can't leave your estate to Jesus. Yes, I get that you love the Lord, but I'm afraid if you want to bequeath your estate to Jesus, you need to route it through an earthly religious institution.'"

"I guess when I think 'lawyer' I think of Perry Mason, always defending the innocent," Lucretia said. "I don't think of a bored lawyer looking forward to retirement. I keep my law license, but never really practiced law. I realized near the end of my third year it just wasn't what I wanted, so this … it's surprising, Master."

"I'm sorry to break your bubble," Josiah said. "I haven't handled a criminal case since I worked for the DA right out of law school. Mostly, what I do is boring stuff that pays well. But believe me, my passion is here, Lucretia. I decided over the weekend that I'm going to start tapering things off at the law firm. I have eight associates working there, and will probably name Louis Taylor – he's the most senior of them – partner, and in a year or hopefully far sooner, managing partner. I never understood workaholics, to be honest. I've made a good pile of money, and will continue to do so through the firm. I want to enjoy it and not be a bored-to-death suit in that office building."

"I'll sure be glad to be here serving you, Master," Lucretia sighed.

"We'll talk more as the week goes on," Josiah said, and gave her rump a light smack that elicited a coo from her. "Get some sleep now. I'm going to talk with the others each for a bit, and then I'm going to go to bed."

"Hey, honey," Josiah said a moment later when he walked into Molly's room.

"Master, tonight … I'm glad you love us, Sir," Molly said. "It's a strange family, but … it's family and feels right. And … Sir, please be harder on me on my Hell Day than you were on Lucretia."

"Why?" Josiah asked.

"Master, I think I'm going to be glad we have Darla, but she put my mind in motion today," Molly said. "One drunken indiscretion and look at what that poor girl threw away, at what she lost, at how devastated she is. I'm glad you forgave her for her white lies, by the way."

"White lies?" Josiah asked.

"Sir, those lies weren't calculated to harm you or anyone here," Molly said. "If they were intended to harm anyone, it was only herself, Master. Anyway … I see how easily I could have thrown away this marriage, what I put at risk for … well … just cheap thrills. I know I'm not as pretty as the others, or as young, and I'm pushing an extra twenty pounds of belly I need to shed. I guess I had kind of

213

a midlife crisis. In some corner of my mind, I needed to know men ... women too, in several cases ... desired me, found me good enough, and so I turned full slut."

"Did I make you feel somehow insecure?" Josiah asked.

"Master ... I made me feel insecure," Molly said. "Yeah, we fucked plenty. But I knew your heart desired someone kinkier, more submissive than me, and I guess a huge snowball of insecurity gathered around that one little kernel. But I realized when I was blowing you after your first session with Darla that I'd wronged you in too many ways. I won't do it again, Master. Punishing me from that aspect is unnecessary. But you know how this is somewhat of a penance for Darla, since her marriage is ashes now?"

"Yeah," Josiah said. "Our marriage remains intact, even stronger, but you still ... your heart needs the penance."

"Now more than ever, Master," Molly said. "Sir, give me at least two Hell Days, back-to-back. And ... Master, I know every lash means you love me. Give me a lot of love, please. Please show me what I'm worth to you."

"I'll consider that," Josiah said. "But it'll be under Leigh's supervision, Molly. Punishment is one thing but I'm not going to kill you or permanently harm you."

"Master, I begged you the other night to brand me like I was no more than a calf," Molly said. "Don't hesitate to scar me, please. It'll be something I'll wear with honor, Sir."

"I'll probably go that far," Josiah said. "Tomorrow, I'll want you and Lucretia to go into town and bring Darla's car back here – it's parked behind our special office – and while you're out, get the other supplies you mentioned."

Molly chuckled. "I see your wheels turning, Master," she

said. "You have more evil in mind for us, don't you?"

"Maybe," Josiah allowed.

"Definitely," Molly countered. "I can think of a number of evil ideas just right here, Master, to humiliate us and make us perform."

"Maybe," Josiah repeated, dramatically shifting his eyes and grinning.

"Who's the smartass now?" Molly giggled.

"I have no idea," Josiah said. "Get some sleep. I'm going to visit Darla and then take Leigh with me to the big house."

"I'll be a while getting back, Master," Molly said. "I ... I'm going to get a gift for the whole family, Sir."

"What is it?" Josiah asked.

"Not telling," Molly grinned. "But if you don't like it, throw in a third Hell Day, Master."

Darla squeaked in surprise when Josiah walked into the room, and looked at him with wide eyes. "I don't knock before entering rooms," Josiah announced. "Slaves have no privacy from their masters."

"Not even the bathroom?" Darla asked.

"Not even the bathroom," Josiah said. "Look, I'm going to have my dick all the way up your ass tomorrow at least twice, and maybe three or even four times. I know what's in there, so who do you think you're hiding it from?"

"God," Darla said, and blushed dark red. "Point to Master."

"How are you with this?" Josiah asked.

"Not to sound flip, but compared to what?" Darla asked. "Master, this is like I walked through the looking glass. Down is up, up is down, I'm owned property, about to be buggered for the first time in my life. I was horsewhipped today, by my own request. I'm wondering if I've gone mad, or maybe I've finally gone sane."

"Sounds like you're having second thoughts and want out," Josiah said.

"Sir, I want to stay here, please," Darla said in a firm tone. "Second thoughts? I'm having those, Master. I'm scared to death of tomorrow. But there's a strange peace. I … I hid a lot of things from Tim, and for that, I always felt … hunted, I guess. I shouldn't have seduced Marvin that night, I knew it was wrong. But … Master … I'm trying to think how to say what I think you need to understand, Sir." She paused and took a deep breath. "Tim is a career soldier. We had a talk earlier today, when you were out and left us all to girl talk. It came up that there is a difference between what you are and what you do. Lucretia is a professional dominatrix, although I think she's hoping you capture her entirely and hold her here. Molly and Leigh are doctors. You're a lawyer. But for you four, that's what you do. What you are is different. You're three slaves and a master is what you are. Is that making sense?"

"Yes, it makes perfect sense because it's the truth of the matter," Josiah said, sensing where this was going.

"Not so with Tim," Darla said. "In a lot of ways he's a wonderful man and deserves a far better woman than me. But what he is and what he does are one and the same. He's a soldier. Eats, breathes, and shits Army. He cut himself shaving one morning and I was half surprised he didn't bleed OD green. He's a smart man, maybe even brilliant. Did you know they do a lot of schooling there in the military? He has a master degree, and we met in a college class."

"I actually did know that," Josiah said. Senior officers all went to a college at Fort Leavenworth in Kansas and exited with the equivalent of a master degree, he remembered learning at some point.

"But beginning at West Point, they're brainwashed, Master," Darla said. "There's the right way, the wrong way, and the Army way, and you'd better damned well do it the Army way, no matter what, or look out below. I honestly think the quartermaster should handle marriage and just issue wives to officers. We need a boot camp to train us in the Army Wife Way." She laughed, but without humor.

"You're not the first Army wife who's said something like that to me," Josiah said. "But you are the first one who's said it while stark naked and enslaved to me."

Darla laughed at this one. "Master ... I need to ask you for something," she said after a moment. "Don't let me run away. Don't listen when I beg you to stop. That's just me being a coward, and God hates a coward, I've always heard. Fortunately for you, nobody's going to come looking for me here, Sir."

"Explain that, please," Josiah said.

"Master, my parents disowned me over Tim," Darla explained. "I don't have a job and didn't even have friends at the base there. I ... God, I sound arrogant when I say this, but here goes. I know I'm a beauty, blonde, blue, tall and long-legged, a good figure, and men look at me. The downside of it is the other wives around the base, whether married to lieutenants or colonels or generals, saw that too, and wanted nothing to do with me. If anything, when word is out I'm gone, there'll be a hearty hallelujah offered up throughout the base. I don't have a job that's going to wonder where I am. I can go completely off-grid and nobody's going to know, Sir. So please ... I think what the army does in boot camp makes sense, cloistering those recruits until they're turned into soldiers. No clothes for me, no car, don't let me off the grounds for ... I'd think at least two months, perhaps as long as six, and not then without supervision from you or one of my sisters. Don't trust me, but make me earn it, Master. And ... use my asshole a lot, Sir. In my mind, it kind of tells me my pussy isn't worth it to you."

"If I wasn't spent from using Lucretia so much today, you'd already have it in there," Josiah said.

"Master, if I displease you in any way, if I don't push back like Lucretia does, or if there's even a hair out of place, crush me for it, Sir," Darla said, and came off the bed, and went to her knees, groveling. "Make me into a woman, into a slave, everyone in this family will think is worthwhile, Sir. Because right now I'm just a shitty slut."

"It begins in the morning," Josiah said. "And I generally agree that slaves here are denied clothes, except when they're necessary, like work boots or gloves, although I've decided collars, working collars, will go on all four of you so that when one of you should be walked by a sister, it happens immediately."

"God, that was sexy, having to do that," Darla said. "I love that I'm not on a pedestal here, that you're not trying to please me for the chance that I'll sleep with you. I've needed this probably since before it was legal for me, Master. So ... while I might curse and beg you to let me go because of my cowardice ... I want you to know right now how grateful I am, Master."

"Get some sleep, slave," Josiah said. "You'll want to be well-rested for the horsewhip and my dick up your ass." Darla shivered and climbed into bed, and wept when Josiah bent down and gave her a tender goodnight kiss.

"Goodnight, Master," she whispered. "God, I could love you so easily."

"Come with me," he said to Leigh, who was waiting for him by the truck. "I want you to be in my bed tonight, honey."

"Oh … thank you, Master," Leigh said, and followed him to the truck. She began to climb into the bed when Josiah told her to get into the cab, and then drove her to the big house, then led her to the master bedroom.

THIRTY-TWO

"Master, I know you're spent tonight," Leigh said. "What can I do for you, Sir?"

"If I wasn't planning to give Darla an awful Hell Day tomorrow, we'd be making love in here tonight," Josiah said. "I considered bringing her here tonight but I don't think she's ready for tenderness, and she sure doesn't deserve it."

"Master, neither do I," Leigh said. "While I could look at Lucretia and tell you really did her right last night, she needed it and deserved some love after ... after Tony's suicide. While I'd love it, I'd rather earn it from you, Master, and I think that means not at all this entire week."

"Your Hell Day will be day after tomorrow," Josiah said. "Molly has requested a double-header, so she's on for Thursday and Friday. Are you working next Monday, by the way?"

"Master, I go in at 3:00 to work two hours," Leigh said. "I have one patient I need to see, but otherwise, no, Sir."

"Okay," Josiah said. "Lucretia has a client next Monday."

"Yeah, her webmaster guy, right? Mark is his name, I think," Leigh remembered.

"Him," Josiah confirmed. "Lucretia likes having an assistant for her dungeon work. So you'll go with her to this session. You are to obey her as you would me."

"I've obeyed her many times, Master," Leigh said. She chuckled. "I still have to remind myself not to call her 'Ma'am' or 'Mistress' here, although that would probably be advisable in her dungeon if I'm to be her assistant."

"Yes it is," Josiah said. "I'll ask her tomorrow, but she might want to get you into fetish attire so you look the part. I somehow doubt a scrub suit is going to do the trick there."

"I suppose not, Master," Leigh said. "A physician in attendance might scare the poor bastard in the wrong way."

"Smartass," Josiah laughed. "I don't know what she does with him, but it should be interesting to hear of it."

"How much am I to participate, Master?" Leigh asked.

"You are to obey Lucretia as you would me," Josiah repeated. "If she wants you to cane his balls, you are to do so."

"I've had boy toys before, submissive men, friends with benefits," Leigh said. "I've laid more than one cane stripe in my time, Master."

Josiah stripped naked and laid on the bed, on his belly. "Massage me," he ordered. "Your master deserves some pampering."

"He does indeed," Leigh agreed. "He's such a wonderful man, such a wonderful master to us." She straddled his body and began kneading his shoulders and arms. "We wouldn't want Master too stiff here to punish his slaves, now would we?" she asked, and began working his entire body until Josiah fell sound asleep under her soothing touch. Leigh would have been surprised to learn this was the first time Josiah had ever been massaged.

THIRTY-THREE

"Out of bed," Josiah said to Darla, waking her long before sunrise. "Get your ass to the kitchen and prepare breakfast. Now."

"Yes, Master," Darla said, yawning. She went to the toilet and peed, and then rushed down the stairs and began preparations. Leigh, at his order, went and woke Molly and Lucretia, and they all went to the kitchen. Darla, given no other direction than to prepare breakfast, went Southwestern and made breakfast tacos, a huge pan of scrambled eggs, crumbled sausage, bacon, cheese and salsa, and even found and diced up a few onions and jalapenos for whoever wanted them, very carefully scrubbing her hands afterward. Coffee was ready in the pot and orange juice and milk were sitting out for those that wanted it.

Josiah thought about being critical, but the truth was, the breakfast was outstanding, and he ate four of the tacos, stuffing himself, a thing he seldom did at breakfast. "Master, I know it's Darla's Hell Day, but I have to say this is a tremendous breakfast, Sir," Lucretia said.

"Delicious," Molly agreed, midpoint through her third taco.

"It is a good effort," Josiah allowed. Darla blushed.

"I figure Master and Sisters should be well-fed before delivering my fate to me," she said.

"That brings us to your fate. "Lucretia, I want you to put a collar and leash on Darla and walk her to the post. Darla, how are

222

you to crawl?"

"With my nipples in the dirt, Master, and lashed by my sister if they come off the dirt until ordered otherwise," Darla answered.

"That's correct," Josiah said. "Now, after Darla is horsewhipped and I have her working, Molly and Lucretia are to go into town and get Darla's car and ... where is your hotel key, Darla?"

"At the warehouse, along with my phone, Master," Darla said.

"Okay, I want you to go to the hotel and round up her luggage to bring here," Josiah said. "Darla, do you have work boots of any kind in that array?"

"No, Master," Darla said.

"Your shoe size?" he pursued.

"Eight, Sir," came the answer.

"Master, that's my size," Leigh offered. "We got me boots yesterday, so if she needs them right after her whipping, Molly could just get a pair for me at the Red Wing store."

"Go get them and take them to the whipping post," Josiah said. "One of you will bring Darla's car here and the other can round up the luggage and do the shopping."

"A request, Master?" Darla piped up.

"What is your request?" Josiah asked.

"Master, take my car away from me, please," Darla said. "Park it in that warehouse so I know there's no chance of escape for me in case I turn coward, Sir."

"Granted," Josiah said. "Park her car at the warehouse,

girls."

"Master, may we take my car instead of the truck?" Molly asked.

"Molly, if you mean that little black Infiniti, my stuff won't all fit in it," Darla said.

"We can take my car," Lucretia suggested.

"It's that big Land Rover over there?" Darla asked, and Lucretia nodded. "Yeah ... that would probably work."

"Just take the big van," Josiah suggested. "I doubt her stuff will take up that much room."

"That would work, Master," Molly said.

"Also, while you girls are out, go get collars and leashes, four of them, for walking one another. I want them all the same, and all new," Josiah ordered. "And straps for you to use on one another. And the enema kits."

"Fortunately, those places are all near one another," Molly said.

"Leigh, whenever I bugger your sister today, you're in charge of cleaning me," Josiah said. "I will probably make that assignment from now on for the last girl who went through Hell, but I think Lucretia has earned a bit of off-campus time."

"Master, I ... I'll do whatever you order me to do, Sir," Lucretia said. "I don't see leaving this place as a privilege, except that it serves you. And it serves this family. If it's most appropriate that I stay and keep your schlong washed, that is a privilege to me too."

"No, I want you and Molly to do these errands today," Josiah said. "Leigh, walk Molly to the track. We'll be along shortly."

"Yes, Master," Leigh said, and buckled the collar and leash to her new sister. "May I put her on all fours once we're off the porch, Master? I ... I think going down stairs would be too dangerous, Sir."

"Yes," Josiah decided, and also decided to add a ramp to the porch so a crawling slave could be kept crawling. "Dismissed to the track."

"Come, Darla," Leigh ordered, tugging the leash. Blushing, Darla followed her sister outside. Two minutes later the sound of leather smacking rump, punctuated with Darla's pained yelps, could be heard.

"We'll ride over in the truck," Josiah said. "You two both go choose clothes to wear into town. Roll them and put them in the truck. Once I've finished buggering Darla – I want it witnessed by all her sisters – you'll get dressed and get moving."

THIRTY-FOUR

"Darla Morris, you are beginning your Hell Day with a punishment for lying to me, coming to me under false pretense," Josiah said. "You will be lashed forty strokes and buggered immediately thereafter, and will then be walked to your work assignment. If your work isn't to my satisfaction, you will revisit this post. Do you request a gag to protect your teeth?"

"I ... Master, I don't deserve one," Darla said, barely above a whisper. "I deserve to be humiliated by screaming and lashed extra if I beg mercy, Sir."

"Very well," Josiah said. "Forty lashes." He lashed into her still-welted back, and Darla cried out, forcing her slim figure to the post, doing her best not to disappoint her master. He lashed her again, and again, driving the whip into her as she howled her agony, her body slickening in a coating of sweat as she sobbed. The lashing went on for about ten minutes before she'd endured all forty, bleeding from several of the wounds.

Leigh approached her and examined the wounds. "Master, I think three of them will become scars, Sir," she announced, pointing to one of them. "This one in particular."

"Th ... Master ... thank you," Darla said. "Marked for life. I deserve it, Sir."

"You're welcome," Josiah said, seeing Molly and Lucretia looking at the scene, transfixed.

"Scarred," Molly said, seemingly unaware she'd spoken aloud.

Darla shrieked at the burning coagulant, and weakly positioned herself for the next step once Leigh took her off the post, offering her ass to Josiah's use. Josiah undressed, and Lucretia went to her knees and sucked him to full hardness, and then Josiah removed Darla's plug, set it aside, and grasped her hips, putting just the head of his penis into her bottom. She quivered, trying to brace herself, and cried out as he rammed hard into her, but remembered to push back, impaling herself fully on her master's member as her show of submission and devotion. Even plugged overnight, her anus remained toned and tight, and Josiah knew he wouldn't last long inside her, so he plundered her hard and furious, excited all the more with her cooperation, and then exploded deeply into her bowels while she sobbed and shuddered. He sensed she was fighting off a cum, but didn't think she'd undergone an orgasm unless she did so very discreetly.

Leigh knelt before him to clean his slowly shrinking erection while Lucretia and Molly dressed themselves. As Leigh took his member into her mouth, Lucretia and Molly came to attention. "Dismissed to your errands," Josiah ordered, and they got in the van and left.

"Put socks and boots on, slave," Josiah ordered Darla. She groaned as she rolled to a sitting position, but got her feet into socks and boots. "Leigh, walk her behind me," Josiah ordered next, and marched off to a fallen tree two hundred yards away, beside which a hand saw was waiting. The crawl took a while, punctuated twice by flurries of lashes from Leigh's strap accompanied by Darla's yelps, but they got there eventually.

"Darla, you're going to saw this tree into shorter lengths for firewood," Josiah said. "There is the saw. I want each length about as far as it is from your elbow to your middle fingertip. Get to work and I'll look in on you later."

"Yes, Master," Darla said, and began sawing after measuring her first cut.

"That should keep her busy for a while," Josiah said as he and Leigh walked away.

"I hope she doesn't go swimming again," Leigh remarked.

Josiah led Leigh to the truck and filled an ice chest with ice and a flat of water, and took it to Darla, and then drove Leigh to the big house.

"Tomorrow's your Hell Day," he said, and Leigh trembled, but Josiah noted the telltale signs of her heightened arousal. "Come with me."

He led her behind the house to the pool, a big pool, and stripped naked, and then dove in, and ordered Leigh to join him. She smiled and did exactly that, executing a graceful dive into the soothing water. "Thank you, Master, but why the kindness?" Leigh asked as she broke the surface.

"You've been doing well to this point, and once in a while I'll treat one of you better than the others, just to remind you what it is to enjoy my esteem," Josiah said. "I'm going to make love to all of you, so you don't wind up thinking all I care about are your assholes."

"If you weren't reserving yourself for Darla today I'd offer you any hole I have, Master," Leigh said. "Sir, for mine, I have an idea to run by you, a request."

"What is that?" Josiah asked.

"I need the cruelty, to remind me I'm being punished too, Sir," Leigh said. "And it would ... push me through more new territory. After you horsewhip me – I guess I'm getting about what Darla got, and deserve worse – but afterward, make me ride you reverse cowgirl, anally, and lash my back until you cum. It'll be tender and I'll be in agony, and it will remind me what I am, being forced to impale myself on you rather than feeling like you just took me. Force me to … well … to participate in my own doom, Sir. Besides, why should you be the one expending the effort?"

"I have to say I like how you think," Josiah said. "Maybe I should make Darla do that, but … no. I want the others to know this is entirely your idea, and see a higher example made." He pushed Leigh against the edge of the pool and kissed her deeply and longingly, knowing it wasn't cheap words when he told her he loved her. He loved them all, probably even Darla, he knew deep in his heart. She groped him, hardening him, and he growled into the kiss.

"God, I want it so badly, Master," Leigh breathed.

"If you make me cum, I'll have to beat you," Josiah said. "And I'll let Darla beat you too for stealing from her."

"It's almost worth it, Master," Leigh said, but let his hard member free and sighed. "Almost. God, I can't believe the whirlwind in my head about tomorrow, Sir."

"Explain it," Josiah ordered.

"Sir, I know I'll cry and scream," Leigh offered. "I know I will very probably bleed and just might bear scars from tomorrow. I'll be humiliated, broken. I'll have to ride you and be whipped more if you decide to adopt my suggestion. I dread it, Master, but I want and need and deserve it just the same. It's only been a few days, but I've spied on you and Molly for nearly two years now, Master, and this place … Sir, it's felt like home to me for months now. I think in some really weird way, you've felt like Master to me for at least that long. So it feels right, Sir. I'm scared and aroused all at once and can't wait until you've turned me inside out, Master. I want to be totally under your will, and tomorrow really starts me on that road,

Sir. So I envy Lucretia and Darla. I understand why they were ahead of me, Lucretia on the heels of her grief and in a different way, the same for Darla, but ... anyway, I'm babbling now, Master."

"I love hearing how you slaves think," Josiah said. "Okay, I'm going to ask you one final time here. You freely and fully consent to all I might do to you?"

"Master, if you wanted to hang me I'd tie the noose, Sir," Leigh said, looking directly into his eyes.

"I won't get that extreme," Josiah said, but took her meaning, and kissed her again. "Alright, out of the pool. I need to handle a few things here. Get us towels from the pool house."

Leigh went to the pool house and got two thick towels, one for each of them, and when Josiah rose from the pool, she toweled him dry. "May slave dry herself as well, Master?" she asked, and Josiah nodded.

"I'm going to handle some stuff on the computer," Josiah said. "Go check on Darla. Take the truck and there's an empty trailer in the wood barn, or should be. Hitch it up and take it over there so the wood can be loaded into the trailer as she cuts it. Make sure she's staying hydrated. I don't want another heat exhaustion event from her."

"I understand, Master," Leigh said. "Should I return here, then?"

"Yes," Josiah said.

Leigh drove the truck to the barn and connected the trailer, and then rolled it out to where Darla was working. She found Darla sitting on the ice chest and drinking a glass of water. The saw was in the tree, after she'd gotten eight or so inches into her first cut. The tree itself – Darla had started at the bottom – was about two feet through the middle at that point.

"God, I am in so much trouble," Darla cried. "That saw is stuck like chuck in there."

"I shouldn't, but let's see if we can get it out of that groove together," Leigh said. She and Darla both grabbed the handle and the saw barely budged. "Jesus, it's jammed, alright, Darla."

"God, I'll probably get another fifty lashes," Darla wept. "I know I bought this and agreed to it, but this is so unfair!"

"Give me a moment, I think I might be able to help here," Leigh said, and went to the truck. There was an old four-pound hammer in the bed of the truck, and Leigh brought it and gave it a good underhand whack, moving the saw an inch or so. And then she whacked it three more times and the saw popped free.

"Thank you so much," Darla said. "You saved my life, Leigh."

"You're welcome," Leigh said. "Look, here's what you need to do, honey. Saw at an angle where you have a vee-shaped groove going, so this doesn't happen so easily. I'm going to have to tell Master about this, so maybe he'll have a better solution. But if I was you, I'd start with the thicker branches, like this one. In fact, what I think I'd do is saw it off close to main stalk of the tree and then saw it to shorter lengths."

"I was trying to prove myself and, yeah," Darla said. "My old man used to say it was letting your mouth overload your ass, and here I did just that."

"I think we all want to please Master," Leigh said. "I need to unhook the trailer. I think Master wants the wood you cut going into the trailer, though."

"Okay," Darla said. "Thanks again, Leigh."

"You're welcome," Leigh said. Darla got busy sawing through a thick branch, one about seven or so inches thick near the main body of the tree, and Leigh lowered the jack and unhooked the trailer, and then drove off to the big house.

Josiah, bored, had been online looking at news sites, but nothing interested him, and he debated doing some fishing again. The fish Leigh and Molly had caught were entirely devoured, without a single leftover fillet, and sounded good to him, although he decided to try to catch a mess of bass and grill them. He went out to the porch, and as soon as Leigh arrived, he directed her to the barn for fishing tackle, and then to the pond. An hour later, they'd hauled out ten good-sized bass, and Leigh filleted them while he watched, surprised at her talent at the task, and asked about it.

"I never did this before in my life until I was here with Molly," Leigh said. "But you learn careful skills with a knife in the anatomy lab in medical school, Master. I guess that sounds gross, but the skill set is about the same, Sir."

"Let's get these to the cabin and I'll get the grill going," Josiah said. "I think Molly got some corn on the cob. That'd go good with this."

"She did, and it would, Master," Leigh agreed. "Master, I … I might be in trouble."

"What happened?" Josiah asked.

"Sir, Darla's saw got completely jammed in that tree," Leigh said. "She couldn't get it unstuck, and neither could I, until I got a hammer from the truck and knocked it out of that groove."

"She went back to work then?" Josiah asked.

"She did, Master," Leigh confirmed. "She'd started near the

base of the tree, where it was thickest. I suggested she cut on the branches so she could show some progress. If I overstepped, I'm sorry, Master."

"Get in the truck and let's go see her," Josiah said.

Darla was just finished sawing through the branch she had begun when Leigh left her, and went to her knees, measured, and began sawing the first log from it. Josiah spotted where Darla had gotten stuck earlier. "Jesus, she got deep into that one, didn't she?" he said to Leigh as he parked the truck.

"She's a hard worker, I'll give her that," Leigh agreed. "I swear, I feel like everyone here is setting the bar higher and higher for me. I am so going to be in deep shit tomorrow."

"I'm about to bugger her again," Josiah said.

"I don't blame you, Master," Leigh said. "Jesus, that's a hot body she's got."

"Attention!" Josiah called out as he got from the truck, and Darla came to attention, red-faced and sweaty on the humid day.

"Your master is horny again, slave," Josiah said.

"Shall I assume that position, Master?" Darla asked.

"Drop the tailgate of the truck and bend over it," Josiah ordered.

"Yes, Master," Darla said, and did as bidden, grasping toward the hinges of the tailgate to force herself to hold her place. His first use of her back there had hurt, and she was still very sore from it, and guessed this was going to be hellish. As it turned out, she was a good guesser, and cried out as he plunged into her, his hips slamming into her ass, and bruising her hips a bit against the steel tailgate. Darla, in this position, was unable to push back, so remained in place to take what he gave, crying as he plundered her back there, and glad he didn't last long before spewing his seed into her.

"Thank you, Master," she groaned when he drew out of her.

"Jesus, tomorrow," Leigh moaned to herself.

"Leigh, walk her back to the cabin," Josiah ordered. "I'll see you there soon."

"Yes, Sir," Leigh said, and took Darla's leash while Darla went to all fours, groaning sorely. Josiah drove off in the truck, circling first toward the fuel tank he kept on the property and filling the tank of the truck, and then he drove to the cabin, letting Leigh walk Darla back. At the cabin he lit wood in the pit and gave it time to heat up, and then set up an outdoor cooker and a pot of water to start boiling, and set the corn and a paper bag on the back porch. Once shucked, the husks and paper bag could go to the burn pit, he decided, wondering what was taking Molly and Lucretia so long.

Thirty minutes later, the slaves were at the cabin, Darla panting and crying. Leigh dropped Darla's leash and Darla laid on the ground, spent from the effort of crawling so far.

"One of you shuck the corn and clean all the stringy stuff off of it," Josiah said. "It only needs to boil a short time. Basically, once I put the fish on the grill, the corn will go into the water, and they can all come off at the same time."

"Darla, you heard our master," Leigh said.

"Yes, Sister," Darla replied. "A moment to catch my breath, please?"

"Yes," Josiah told her. "Come inside, Leigh."

"What happened out there?" Josiah asked.

"She cramped up once on the way back, Master," Leigh said. "Charley horse in her hamstring. She popped to her feet and lurched around for a while until it loosened up, Sir. She's hydrated but needs more potassium, I think. I'd ask permission to feed her OJ with lunch and maybe bananas, Sir. If I'm in trouble for it, I accept your punishment, Sir, but I don't think the cramp was her fault, necessarily, or could be helped, and I didn't lash her for coming up to her feet. Obviously, her nipples lost contact with the ground, but God knows she'd have been a wreck if she'd kept crawling then and let the cramp take her, Sir. She'd have been no good the rest of the day, maybe a couple or three more days."

"I think you need to give her a more thorough physical soon," Josiah said. "Let's find out if there's an issue with her electrolytes. She looks young and amazingly fit, so what's bringing this on?"

"Honestly, probably just using her muscles in unaccustomed ways, Master," Leigh said. "She is young and amazingly fit, but who the hell spends much time crawling like that, Sir? And I doubt she's ever used a saw like she has today. She probably spent a lot of time in a gym, maybe out at the fort, but ... it's not the same as real-world work, Master. Workouts are symmetrical. Work really isn't."

"No, I suppose not," Josiah agreed. "Okay, it looks like she's starting to shuck the corn out there. Take her a glass of orange juice. I'm going to check the pit and see how we're going with the fire."

Josiah figured he'd be ready to throw fish on the grill in about twenty minutes, and went back into the cabin. His phone rang and he answered it, seeing the number was Molly's.

"We'll be there shortly, Master," Molly said. "The Honda got a flat about a mile into the trip to the warehouse. Her fucking spare was flat, and we had to run off and buy a new tire for her. Anyway, it's handled and the Honda is parked, and we've done the other errands. We should be there in about thirty minutes, Master. The Chevy dealer called and said the Suburban is ready, so we're bringing that back with us as well, Sir."

"Sounds good," Josiah said. "Come to the cabin."

"We'll be there in thirty," Molly repeated, and ended the call.

Josiah opened a Coke from the fridge and drank a few swallows, and then decided to shower. He stripped himself naked and went into the downstairs bedroom for a long shower, and then came out and saw there was a message holding on his phone. He finished his Coke and then listened to the message, from a woman named Elaine, no last name given, interested in his beadle services. He'd call her after lunch, he decided, already mostly deciding that he simply hadn't the time to take on a client for at least the coming week.

He looked at the clock and decided to wait until Molly and Lucretia were back before starting the fish. They arrived a minute or two before Molly estimated, and Josiah put the fillets on the grill, and told Darla to put the corn in the pot. Minutes later the fish and corn were ready, and Leigh came out with platters for both, and tongs for Darla to dip the cobs from the pot.

THIRTY-FIVE

"Drink more orange juice, Darla," Josiah commanded when she finished devouring a fillet and most of a cob of corn. "Those charley horses generally mean you need electrolytes, slave."

"Yes, Sir," Darla said, and refilled her glass with juice, and reloaded her plate with another fish fillet and another cob of corn. When the meal was done, there were only three fish fillets left, and only two cobs of corn.

"I brought things for us, Master," Molly said. "Thank you for sending Lucretia with me, Sir. As it turns out, she was a good sounding board."

"It was fun," Lucretia grinned.

"So what did you bring to the family?" Josiah asked.

"First, I got enema kits for you to clean us out or otherwise torment us, Master," Molly said. "But that's no surprise, I know. Second, per your orders, I got good collars and heavy leather leashes for all of us, and got laser-engraved tags for all of us."

"Why the tags?" Josiah wanted to know.

"Sir, I think we're likely all in this for the long haul," Molly said. "I ... Master, we entertain out here from time to time, and I guess you won't want us clothed. The collars let guests know first that you own us, and second, who we are." She blushed, and Josiah smiled.

237

"Like for the races coming up?" Josiah asked.

"Yes, Sir, that, and other similar events," Molly said. "I think it's powerful, and puts us in our place, being naked, and I think it will be that much more so when we're entertaining out here."

"I like it," Josiah said. "Good call, Molly."

"That's not all, Master," Molly said. "Lucretia gave me her counsel there, but we were pretty much in agreement on it. By the way, I got work boots for Leigh, and new ones for Lucretia and for me, Sir. The Red Wing store was delighted. Anyway, the big thing I got, something that occurred to me last night …"

"Going to keep us waiting with bated breath?" Josiah asked.

Molly grinned and opened a box she'd brought in, and from it produced strap-on devices for the four slaves, with a wide array of appliances. "I figure if you want one of us used hard, we should all participate, so the errant sister feels the weight of the entire sisterhood on her, Master. You're a horny one, for sure, and use us often and well, but imagine one of us having to be glory hole for all her sisters after you're done with the slave."

"Oh, God," Leigh moaned. "Me first!"

"Hey!" Lucretia said. "What about my black ass?" She tried snarling but it ended in a bark of laughter. "Shit fuck, I can't even bluff you girls now."

Josiah laughed, pleased, but noticed Darla's look of outright dismay as she began to cry, which ended the jovial exchange as the others looked at her in confusion and concern.

"What has you crying, Darla?" Josiah asked. "Take a drink and calm down, then talk to us," he added in a calm voice.

"Master … I thought I was ready for this," Darla said. "I

deserve it and I'm not thinking of leaving, but please don't let my sisters do this to me today, Sir. It's all I can do to keep sane knowing you're probably going to horsewhip me more and have me walked more, and probably bugger me another time or two. I don't think I could take being the glory hole right now, Master."

"No, not on your first Hell Day," Josiah agreed. "Darla, most of the time around here, sex will be for the mutual pleasure of all involved. Right now you're being broken and punished, but imagine all of us lined up to fuck your pussy. Or having to ride each of your sisters cowgirl. Or putting on your own device and riding one of them."

Darla gaped at him, and then frowned. "I'm sorry, Master," she said. "I just made an ass of myself. With your permission, I'll go to the whipping post. May I ask how many strokes this time, to try to mentally prepare, Sir?"

"All four of you, kneel upright," Josiah ordered.

"Master, before you collar us, may I speak?" Molly asked.

"Sure," Josiah said. "You have the floor."

"Sir, I would ask that you give me the rest of Darla's Hell Day, and give her another Hell Day later," Molly requested. "I can see she's in a really low place with this, and I wonder if it wouldn't benefit her to spend a day or even two or three easing into this before really hard-breaking her. By the look on her face, I don't think this is helping her today but only damaging her. Maybe if she saw examples made of the others here – she only caught a glimpse of it yesterday with Lucretia – she'll have a better grasp?"

"Granted," Josiah said as Darla gaped, stunned. "Darla, your Hell Day is postponed, and your sister Molly will endure the remainder of this one in your stead."

"Thank you, Master," Molly said softly, and then knelt upright. A moment later, Leigh and Lucretia joined her, and then Darla, weeping anew, but for different reasons.

Josiah opened the box of collars, all identical but for the tags Molly and Lucretia had already placed on them. He decided to make a point by beginning with Darla. "Darla, custom holds that the collar is an ultimate symbol to others of your status as owned property of your master," he said. "Do you accept my collar and ownership?"

"God, yes, Master," Darla said, trembling. Josiah placed the collar around her neck and fastened it in place. The collar was simple stainless steel chain links, like a really big watch band. It had a ring for a leash and another ring for the name tag, which was already on it, of simply her first name.

"Thank you, Master," Darla said in an emotional whisper.

"You're welcome," Josiah said. He knelt down and gently kissed the beautiful young woman, and then stroked her hair, and retrieved Lucretia's collar from the box.

"Lucretia, do you likewise accept my mastery over you and ownership of you?" he asked.

"I do, Master," Lucretia said, and Josiah saw she was likewise struggling to hold her composure as he fastened the collar to her. "Thank you, Master," she said with a hitch in her voice.

"I love you, Lucretia," Josiah said, kneeling down and kissing her.

"God, I love you too, Master," Lucretia returned, barely able to speak.

"Leigh, this will be your collar," Josiah said a moment later. "Do you likewise accept my mastery over you and my ownership of you?"

"For the rest of my life, if you'll have me so long, Master," Leigh said. Josiah fastened her collar and kissed her too, resting a hand briefly at the flare of her hip. He rose and retrieved the fourth and final collar from the box, and saw Molly was openly crying with the emotion.

"And Molly, do you accept my mastery over you and my ownership of you?" he asked.

"I do, Master," Molly said. "Forever and always, Sir." Josiah collared Molly, and then gently kissed her too while she struggled not to weep.

"Master, I brought a gift too," Lucretia said. "May I go to the van and get that box?"

"You may," Josiah decided. He was thinking about something, and had mostly arrived at his decision.

Lucretia returned a moment later with a big bag and produced its contents of four bondage belts, well-made leather belts, lockable at the buckle, with rings surrounding it so that a slave could be cuffed in all kinds of ways to it. And she produced four identical and painful-looking straps.

"More bonding, and bondage I guess," Lucretia said, and smiled. "Master, we would each wear one, with a strap hanging from it. That way a slave who needs to be walked hands her strap to the sister walking her, but meanwhile she has that reminder hanging on her hip at all times, Sir. And, obviously, the belts can be used for different handcuff positions as well. I also bought carabiners for the straps to hang, and handcuffs for us all, so each of us has a set on her belt for immediate use when you need to cuff one of us for one reason or another."

"Thank you, Lucretia," Josiah said. "That was very thoughtful of you."

"I got size medium for everyone but Leigh," Lucretia said. "She's petite and pixie like and cute and we all hate her so I got her a small." She grinned, Molly laughed, and Leigh giggled at this one, and then Josiah laughed, amused.

"Jesus, here I'd swap my left tit to be your height, as exotic as you, and you're jealous of my shrimp ass," Leigh said, shaking her head in amusement, then turned serious. "Thank you, Lucretia. I'll wear mine proudly."

"Well, I figured I owed you and Molly for all the doctoring I'll have coming my way," Lucretia said, keeping the mood light. "God knows I seem to be a problem child here, right?"

"I love your black ass, did you know that?" Leigh chipped in, and she and Lucretia laughed before Lucretia knelt before Leigh and kissed her, and then circled her waist with the belt, locking it in place on her.

"Master, the bat belts unlock with a standard handcuff skeleton key, by the way," Lucretia said, kneeling.

"Leigh, pick a sister and put her belt on her," Josiah ordered. Leigh smiled and went to Darla with a belt. She cinched it around Darla's waist and locked it onto her, and then kissed her lips.

"I love you, Darla," Leigh said. "I think you're going to make us proud sometime soon."

"I doubt I ever will," Darla said in a glum tone. "But I love you all and I'm grateful to you all."

"Darla, pick a sister and put her belt on her," Josiah ordered.

Darla chose a belt and knelt before Molly, and then locked

the belt in place around her waist. "Molly, I love you," she said. "I … I … I don't know how to thank you for taking my Hell Day. I hope you can forgive me someday."

"I love you too, Darla," Molly said, and kissed her young sister. "And it's okay. Some days you're the windshield and some days you're the bug, right? We'll see whether I'm a windshield." She smiled bravely and kissed Darla again, then raised her voice just a tad. "Master, may I approach Lucretia with her belt?"

"You may," Josiah said.

Molly knelt before Lucretia and snapped her belt in place, and then longingly kissed the exotic woman. "I'm glad I got to pick you," Molly said. "Of all of the slaves here, you're the one I respect the most, and the one I most want to emulate, Lucretia." She pressed her body against her sister's, and grasped Lucretia's ass with both hands, and Lucretia hissed a bit and groaned. "Get used to it. I love your ass."

Lucretia grasped Molly's ass too, and Molly moaned. "I love your white ass too, Doc," she said, and the two kissed a third time. "When Master lets us, I am *sooo* going to fuck your brains out."

"God, I can't wait," Molly whispered.

"You're going to have to wait," Josiah interjected. "But not for long. "You four line up." Josiah sat on a chair and set out the straps and cuffs as his slaves got in a line. "When I call your name, you will approach me. Lucretia, you first."

Lucretia approached Josiah and stood at attention, and he attached the strap to a ring along her right hip, and then had her about-face, and attached a carabiner with handcuffs through it to the ring at her back. He next had her kneel, and attached her leash to her collar. "You will return to the line and stand at attention," he ordered. Lucretia obeyed, and Josiah admired how sleek and sexy she was with these accoutrements.

"Darla, approach," he ordered next. She trembled and wept as he attached strap and cuffs to her belt and leash to her collar, and decided she would be his bedmate that night.

"Thank you, Master," she said, but seemed far the more sad than pleased.

"Rejoin your sisters," Josiah ordered. "Molly, approach."

Molly approached as ordered, and came to attention while her master fitted her items to her belt and collar. "I love you, Master," she said. "I really can't say this enough."

"You know I love you too," Josiah said. "Rejoin your sisters."

"Where'd Leigh go?" Josiah asked, dramatically turning his head left and right. "Oh, there that petite thing is! Good Lord, stand up, and don't stand sideways or you disappear!"

Darla's expression never changed, but Lucretia and Molly laughed while Leigh blushed and giggled. Josiah took note of this too. Leigh approached, and Josiah fitted her with her equipment as well and ordered her to rejoin her sisters.

"Slaves, assemble off the porch," he ordered. "Wait for me there."

His slaves all exited, and Josiah decided to return the call he'd gotten earlier, curious who Elaine was, and exactly what it was she wanted.

"This is Elaine Connors," Josiah heard when he called.

"Josiah Bailey," Josiah introduced himself. "I had a moment

and decided to return your message."

"I was told you don't conduct business by phone or e-mail," Elaine said. "So I suppose I need to make an in-person appointment."

"What about 6:30 today?" Josiah asked.

"That works nicely," Elaine replied. Josiah gave her the address and decided to take Leigh with him to this appointment, and then went outside.

THIRTY-SIX

"Molly, hand Darla your strap, and get on all fours," Josiah ordered. Molly obeyed while Darla looked uncomfortable as she accepted the strap. "Darla, Molly's taking your Hell Day, so it's only appropriate that you be her handler. You know the crawling protocol. Lead her to the whipping post at the track. Molly began crawling, clumsy and slow.

"Leigh, a client phoned earlier," he said after waiting several minutes until Darla and Molly were around a bend and out of earshot. "I'll want you to go with me so you can perform the physical if need be. But if it's for more than a simple whipping, I'm probably going to have to decline for at least the next couple or three weeks."

"I understand, Master," Leigh said.

"Give your strap to Lucretia," Josiah said. "All fours. Lucretia, walk Leigh to the track."

"It won't be the first time for you to whip me, right?" Leigh said. "Jesus, hate on me all you want for being small, but I'd sell my soul for tits like yours so I don't have to crawl as low."

Lucretia chuckled and took Leigh's leash, and began walking her. They'd barely gone fifteen feet when Leigh howled as Lucretia's strap slashed across her rump four strokes. "Don't do that again," Lucretia warned. "I won't be nice the next time, Leigh." Josiah smirked and went inside to use the bathroom and have another Coke. He knew they'd be a while crawling to the track.

Molly's nipples came up off the ground and Darla ignored it, tugging a bit at her leash as she struggled not to cry. "Darla," Molly said.

"What is it, Molly?"

"Look, we're under orders from Master, and you know if you were in my position I'd be whipping your ass blue for letting your nipples up out of the dirt."

"Molly, I feel bad enough about this already," Darla said.

"Darla, it's time you grew up and realized you're going to have to do many things as a slave that you don't like," Molly said. "And it starts right here, right now. Either you strap me for letting my nipples up, or I confess to Master. I'm probably already taking fifty lashes on that post, and I could easily see him upping the ante to eighty or so."

"How many?" Darla asked, resigned.

"At least ten, probably more," Molly said. "And they better all count."

"Jesus, please don't make me do this to you, Molly," Darla wept.

"At least ten," Molly said.

"What's going on?" Lucretia asked from ten feet away as she and Leigh approached. Molly explained the situation and Lucretia clucked her tongue.

"Leigh, you keep those nipples in the dirt," Lucretia ordered.

"Yes, Mistress ... shit ... yes, Sister," Leigh answered, and Lucretia smirked a bit.

"Call me 'Mistress' again on this property and I'll horsewhip you myself Monday," Lucretia said, then returned her attention to Darla. "Darla, give her twelve hard lashes or I'll give her forty and report this matter to Master. This is how we show love to one another here, by assisting in discipline."

"I hate you," Darla said, and hit Molly with the strap, barely impacting her.

"Give me that strap so I can give her forty," Lucretia said, taking a step toward her.

"I'll do it," Darla said quickly. "I'm ... I'm sorry, Molly," she whispered, and then slashed the strap hard into Molly's upturned ass. Molly ground her teeth and absorbed it in silence, and Darla lashed again.

"Ten more of those," Lucretia said. "Make them hurt, Darla. Discipline is love here, and I'd say you owe Molly at least this after what she's done for you."

Darla glared at Lucretia and resumed lashing Molly, who was sobbing before it was done. "Th ... thank you, Sister," Molly said. "I love you and I'm grateful."

"God," Darla whispered. "Please keep your nipples on the ground, Molly. Please don't make me do that again."

Lucretia held Leigh back and let them crawl a long way ahead. "I don't think she's going to make it, Leigh," Lucretia said. "I've had clients like that before that let their alligator mouth overload their hummingbird ass, get in over their heads, and run like hell when it gets too intense for them. She means well, but she's gutless."

"I wish I could disagree," Leigh said. "The only merit I see in her now is she at least has a conscience. It was a nice touch, threatening forty to Molly if Darla didn't give her twelve."

"I would have done it," Lucretia said.

"You would have had no choice, Sister, and I'm sure everyone but Darla understood the math there, and Molly would have thanked you from her heart for it," Leigh agreed, and groaned. "God, first chance I get, I'm going for breast augmentation. Crawling this low is killing me. May we continue and get this over with, please, Sister?"

"Yeah, let's go," Lucretia said. "I'm sorry. I just … you're the one I know the best here, Leigh, and I needed to get that off my chest before I personally punch that little blonde cunt in her nose."

"This too shall pass," Leigh said, and groaned as she pushed up too far, a mistake immediately rewarded with her own dozen of that evil strap, one that Lucretia knew all too well how to wield and apply very effectively. "Thank you, Sister," Leigh said, angry with herself for her error, and truly grateful to Lucretia for holding her to a high standard.

Josiah arrived at the track about ten minutes after Molly and Darla arrived, and noted that Molly was cuffed to the post already. He understood Molly's motivations very deeply, but wondered if she wasn't gambling away the skin of her back trying to draw to an inside straight.

"Molly, you are to suffer the remainder of Darla's Hell Day, per your request," Josiah decreed. "You are to be lashed forty strokes, and are to be buggered immediately thereafter, and then Darla will walk you to your afternoon's work."

"Yes, Master," Molly moaned. She sensed she had failed in her attempt, and told herself she deserved what she was getting for being so stupid, and wondered how bad this lashing was going to get. But that die was cast, she already knew.

"Slaves, come to attention," Josiah ordered. "I want you all to witness Molly's act of love here."

He slung the whip at Molly's back for her first lash, and she screamed at the agony as he heard a choked sob come from one of the slaves at his periphery. He lashed again, opening Molly's skin, and she screamed anew, and she howled once more at the third lash, panting. Suddenly, Darla rushed in and pressed her breasts and belly to Molly's back, wrapping her arms tightly around Molly and the post, and cuffing her own wrists together with the cuffs from the back of her belt.

"Get out of the way, Darla," Josiah said.

"No, Master," Darla replied in a surprisingly strong and determined voice. "This is my whipping, and I'll take it. God hates a coward, Master, and I know you all hate me, and if you don't, you damn well should. Please continue, Master."

"Darla, remove yourself at once," Josiah said.

"I deserve this lashing, not Molly," Darla said. "Please whip me, Master."

"Darla, here's how this is going to play out," Josiah said, unknowingly taking a page from Lucretia's book. "You have three choices. You can return to the line and let me finish lashing Molly — she has another thirty-seven heading her way — or you can remain where you are and suffer fifty lashes, this forty plus ten for interrupting and defying me. If you choose to remain where you are and fail … if you run away from it, or evade it, or beg for mercy or faint, I will lay eighty lashes to Molly."

"Fifty for me, please, Master," Darla said.

"Have you lost your mind?" Molly asked Darla.

"Maybe I have," Darla said. "But I found my heart. I love

you, Molly, and I'm sorry for how I've been." She opened her mouth to say more but the whip cut her words off as she groaned when the lash crossed her back. Josiah swiped a tear from his eye and lashed Darla six more times before she screamed, but she only hugged Molly tighter as Molly cried for her young sister. The lashing continued, and Darla was a sobbing wreck when it was over, but she had held her place and shielded Molly for all fifty lashes.

"Treat them, Leigh," Josiah said in a husky voice and quickly walked off. Lucretia followed him to the barn while Leigh did her thing.

"Master?" Leigh said.

"Sorry," Josiah told her, harrumphing. "Allergies are a bitch."

"Bull fucking shit, Master," Lucretia said. "You just saw a beautiful thing and you're choked up." She choked down her own sob. "Please hold me." Josiah turned to her, tears running down his face, and the two held one another and wept at the emotion of the moment.

"I think we finally got through to Darla," Lucretia said. "And, God, Molly is a gutsy one. I knew what she was doing when she stepped up, but Goddamn. That was ... I cried all the way through Darla's whipping, Master. And I'm glad you did too, Sir. It tells me the love out here is genuine."

"It is," Josiah said. "Come with me." He led her back to the track and found Molly and Darla in a tight embrace, holding one another and crying while going on about love for one another. Leigh, knowing she would be the fifth wheel there, stood several feet away, silently weeping, until Josiah beckoned her to him and held her while she cried.

"Everyone in the truck," Josiah said. "We're going to the

house."

Josiah had Molly ride up front in the truck while the other slaves rode in back. "Well, that was a cardiac kids moment," he said. "You did good, Molly."

"Thank you, Master," Molly said. "I never thought I would use love and affection as weaponry and be on the right side doing it. Jesus, this is a whole new world we're in. So what happens now, Master?"

"I think the rest of today and tomorrow needs to be a bit more casual for us," Josiah said. "I'm going to make love to Darla, in front of all of you, to seal this deal with her, so to speak. And then the rest of today and tomorrow we're going to orgy, I think. We'll resume Hell Day with Leigh on Thursday. I have a client meeting at 6:30 and I'm taking Leigh with me in case a physical has to be done, but I'll tell you what I told her. If it involves much more than just a straight-up lashing, I'll pass on it or push the appointment back three weeks or so."

"Master, why not take Darla too?" Molly suggested. "It might do her good to see that you trust her enough to take her off the farm."

"I'll ask her, but look at what happened to her," Josiah said. "I don't think she's going to have energy much to want to go out, even if all she does is sits on a chair and looks pretty."

"I think if you gave me ten more lashes right now I'd be done for the day too, Master," Molly agreed. "I love these belts and collars, Sir. I thought it was a nice touch when Darla shielded me. She used her own cuffs to bind her wrists so she couldn't get away. She kept crying she was sorry and she loved me. I think I have a pound of her snot and tears in the back of my hair. But Master ...

she never took her tits off my back, nor her belly. She didn't once try to dodge or escape her whipping." Molly let loose her own little sob. "I'm so proud of her right now. She was a tough nut to crack, but I think she's going to train much easier, moving forward." She was silent a moment. "Master, does this mean we're free to have one another however we want?"

"Until sunrise Thursday," Josiah said. "If you want to be the asshole glory hole for everyone here all that while, take your position and offer up. If Darla wants you all to molest her, have at her. If you —"

"Master, whoever sucks you off after you make love to her, please order me to eat her out," Molly said, and blushed. "I ... we're starting to become two cliques here and you need to break us of that, I'm afraid, but I'm feeling really big-sister about her. And while I love Leigh and Lucretia, they had a relationship pre-existing and seem closer to one another."

"I'm well aware," Josiah said as he parked the truck.

"To the master bedroom," he ordered the slaves when he exited the truck. Josiah stripped naked downstairs and then trod the stairs behind his slaves, who all stood at attention, Molly and Lucretia to the left of the bed, and Darla and Leigh right of the bed.

Josiah sat at the edge of the bed after taking Darla's hand and leading her between his feet, and having her kneel. "Darla, what did you learn today?" he asked.

"That ... that I love Molly, that I love you all," Darla said. "Lucretia, can you forgive me, sister?"

"Of course," Lucretia said. "Darla, there is often somewhat of a crisis of faith in this kind of immersion, and God knows I've been through the wringer too in recent times. We're all having our issues coming to grips with our needs, honey."

"Thank you," Darla said, weeping anew.

"Leigh, what did you think of Darla's action out there?" Josiah asked.

"Master, we talk a lot about love and loyalty here, and I only hope I'd have as much courage and integrity as Darla discovered out there," Leigh said.

"Lucretia?" Josiah asked.

"Master, you saw how I cried," Lucretia said. "I saw how you cried too, ya big softie. It was love in action, loving her sister so much that she wrapped Molly in her own body to shield her from a whipping Molly didn't deserve on her own hook."

"Molly?" Josiah pursued.

"I'll always love Darla for what she did for me," Molly said. "I ... I don't think I ever felt more loved by anyone in my life than I did out there."

"I think it's fair to say we're all proud of you and glad we adopted you, Darla," Josiah said, and kissed Darla.

"Master, it wasn't heroic or brave," Darla said. "It was just doing the right thing. It was my whipping. I had it coming, not Molly. She ..." Darla fell silent a long moment as her eyes widened. "Jesus, you set me up. You knew I'd do that, didn't you, Molly?"

"No, I didn't know you'd do that," Molly said. "I'm glad you did, and I hoped you would and ... I sensed in you what I think you never guessed was there. Did I know you would embrace that courage and strut it out there? No, I didn't. I rolled the dice, and knew perfectly well if you didn't step up and offer yourself somehow, I'd be recovering from forty lashes while ... what did Master have you doing on your work assignment, again?"

"Cutting a tree into firewood lengths with a handsaw," Darla said.

"Then I'd be covered in sweat, sawdust and welts while praying I sawed enough wood not to buy another trip to that post," Molly said.

"You gambled on me," Darla said. "Jesus, you're the one rocking the lady balls out here, Molly!"

"We're sisters, and sometimes that means putting it out there for each other," Molly said. "You're worth it. I hope you see that now. But … I was about to tell you I want to talk privately with you, but no secrets here, right? If Master tells you to do something to one of us, I hope you know now that you are to do it immediately. We're not going to hate you for it. We're all going to have to participate in ensuring we remain enslaved, and Master needs us to be his minions over one another sometimes, honey. So the next time you're walking one of us and tits come off the ground, be harsh, not because you're cruel but because you love this family, your master and whatever sister is under your stewardship. We're not made of glass and won't shatter, honey. Okay?"

"I gather there was a problem on your walk?" Josiah asked.

"It was handled, Master," Molly said. "I'll tell you the details if you like, Sir. I think Darla needed a bit of coaching. She's growing out of her timidity though."

"Do you understand that, Darla?" Josiah asked.

"I … I'm trying, Master," Darla said.

"Give me your strap," Josiah told her. Darla unhooked it and handed it to him, and then bent over and grasped her ankles for the lashing she expected.

"Lucretia, Leigh, Molly, elbows and palms on the bed, legs

straight," Josiah ordered. "Darla, recover."

Darla stood and looked uncertainly at her master, who extended the strap to her. "Give each of them ten harsh strokes to their asses," he ordered.

"Why?" Darla asked.

"Two reasons," Josiah began.

"Darla, the first reason is master ordered it, and that's always reason enough," Leigh said.

"And if you don't, he'll give us each twenty," Lucretia chimed in.

"Make them hurt," Molly said, and chuckled.

"Machiavellian," Darla said, and accepted the strap, deciding to go first to Molly. No fool, Darla knew she was being taught what Tim had always called an object lesson, a practical hands-on lesson in a skill or philosophy. She even accepted that it was a lesson she needed to learn, not only for the technique, but for the sure knowledge that it was okay.

She reared back with the strap and gave Molly a hard stroke. Molly yelped at it, then said in a calm voice, "thank you, Sister." Darla looked questioningly at Josiah, who gestured for her to continue, and she did, striking Molly again, who hissed as her feet drummed a quick tattoo on the floor. But she held her place and calmly said, "two, thank you, Sister." The lashing continued, with Molly counting each stroke and thanking Darla for it, through all ten.

"Recover, Molly," Josiah ordered, and Molly stood. "Your thoughts, Molly?"

"Master, I've been whipped harder, but I heard Darla grunt quietly a time or two," Molly said. "I think more than anything it's just she needs to learn technique. Maybe Lucretia would be the one to teach her, Sir. It hurt, though. If she'd done that the first time my tits came off the dirt, I'd have dragged a set of grooves the rest of the way to the track, Sir. She did okay, and thank you, Master and Darla. Every lash is love. Every lash improves and makes a better woman and slave of me."

"Pick your next target," Josiah ordered Darla. He watched her carefully and could see she just needed practice, to learn to flow with the strap, but that would come in time. He agreed with Molly that Lucretia was probably best suited to instruct her, and decided she would take Lucretia for a walk Thursday. Even at the risk of her own skin, Lucretia wouldn't put up with lenience or bullshit from anyone, probably not even her master, he thought with dark amusement.

Darla stepped up behind Lucretia, and slashed the strap at Lucretia's rump. Lucretia hissed and groaned, but counted and thanked Darla for the stroke, and Darla simply lashed her again, slowly pushing her sister through all ten lashes, counted and thanked on every one.

"Recover and report, Lucretia," Josiah ordered.

"To be sure, it hurt," Lucretia said. "But it should have hurt worse, Master. Like Molly, I don't think it was a lack of effort but one of technique, Sir. If Master wishes, I can make a dummy and train her, Sir."

"Master probably does wish," Josiah agreed. "Darla, give ten of your best to Leigh."

Darla approached Leigh, and lashed her as she had her other two sisters. Leigh, taking her cue, also counted every lash and thanked her sister on every lash. In truth, it felt very submissive to Leigh, who was red-faced and crying by the time it was done.

"Recover and report," Josiah again commanded.

"Either I turned really wimpy or she improved in a huge hurry," Leigh said. "Ten of those on a walk and I'll stone guarantee my nipples would drag the ground even if my nose did with it."

"I'm sorry," Darla said, and Leigh winced.

"Darla, sisters only apologize to one another for wrongdoing," Josiah said. "If you were obeying my decree, you were being trusted to act in my stead, and an apology insults us all. Understood?"

"Yes, thank you, Master," Darla said, and positioned herself for the strap.

"Ladies, she took the position," Josiah said. "Vote."

"Master, I got it the other night for the same thing, but I would suggest there is a fundamental difference in that I've been around this for a long time and I damn well knew better," Leigh said. "I vote no."

"I agree with Leigh," Molly said. "If she does it again, then yeah, tear her a new one. But she's learning and some well-meaning mistakes should be forgiven."

"I also vote no, for all the reasons Leigh and Molly already stated," Lucretia added.

"Darla, recover," Josiah said, and Darla stood, looking at her sisters in disbelief. Josiah approached her, put the key in the belt's locking buckle, and unlocked it, setting the belt aside, and then unclipped her leash.

"Slaves, I am altering our program," Josiah said. "I am about to make love to your newest sister, after which Molly is going to eat my seed from her. I think bonding sometimes requires we're more

258

casual, so while I will require service from you four, beginning now and until Thursday morning when we wake, you are all unrestricted on orgasms and may enjoy recreation and a lot of getting to know one another. However, I am slated to meet with a client in ..." he looked at his watch "... four hours. I planned to take Leigh to the meeting to perform a physical if needed, but would anyone else like to come with us?"

"I would, Master," Lucretia said immediately.

"So do I," Molly said. "I will remain silent, if you wish, Master, but it would feel strange not going."

"Master, I ... I know I begged to be restricted to these grounds, but I'd rather be with family than alone here, if I may," Darla added.

"Very well," Josiah said. "I want everyone dressed and ready at 6:00 to drive to the office." He smiled at Darla. "And now I think it's time to show you that slavery isn't all about suffering, my love."

As though hypnotized, Darla climbed onto the bed and Josiah nibbled her throat while his hands roamed her taut form, caressing her and coming to know her every contour before kissing a trail down her belly and nibbling a trail around her navel while she trembled and moaned low in her throat. He nibbled up to her breasts and teased her right nipple with his tongue and teeth while his fingers drifted southward and found her labia, gliding up and down them. Darla squeaked a bit at his knowing touch but responded soon with low moans of desire until Josiah's fingers found her clitoris and teased it, flickering and circling. He saw goosebumps rising all over her body and smiled as she began twitching, bucking her hips, and mewling, while he nibbled her earlobe, growling low and soft, knowing she was at the brink but afraid. He ordered her to cum in a low and soft voice, and that was all it took for Darla, who cried out and arched her back as she clenched her thighs together, and then suddenly bucked into a fetal position, shuddering as she cried out, and then rolled back into place, sweated and quivering.

"That was a nice try," Josiah said in a confident tone. "But I want to turn you inside out, mine, until you're nothing but orgasm, my love."

"Oh, God," Darla moaned as Josiah kissed and nibbled down her belly to her knee, then up her inner thigh while she began mewling and trembling anew. And then he glided his tongue up her labia while she knotted her fists in the sheets, almost afraid of how intense this was about to get.

And then her clitoris was trapped in his mouth as his tongue went nuts on it, lashing and tormenting her as she clenched his head between her thighs, lost in the sensations he was knowingly delivering her. She mewled louder and began thrashing, shuddering and tightening against the intensity, growing more afraid she might not even survive this unexpected storm of pleasure. She was lost in it, unaware of anything but her clitoris and the oral delight her master was so willingly giving her. And then she clenched her eyes shut and screeched, squirting the bed and bucking in the throes of her climax, not even breathing as her vision tunneled and she gasped for breath against the intensity of the climax her master had thrust upon her.

"Jesus ... fuck ..." Darla gasped. "Oh my God, Master."

"My turn," Josiah said, and slid up her body, kissing her deeply as he slid his erection into her, feeling her slick tightness encasing his member as he drove fully into her.

"Oh, you feel so good, Master, but ... behind, please?"

"A gentleman always obliges his lover," Josiah smiled, drawing from her while Darla got on all fours, spreading her knees and arching her back.

"Hard, Master, please," Darla begged. "Take me. I need ... I need to be dominated here, Master."

"I hope you cum hard for me," Josiah said as he grasped her hips and plundered into her vagina, feeling her pushing back as she bit her pillow, shivering in delight as he took her, and took her hard. She came hard, squirting again on Josiah, and then he erupted deeply into her, groaning and shuddering against his own intense climax before they collapsed together on the sheets. Darla was torn between gasping and sobbing as Josiah took her into his arms, kissed her, and held her while she regained control, shivering in his arms.

"Jesus, you're ... Master, you're amazing," Darla breathed.

"I am," Josiah agreed, and she giggled at this.

"God almighty, I've ... you made love to me, and I finally know what that means, Sir," she said. "Tim ... he usually made me cum, but was in it for himself, really. And other men ... shit, they were boys. I understand that now. Just boys. Please don't ever let me be free, Master. I need you for all of this, the pain, the pleasure, the serving ... all of it."

"And you need to be cleaned out while someone attends Master's needs," Molly said, laughing. "Out of the way, boss. I'm hungry."

"Yes, Ma'am," Josiah joked, chuckling as well until he sat up and suddenly his penis was in Leigh's so talented mouth while Lucretia plundered her with a strap-on, thrusting hard into her until she spit out his member, wrapped her arms around him to brace herself, and screeched through her own climax, while Josiah held her head, stroking her hair. But Lucretia was far from done, still thrusting and grinding at her sister, and Josiah smiled at her as she kept driving in and out, grinding hard, until Lucretia arched her own back, just like Josiah did, and howled out her own cum, bucking and shuddering while Leigh, helpless against it, held tight to her master and came again, finally sliding from him to the floor, groaning as she tried to assemble herself.

But Lucretia, in a frenzy, needed more, and slid onto the bed, positioning herself under Molly and orally pleasing her while Molly ate Josiah's seed from Darla, who was begging and pleading to cum. Josiah rolled near her, and whispered in her ear that she was to cum as hard and often as she pleased, and that was all Darla needed to hear as she screamed through another orgasm, and Molly screamed into Darla's vagina as she had her own bone-wracking climax. Josiah smiled, pleased, as his frenzied slaves collapsed in various states of exhaustion. He lay on the bed, setting the alarm for 5:00, and in a moment was snoozing. Leigh climbed up onto the king-sized bed, and all five slept in a tangle of limbs, love, and passion.

THIRTY-SEVEN

"You're Elaine?" Molly greeted the woman as she entered the office suite.

"I am, and these are Marvin and Beth," Elaine said. "My miscreants require punishment, and I'm currently unable to impart it." She pointed unnecessarily to the sling encasing her right arm.

"Master will be along in a moment," Molly said. "The conference room is through there. Would you like any refreshments?"

"Nothing for my slaves," Elaine said. "But if you have a Coke, I think I'd drink it."

"I'll bring it right in," Molly said. "Master sent me ahead to get the office opened up, lights on, that sort of thing. He got caught in traffic, but will be here in probably no more than five minutes."

"Thank you," Elaine said to Molly, pointing her slaves into the conference room and taking seats along one side. In a moment, Molly entered with a Coke and two file folders. She opened the soda and asked Elaine if she would like a glass, and Elaine declined, accepting the bottle and drinking deeply from it.

Molly sat across the table in the conference room and opened one of the folders. "Has Master explained to you how this all works?" she asked.

"No," Elaine said. "He's ... I'm sorry, I didn't get your

name?"

"Oh," Molly said. "I'm sorry. I'm Molly, Ms. Elaine."

"Molly," Elaine repeated. "I should have known. The pain pills have me addled too much lately. I heard about you through … well … a former client, who tells me your master's results were highly satisfactory."

"May I ask who?" Molly asked.

"I don't think I should say," Elaine answered. Just then, Josiah entered and smiled at her.

"I'm Josiah," he greeted her. "I couldn't help overhearing. On my way here, Martin called me and gave me the heads-up that he'd referred you to me. He … about two years ago he had a wing in a sling like yours and sent his slave Lorie to me for correction. I'm glad he was so pleased he referred you."

"He says there was a day-and-dark difference in her when he got Lorie back," Elaine said.

"What happened to your arm?" Josiah asked.

"A stupid damn thing," Elaine snorted. "I was going down the stairs in the dark – I decided on a nightcap one night three weeks ago – and didn't see the cat sleeping on the third step. I stepped on it, the cat screeched and leapt, and the end result is I went tumbling like Jack and Jill, and cracked my elbow and sprained the shoulder. They're trying rehab on it but the doctor tells me probably I'll need surgery, and my arm is out of the game for maybe as much as six months. Meanwhile, my left arm is stupid. I swear, some days I think it could fall off of me and I might be a day or so before I noticed, and might decide I'm better off without the thing. They say lefties get killed far more often than righties, and I damn well see why."

Just then, the door opened, and Lucretia came in, followed by Leigh and Darla. Elaine gaped at them, and then Beth leapt to her feet. "You!" Beth hissed.

"What is this?" Elaine asked in sudden anger. "Some sort of a joke on me?"

"I beg your pardon?" Josiah asked, confused.

"Master, if I may?" Darla asked. Josiah gestured for her to speak. "The man there is Marvin. Captain Marvin Jackson."

"Holy shit," Josiah breathed, shocked.

"What the fuck is going on here?" Elaine demanded, not at all mollified. She noticed Beth and glared at her. "Beth, sit down. And I don't want to hear a peep out of you or Marvin until I tell you to speak."

"Yes, Ma'am," Beth said, and sat, but glared daggers at Darla.

"Master, should I leave?" Darla asked, looking distinctly uncomfortable.

"Maybe we should," Elaine said. "She sluts around apparently without consequence, and for that, my two slaves are in deep trouble with me."

"Without consequences?" Josiah repeated as his own annoyance rose. "Darla, remove your blouse and show them consequences."

"Y … Jesus …" Darla stammered.

"Darla, if I'm correct, our guests have all seen the photographs, and at least Marvin has had the privilege of connubial congress with you. In other words, the cow is out of the barn. Remove your blouse," Josiah repeated.

"Yes, Master," Darla said. She'd foregone a bra and had chosen a dark blue blouse from her wardrobe, to conceal her marks that would have shown through a sheer white garment. She unbuttoned the blouse and slid it down her arms, and then folded it and put it on the table, and then about-faced to show her back to their guests.

"Looks almost like hamburger," Elaine said, nodding her approval. "But I still have more questions than answers."

"Actually, so do I," Josiah said.

"I know you too," Beth blurted.

"Beth, how deep are you trying to dig your hole?" Elaine asked in an irate tone.

"I'm sorry, Miss, but the ... she ... I've seen this other woman somewhere before," Beth said, and then fell silent.

"Which?" Josiah asked. Elaine looked thoughtful for a moment and then gestured to Beth.

"The ... well ... the black woman, Ma'am," Beth said. "I've seen her somewhere. And it's something to do with S&M, ma'am."

"I don't doubt you have," Elaine said. "Josiah, my Beth has a nearly eidetic memory and if she says she's seen your woman somewhere before, it's a safe bet she indeed has. But we have a lot to discuss here, I think. Are you willing to just tell me who she is?"

Josiah gestured to Lucretia to speak. Lucretia nodded. "I'm Lucretia —"

"St. Cyr!" Beth exclaimed. "That's who you are! A professional dominatrix in this area."

"Well, that's ... yeah, until recently," Lucretia agreed.

"Ma'am, permission to speak freely?" Beth asked.

"You haven't stopped so far," Elaine said, sounding exasperated, but Josiah sensed a bit of humor in her tone nonetheless.

"Thank you, Ma'am," Beth said. "I was researching dominatrices about three years ago and came across your site, Ma'am. I —"

"I'm Josiah's slave," Lucretia interrupted, and Josiah saw Elaine's brows raise at this, and ... something ... flit across Elaine's face. "I am discussing with Master whether I should close up shop as a dominatrix, Beth."

"Wow, you must be something," Elaine said. "I remember coming across that profile and asking questions, now that it's come up. Lucretia and her boy Tony enjoy a certain level of notoriety for her ownership and skills, and his devotion. How did you seize her, Josiah? And do you own Tony as well? I hear he's one hell of a specimen."

Josiah frowned, and started to answer, and then noticed Darla was still in position with her back turned to them. "Darla, leave your blouse off, but sit beside me," he ordered.

"I must add that the photos don't do her justice," Elaine remarked. "She's a show-stopper, that one."

"Thank you," Darla said, and blushed a bit. Josiah didn't miss Marvin's eyes riveted to Darla's nakedness, and wondered if it would be bad or good to accept this pod as clientele.

"Before we go further, may I speak?" Lucretia asked, and Josiah nodded. "Josiah and I will each need a dollar apiece from each of you. Before you ask why, I'll answer the question. He and I are both attorneys at law, and we cannot reveal what our clients might tell us as their attorneys, so we're all protected."

"My wallet, Beth," Elaine ordered, and Beth produced a wallet from her purse, and unzipped it, then handed it to her owner. "Aw, fuck it, here's a ten. Credit my account with the change." She dropped the ten on the table, and Josiah nodded.

"So tell me about Darla," Elaine pressed.

"Master, I paid you my dollar too," Darla said. "So if you're worried about a conflict, I authorize you to discuss with the lady what has transpired between us in recent times. She's seen the marks on my back and is sure to know I've been thoroughly whipped, but I … I think she has every right to know since this seems to involve both her slaves, Sir."

"Very well," Josiah said. "Last week, Darla's husband brought her to me and hired me to punish her for several excesses involving alcohol and marijuana. He was concerned that she was behaving as a headstrong child and that it might be damaging. For reasons I'm sure you can assemble on your own, her conduct had begun to worry him about his own career. So this past weekend, she was a guest on my estate to be punished, and then Sunday I sent her home, per her husband's request. She had to walk home in that storm, in fact."

"He already knew she'd been fucking my husband?" Beth asked, and glared first at Darla and then at Marvin. "How many times did you fuck her, asshole?"

"That will be enough from you, Beth," Elaine said. There was steel in the tone, Josiah noted.

"He didn't know about Marvin, not at that point," Darla said. "And it was only once with him, Beth. Just that one time, but I'll get to that when or if Master permits me to tell my tale."

"So Darla phoned me yesterday, reporting that she needed a week-long session or three weekends, as my schedule permitted," Josiah continued. "I agreed to bring her to my facility, gave her a severe whipping, and then let her associate with my slaves while I took care of a few things, including a phone call to her husband since things seemed wrong, somehow. Frankly, her story was too pat, tied neatly in a package complete to the bow. She'd told me he was deployed, but that proved a lie, and things came unraveled for her in a hurry. Apparently, Tim got a photograph of Darla and Marvin having sex, and while she was on my place being put through her paces over the weekend, he moved her things to a residential motel and when she returned home, he handed her the keys to her car and ejected her from his life.

"So anyway," Josiah went on, "I confronted her, with Tim beside me, and she admitted her guilt. Her initial plan was to try to keep me in the dark while I held several sessions on her throughout the year, and upon his return from deployment, in order to present him with proof of extended penance she had done, to win back her marriage. He made it plain on no uncertain terms that the marriage was over, and he didn't want her back. He was planning to file for immediate divorce, and Darla was persona non grata with him, now and forever."

Josiah paused and saw Beth nodding and frowning, and wondered what was going on with her, and resolved to have answers before accepting her as a client.

"Anyway," Josiah continued. "Darla begged me to punish her anyway, to keep and own her for her own sake and betterment. She was eyes-deep in self-loathing, and my other slaves agreed to give her the chance to earn a place in my family. Yesterday, she took forty lashes of the horsewhip, and today she endured ninety of them, and until further notice she is mine, a part of my family. Beth, I gather you're Marvin's wife and sent the photographs to Tim?"

"I am and I did," Beth said, looking ashamed.

"Well, if you were trying to destroy her marriage, you can sleep happy tonight," Josiah said. "Tim hates her now."

"Which is why I'm here with them," Elaine interjected. "I'm sure you know how complicated these kinds of polyamorous relationships can be, Josiah."

"I am well aware," Josiah said.

"I mean, here you are with collars on your wife, a dominatrix with a wide reputation for her skills with her own clientele, a woman I don't know, the pretty little blonde there, and the woman who seems to have become an unwitting catalyst in the problems I'm facing now," Elaine said. "Part of me thinks I accidentally stumbled over the most perfect man in the world to act in my stead, but part of me worries I'm lighting the fuse to disaster."

"I suppose it depends upon what it is you want of me, and the objectives to hope to accomplish," Josiah said.

"If I question your Darla, will she give forthright answers, sparing nothing?" Elaine asked.

"When I question your Marvin and Beth, will I have the same?" Josiah returned.

"Beth, Marvin, you will only make your situation worse by lying, and worse still by evasion," Elaine said. "Is that understood, slaves?"

"Yes, Ma'am," her slaves answered in unison.

"Darla?" Josiah asked.

"I understand, Master," Darla said. "There's nothing I want to hide anymore, Sir."

"Darla, your recitation of the events of the night in question, please?" Elaine asked.

"Ma'am, I'm going to say this up-front," Darla said. "I was drunk and I was high, Ma'am. But those aren't excuses, they don't wash. I remember that night, and while perhaps my inhibitions were lowered, I acted of my own free will."

"Understood," Elaine continued. "Continue."

"Ma'am, the bar was called the Slippery Member," Darla began. "I was angry with Tim – I love him and all, but while I think he's a good man and probably a very good soldier, he was a lousy husband, far more interested in his career than his wife – he'd eaten my ass about my habits and tendencies, and I was angry with him, and in the grand tradition of a stubborn teenager, I went fully defiant. My God, I was the perfect hausfrau for him. Every day, all the dishes weren't just washed but polished. I changed the sheets daily, pressed his uniforms, sucked his dick, I did everything I could to make him happy. But his wife and mistress were one and the same: his career." She sighed. "I was – I am – really a whiz in the kitchen. Whip me for bragging if you will, but I'm damned good in there. But every night for a week, Tim promised he'd be home in time for supper, and I cooked a beautiful and delicious supper, all for him to not call home and to arrive, too often with booze on his breath, long after it all went cold, and on two of those nights, even after I went to bed crying."

"What did you know of Marvin when you and he had your affair?" Elaine asked.

"Ma'am, it was one time," Darla said. "I'm not excusing or reducing what I did, because I deserve what I'm getting, including having my back turned into hamburger, as you put it. For the record, I haven't seen my back, how it looks, but I deserve all the tears I'm going to cry, all the scars I might wear, all the humiliation I might undergo. Ma'am, if Master told me to face that door and take another lashing right now in front of you and your slaves as more atonement, I'd do it without objection or evasion. But it was a one-night-stand, Ma'am, not a longer-term 'affair' as I take that word to mean."

"Fair enough," Elaine said. "What did you know about him?"

"Only that he was handsome and we were both horny," Darla said. "By his bearing, I guessed he was military, but Ma'am, he was in civilian clothes. I was stoned and drunk all at the same time and my hormones were riding high."

"So he took advantage of you?" Elaine asked. "He got you bombed out of your head and raped you?"

"No, Ma'am," Darla said. "I wasn't forced into it. I knew what I was doing, although obviously I had no inhibitions at the time."

"Did you know Marvin is married?" Elaine asked.

"I don't remember seeing a ring, or any mention of a Mrs. Jackson, Ma'am," Darla said.

"And you then became Josiah's slave?" Elaine pursued.

"I slept with Marvin a couple weeks before Tim finally had enough and came here with me for Josiah's services," Darla said. "I'd met him a few weeks before that at a local munch, but at that point I couldn't even term him an acquaintance. He picked me up at quarters Friday and punished me over the weekend, although I didn't successfully complete the punishment, and figured I would be sent to him again."

"How did you fail the punishment?" Elaine asked, looking interested.

"A big part of it was hard labor, Ma'am," Darla answered. "I had to dig a pit, or at least work at digging it. And I worked hard, probably too hard, and came up with heat exhaustion. Molly medically disqualified me from activity Saturday for twenty-four hours, and by then it was time to go home. He drove me to … to where my clothes were … and I had to dress. And then he drove me to a diner in the rain and I had to walk the final ten miles home. I don't think anyone anticipated the storm we got, but that was a harsh punishment in its own right."

"Medically disqualified?" Elaine asked. "You let your slaves do this, Josiah?"

"Ma'am, I'm a physician," Molly said. "In that role, I rendered a medical decision based on many long years of being a physician."

"I see," Elaine said, brows raised.

"Ma'am, Master has never had a client that I didn't approve medically after a physical exam," Molly continued, struggling to keep her tone neutral and not let her annoyance show with this arrogant bitch, but she was rapidly building a large dislike for Elaine. "He relies on my expertise and if I order something stopped on the basis of that expertise, it stops."

"I seem to have pissed you off somehow, and I'm sorry," Elaine said, sounding sincere. "I've met any number of people in and around S&M, but I don't think I've ever met a physician slave. You're a rare find. If you don't mind my asking, do you also have that right when you're the one being punished, to stop it for medical reasons?"

"He owns two physicians," Leigh said. "So when one of those physicians is under the lash, the other still has a thumb on the stop button. Sometimes, if there's doubt or a question, the slave is monitored with ECG and a blood pressure machine throughout a session."

"I have to say I'm very impressed," Elaine said.

"May I question yours as you've questioned mine?" Josiah asked.

"Of course," Elaine said. "Marvin, Beth, you will answer all questions Josiah asks you, fully and truthfully."

"Marvin, you knew that Darla was married to a colonel at the base?" Josiah asked.

"Yes, Sir," Marvin said. "As I'm sure you know, she's ... she stands out and draws notice, Sir. And Colonel Morris is ... we work in the same department, but I'm not his subordinate. But he's a pure asshole, Sir, chews anyone's ass for any reason at any time, a real tyrant, and ..." he trailed off, as though assembling an answer. "Sir, I'm married to Beth, but it's not an easy marriage, in large part because of our careers. I'm a captain out there and she's a first lieutenant, but Mistress has forced us both to resign our commissions, and we're out of there soon. Anyway, Beth and I got into a fight and I stormed out of the house and off the base, mad at her. And I went hunting, Sir."

"Hunting?" Josiah echoed.

"For ... I guess for revenge sex," Marvin said. "And I saw Darla at the Slippery Member and thought it was a great two-fer, so to speak."

"Jesus," Josiah said, disgusted. "So you pursued her, seduced her, all to enjoy revenge on your wife and on Colonel Morris, without a thought as to who would be harmed by your dick and its forty seconds of glory. And now, Colonel Morris is disgusted, angry, and heartbroken, and a marriage lies in shambles, and I would guess your marriage with Beth is going to take a lot of work, if it can even be repaired, and by the look of your Mistress, she'd really like to cut your nuts out for this stunt."

"Sir Josiah, Marvin behaved despicably, but so did I," Beth suddenly said.

"I gather you're the one who sent the photos to Colonel Morris?" Josiah asked.

"I did," Beth admitted.

"Why?"

"Because I felt hurt and threatened by her," Beth said.

"Threatened how?" Josiah asked.

"Look at her," Beth said. "She's beautiful, poised ... she could be a model for Victoria's Secret, for God's sake. I freaked out, worried she'd steal Marvin for her own, and that Marvin would happily throw me overboard for her if she crooked her finger at him."

"Do you see your logical fallacy?" Josiah asked.

"I did when Mistress Elaine pointed it out to me," Beth said. "That upending her marriage really made her the greater threat since she could pursue him more successfully if divorced or separated. I knew who she was. I'd bet if I did a poll on the base, probably three fourths of the people there, male and female, would at least remember seeing her. Most of those would have found out precisely who she is, Sir. Women tend to be really hateful and jealous of the beautiful ones like Darla, and ... in my case, I behaved stupidly. And even if it hadn't been stupid, it was simply wrong to hurt so many innocents with it. Thank God she and Colonel Morris didn't have children, I guess. Sir Josiah, I guess what I'm saying is that Marvin and I are both guilty of fucking this up, and that the wrongs were done to your slave, and by extension, to you. I know we're going to be punished harshly for it, and we deserve that. But for my part in it, I do apologize."

"So do I, Sir," Marvin said. "Beth … she and I have our problems, Sir, but I agree with everything she said, Sir."

"Josiah, perhaps you and I could talk privately?" Elaine asked.

"I think we should," Josiah agreed, then fixed his glare on his four slaves. "You may discuss anything you wish in here with one another. You may express anger or disgust, and you may enjoy refreshments from the fridge there. But there will be no violence and no raised voices. Do I make myself clear?"

"Yes, Master," his slaves all said, in nearly perfect sync.

"The same goes for you, Beth and Marvin," Elaine said. "And since Josiah has been so generous about letting you see Darla in such humiliation and intimacy, return the favor. I want both of you naked as birth, this instant. From what I understand, that would be happening soon anyway."

"Jesus," Marvin moaned as he stood and turned his back, and then removed his shirt and shoes, and then slid his pants off. He wore neither underwear nor socks. He was of average build and his only scar was an old puncture wound on the back of his left thigh.

Beth, similarly, wore neither bra nor underpants. She had a more appealing figure than her clothing seemed to indicate, a nice hourglass design with a fairly plump rump and 34-C breasts, all on a 5'5" frame. Her mousy brown hair was limp, but clean. In all, Josiah thought she was an attractive specimen who simply needed a trip to the hairdresser.

"Same for you, slaves," he decided. "You may as well all sit equally in here, right?"

His slaves began stripping naked when Elaine ordered Marvin to turn around, and he did so, displaying an erection that looked almost painfully hard. Lucretia smirked at it. Darla didn't look at him. Leigh and Molly simply didn't seem to care.

"Marvin, I'd better not learn you used that pathetic pecker of yours while you're out of my sight," Elaine warned. "Josiah's girls have my every permission to tease you, even to make you cum, but if you do, I'm going to kick your balls so hard you'll sing soprano for a month."

"Wait for us," Josiah ordered, and left with Elaine for the office in the suite.

[To be continued]

AFTERWORD

This was the first installment of four or perhaps five of this novel, an epic work that has extended well beyond 350,000 words. It has become my magnum opus without me realizing it would be so when I began.

I want to say thank you a thousand times over to my PA in this endeavor, Lee Ann Kanowsky, who has been nothing less than a godsend through all of these hours we poured into having this book ready for you. I am also deeply grateful to hundreds of friends and fans who offered me so many words of encouragement as this novel grew closer and closer to completion and publication.

And to you, Dear Reader, I also offer my humble thanks. Without you, publishing would be pointless, and I genuinely hope you've thoroughly enjoyed this novel thus far, and will enjoy those volumes soon to follow.

LXB

ABOUT THE AUTHOR

Lucas X Black lives in the southern US, where he writes full time in and among stumbling about the house and muttering random lines from such movies as *Monty Python & the Holy Grail,* often ranting about silly English kah-niggets and farting in their general direction. If you wish to follow him for news and events, he may be found here:

Facebook:

www.facebook.com/Author.LucasXBlack

Twitter:

@lxblacktx